Praise for *Some Boys*

"Blount hits home with this novel…*Some Boys* belongs in every YA collection."

—*School Library Journal*

"You will be satisfied at the end of this powerful work."

—*RT Book Reviews*

"A largely sensitive treatment of an emotionally complex topic."

—*Kirkus Reviews*

"A bold and necessary look at an important, and very real, topic. Everyone should read this book."

—Jennifer Brown, author of *Thousand Words* and *Hate List*

"*Some Boys* is an emotional and heart-wrenching story that sheds light on rape and bullying."

—Christy's Book Addiction blog

"*Some Boys* is smart, heartbreaking, horrifying, and courageous… A must-read."

—Confessions of an Opinionated Book Geek blog

"This book did quite a number on me…made me FEEL, and feel really strongly."

g

Praise for *Send*

"Dan's likable first-person voice rings with authenticity...this offering may be relevant for those looking for more books on the ever-important topic of bullying."

—*Kirkus Reviews*

"Blount's debut novel combines authentic voice with compelling moral dilemmas...raise[s] important questions about honesty, forgiveness, the ease of cyberbullying, and the obligation to help others."

—*VOYA*

"A morality play about releasing the past and seizing the present... the ethical debates raised will engage readers."

—*Publishers Weekly*

"Read. This. Book."

—Fiction Folio blog

"Emotional, dark, and real, *Send* will not disappoint."

—Singing and Reading in the Rain blog

Praise for *TMI*

"A great page-turner to savor during the last days of summer."

—Seventeen.com Book Club

"[A] tech-driven cautionary tale...Blount addresses the potential perils of online relationships and the sometimes-destructive power of social media without proselytizing."

—*Publishers Weekly*

"Blount has a good handle on teen culture, especially the importance of social media...realistically expressed...[and] honestly portrayed."

—*School Library Journal*

Also by Patty Blount

Send
TMI
Some Boys

NOTHING LEFT TO BURN

PATTY BLOUNT

sourcebooks
fire

Copyright © 2015 by Patty Blount

Cover and internal design © 2015 by Sourcebooks, Inc.

Cover design by Vanessa Han

Cover image © Mohamad Itani / Trevillion Images

Sourcebooks and the colophon are registered trademarks of Sourcebooks, Inc.

Published by Sourcebooks Fire, an imprint of Sourcebooks, Inc.

P.O. Box 4410, Naperville, Illinois 60567–4410

(630) 961–3900

Fax: (630) 961–2168

www.sourcebooks.com

Library of Congress Cataloging-in-Publication Data

Blount, Patty.

Nothing left to burn / Patty Blount.

pages cm

Summary: Desperate for forgiveness from his father, Reece, who survived a car wreck that killed his brother, joins the grueling cadet program at his father's firehouse and grows close to fellow cadet Amanda until she is implicated in a string of arsons.

(13 : alk. paper) [1. Fathers and sons--Fiction. 2. Fire fighters--Fiction. 3. Arson--Fiction. 4. Love--Fiction.] I. Title.

PZ7.B6243No 2015

[Fic]--dc23

2015009890

Printed and bound in the United States of America.

VP 10 9 8 7 6 5 4 3 2 1

For Amanda Pitcher, who makes me feel like the best author who ever was.

Prologue

Home is where the heart is—unless you're me.

My steps slowed on my way to the front door, the ball of ice in my gut abruptly melting into this floe of guilt the second I heard their raised voices, every word pounding another stake through my heart.

"…can't throw out all of his stuff. I won't let you!" Mom shouted.

"Why? You think he's gonna, what, rise up from the dead and say 'Thanks for keeping my room the way I left it?' Stop dreaming, Abby."

"I'm not dreaming, John. I'm grieving. Just like you and Reece."

Dad snorted.

I couldn't actually hear him snort, but that's what he usually did whenever he heard my name. I mean, that's what he *used to* do. Lately, he did this thing where he'd hesitate for a second, like he was swallowing back a curse.

"That…kid. What the hell were you thinking, letting him drive at fifteen?"

And there it was, Dad's favorite fill-in-the-blank Mad Lib. You had your pick—*goddamn, stubborn, thoughtless, careless, skinny, weird, freaky*… Extra points if you added a vulgar expletive.

I shut my eyes and gulped back the scream that had clogged my throat since Matt died, since I…killed him. I tugged on Tucker's leash and turned away from all the shouting and the grief and the hate and just kept walking.

"Hey, Reece."

I jerked and found myself sitting on Alex's front steps with no memory of walking the three blocks to his house. Tucker's leash was still gripped in my hand. A lifeline. "Hey, man."

"Whoa. What happened?" Alex took one look at my face and sat next to me on the top step, iPad forgotten in his hand.

I shook my head. "My parents."

He blew out a breath, fanning the hair that was always in his eyes. "Oh. So I guess that means you didn't talk to your dad?" he asked with his usual precise diction.

I hunched my shoulders. Tucker whined at the jerk on his leash.

"Reece. You *have* to talk to him. You promised—"

I shot to my feet. "I *know*. It's just…he's not the easiest guy in the world to talk to." Or be near. Or be related to. Oh, he didn't beat us or anything like that. He just…didn't care. "I'm writing a note."

Alex didn't say anything. He just reached down and scratched Tucker's head. The dog climbed up the steps, put his head in Alex's lap, and stared up at him with big happy eyes, grateful for the attention. I tried not to be insulted. "Can I hang out here for a while?"

Alex grinned and handed me his tablet. "Up for some chess?"

What the hell. I shrugged, unlocked the device, started a new game, and moved my pawn. Alex made his opening move. We were silent, just passing the tablet back and forth between us. Soon, the screen flashed, and Alex sighed.

"Draw."

I shot him a questioning look. Since we'd met in chess club in fourth grade, I'd beaten Alex Boyle only eighty-six times. For us to reach an impasse during a game was statistically more improbable than winning the lottery. "You throwing games now?"

His eyebrows shot up, and he shook his head. "No. But I was trying out a new mating pattern."

I nodded but didn't ask which one. It didn't matter.

He closed the iPad's cover and gave Tucker a head pat. "So you're writing him a note?"

It wasn't the worst idea I'd ever had. Notes kind of had the last word, didn't they? Dad couldn't interrupt a note or stalk off while it was still talking. "Yeah. It's cowardly, I know. But at least I'll get it all out."

Alex suddenly grabbed my shoulders. "Reece, please don't leave. Just write the note and tell him off for the various things he's done. You'll feel better, and who knows? Maybe he'll change."

I laughed. The idea of my dad *changing* was even less likely than winning the lottery. "No. No, I have to go, Alex. It's not just my dad. It's Mom too. She looks at me and sees Matt and—" I broke off, swallowed hard. I was a year younger than Matt but looked just like him. "I hurt her." And that was unbearable. "I hurt her every time she looks at me."

Alex watched a car drive down the street, his lips pressed into a tight line. He didn't say anything, didn't try to talk me out of it. He knew me better than anybody, but even he didn't know how bad it had gotten with Mom crying all the time, Dad yelling at her for crying. I knew it was my fault, knew they needed time so they could heal. Time without me around to remind them of all the bad shit.

I turned to my best friend. "Could you take care of Tucker for me?"

Alex's head whipped around. "You're not taking him with you?"

"Um, no." I quickly looked away. "I don't want him there with me." Definitely not.

"Reece, you've had him since he was born. You can't leave him behind."

Tucker's ears twitched, but he didn't move from his spot, curled at Alex's feet. "He likes you. I know he'll be in good hands."

Alex stared at me, mouth open, and eventually nodded. "I will see what I can do."

I shut my eyes and let my shoulders fall. That was one less thing to worry about. I knew my mother wouldn't want to take care of Tucker after I was gone. I stood, walked down the porch steps, and snapped my fingers. Tucker immediately stepped to my side. "I should probably go. Thanks for the game. And the talk."

Alex smiled, stretching the freckles that dotted his face. "Let's get something to eat. I'll buy."

I was happy to delay my return home. After he dropped his iPad on the hall table and grabbed his keys, Alex walked with Tucker and me to Main Street, where we bought a few burgers and ate in the park, Tucker's leash fastened to a bench. Tucker watched a game of Frisbee, tail wagging, wishing the disk would fly his way just once so he could snag it out of the air. In the distance, the fire alarm sounded, and a few minutes after that, the sirens wailed. I watched for the trucks, heart twisting in my chest.

Matt would have been on one of them, if he'd lived. He'd been a junior squad volunteer since he was twelve years old. At seventeen, he was finally allowed to work an actual fire scene and become a full-fledged volunteer with the Lakeshore Volunteer Fire Department. He'd turned seventeen in November.

And died in December, the day after my sixteenth birthday. It was April now, and the hole Matt left just kept getting bigger and bigger and—

"Reece. Reece!"

I stared at Alex, wondering why he kept shaking me.

"It was an accident, Reece. You know it was."

I laughed. *Accident* was a funny word, a word people slapped onto events and incidents with one breath and then looked for somebody to blame with the next.

That would be me.

But me? I blamed my dad. If he'd done one thing, just one thing for me the way he used to do for Matt, I never would have asked my brother to show me how to drive in the snow. And Matt would still be alive today.

Suddenly, I couldn't wait to get home and finish my note. I had sixteen years of Dad-related crap to unload. It wouldn't be a note; it would be a manifesto by the time I was done. For the first time since Matt died, I felt something pretty close to relief. I'd finally be able to fulfill the promise I made to my brother while the blood drained from his body. I would have promised him anything in the world to stop the blood.

Don't you give up, Reece! Promise me. Promise you'll fix things with Dad before you do anything.

I promised. I had to. My brother was the only friend I had until I was nine years old. Even though I knew *fix things with Dad* was about as likely as me winning the Heisman Trophy, I'd do this last thing for my brother, and then I would go and let my parents live their lives without me around, constantly reminding them of what they'd lost.

"Well, I guess I stalled long enough," I said when Alex crumpled up his wrapper and pitched it into the trash can. The shot went wide, and Tucker tried to grab it, but his chain jerked him back.

"I'll walk back with you. We can watch some *Doctor Who* on Netflix."

I snorted out a laugh. *Doctor Who* was the best emotional anesthesia I knew. My chest tightened when I thought about leaving Alex behind. I would miss him as much as I missed Matt. But there was still time.

When we reached my front door, I blew out a loud sigh, relieved I couldn't hear my parents' raised voices. We stepped inside, and I unfastened Tucker's leash and hung it on the hook by the door. "Mom?"

A throat cleared. "In here."

We found her in the kitchen, staring into a cup of coffee. She lifted eyes that were swollen and red and huge inside a face that was pale and lifeless. "I didn't make dinner, but there's some leftover pasta from last night if you want to reheat it."

I shook my head and glanced at Alex. Something was wrong—off—*worse*. "No, um, we ate. We'll just watch some TV."

"Oh. Hi, Alex." She blinked up at him, just noticing his presence.

"Hi, Mrs. Logan."

She continued to blink and then jumped up. "Sit, sit. I'll reheat some pasta."

"Mom, it's okay. We already ate."

But she was busy pulling plates from a cupboard and a plastic container from the refrigerator.

"Mom. Mom?" I took her shoulders and turned her around to face me. "What's wrong?"

She sighed heavily and shook her head. "Your father," she said, her face blank.

I braced for it—whatever thing I'd done to piss him off this time. "What?"

The blank expression disappeared, and her face turned stony and tight. "He's…gone. He's decided to leave. He doesn't want to see either of us again."

I forgot how to breathe. I opened my mouth, but the air just wouldn't move. My ribs crushed my lungs, and little black and white dots filled my visual field. System offline, reboot.

When I was little, I used to have these episodes. Everything in the entire world, every fear, every worry, every *thing*, coalesced into a single point deep in my chest, and I couldn't keep it inside. Matt was the one who'd taught me how to beat these episodes. He'd asked me silly things like "Why did the chicken cross the road?" (It didn't. The road merely passed beneath the chicken.) and "Why did six hate seven?" (Because seven was hungry and *eight* nine.) and if I'd been able to breathe, I'd have laughed. It helped. He told me jokes and riddles and had me answer questions, because concentrating on him helped me forget about the pressure blocking my systems.

But without him, only one thought kept replaying in my head.

I promised. I promised. I promised.

He wasn't supposed to go. *I* was.

Dimly, some corner of my brain realized if I could think about the promise, then I could think of questions Matt would have asked. I focused on chess openings in alphabetical order. By the time I got to the Evans Gambit, I could breathe again.

"Reece. Reece!"

"I'm okay." My voice was nothing but a wisp of air. I blinked and found Mom crying next to me and Alex leaning over me. Somehow, I'd ended up in the chair Mom was in when we arrived.

"Oh, honey, I'm sorry," she whispered, folding me up in a tight hug.

"Not your fault." It was *his*. I pulled in a deep breath, trying not to pant, trying not to obsess about the damn promise. Mom pulled back and just stared at me.

"I won't lie to you. Things have been really hard since Matt"—she paused, swallowed hard, and then finished the sentence—"died."

My stomach rolled, but I waited for Mom to make her point.

"Things have been hard for all of us, Reece, but they've been really hard for your dad."

I blinked. Did I hear her right? Did she just make a fucking excuse for him?

"He can't talk about it. He can't face it. He can't even look at Matt's things. He's in complete denial."

Oh, how terrible for him.

"Give him the time and space he wants, and maybe he'll—"

My sound of disgust stopped her from finishing the sentence. She raked hair off her face—it was wild and sticking out all over—and put up her hands in a gesture of surrender.

"No. Forget it. Reece, the truth is your father will never change. Let him go. We'll be fine without him." Her voice cracked, and she pressed her lips together. "You boys go watch your show. I'm going upstairs to soak in a hot tub."

We listened to her footsteps climb the stairs and creak over our heads. Alex pulled out the chair next to me and sat down with a sigh. "Reece, you okay?"

It was a rhetorical question. *Okay* was a state of being that I hadn't felt in a long time, and he knew it. I was tired, tired of hearing excuses for my father, tired of being treated like a freak because I wasn't Matt, tired of myself.

I shook my head, and he stood up. "Come on. Let's watch TV, get out of our heads for a while."

Alex had the uncanny ability to compartmentalize his world. We'd watch TV, and some part of his highly evolved brain would be working on chess gambits, SAT practice exams, and plans for the hovercraft he was bitterly disappointed to not yet have. Halfway into the first episode, Alex suddenly turned to me with the familiar gleam in his eye and twitch in his lip that I knew meant he had a theory.

"Reece," he began, appraising me from head to toe. "What does your dad love beyond all things?"

I considered that for a moment. Half an hour ago, I'd have said my mother, but what the hell did I know? "Firefighting," I finally answered.

Alex clapped his hands. "Yes! Exactly. It's something he'd never quit, right?"

Slowly, I nodded, not quite connecting the dots. "Right."

"What if you were to join the junior squad?" When my jaw dropped, Alex stopped my protest with a raised hand. "Just listen. He's a career firefighter. Loves it so much, he hired extra crews for his business so he could spend more time volunteering. If you signed up, he couldn't walk away from you. He couldn't ignore you. And he couldn't kick you out—not unless you did something so terrible, he'd have no choice."

I was six foot two and a hundred and fifty pounds if I wore clothes on the scale. "I'm not…physical enough for that."

He waved a hand. "Matt didn't get ripped until he was, like, sixteen, and you're taller than he was. You put the effort into training, you'll be able to do it."

"Maybe, but he'll never sign the permission form."

Alex inclined his head. "True." And then he grinned. "But your mom will. Especially if you ask her now."

My eyes popped wide. He was right. She was so pissed at my dad, she might do anything if she thought it would upset him back. "I like the letter idea better."

Alex shook his head. "Write it if you need to get it out, but a letter now won't make an impression. He's already gone. You need to get inside him, Reece." He tapped his temple.

"Yeah." I reconsidered. "Yeah, where he lives."

Alex smiled. "Exactly."

Chapter 1
Reece

Dear Dad,
I promised Matt I'd do this. I know it'll piss you off, but a promise is a promise, and I can't let him down.

Baring your soul wasn't as easy as I'd thought. There was so much I wanted to tell Dad. Remind him about all those times he'd said no, every time he'd made me feel less important than my brother. Every time he'd made me cry and wish I were Matt instead of me. There were *years* of pent-up resentment that could fill entire reams of paper, yet I'd managed to scrawl just a few lines. Somehow, the right words were impossible to find—if they existed at all.

I folded the crisp white sheet of paper into thirds, then folded that in half, tucked it carefully into my pocket, and thought about abandoning this entire pointless idea. But I had no other options. I sucked in a deep breath, tried to ignore the pounding of my pulse, and left the car.

It was time.

At the entrance where the roll-up doors were all the way up, I stopped and took a good look around. Red trucks gleamed in the light.

I could hear guys busting each other's balls, laughing hard and cursing loud. The slight scent of mildew tickled my nose when the April breeze blew my way. The fire station was every little boy's fantasy, including mine. But I learned a long time ago that it did no good to dream.

Then I saw Amanda Jamison, packing nylon rope into a bag, and just watched. In her station uniform, the lean muscles in her long limbs flexed when she strode to a truck to stow the bag. I knew Amanda from school. Knew the blond hair she wore scraped viciously back and twisted into a knot at her neck was straight and smooth, reached past her shoulders, and smelled like lemonade. Knew I had no shot with her. She'd never said so much as "hi" to me.

She'd had a thing for my brother.

She caught sight of me, turned, and didn't notice her rope bag tumble out of the truck. "Matt? Oh God. Matt."

Matt. My shoulders sagged. Okay. No turning back now. I swallowed hard and walked into the house where I had never been welcome. It took only three steps for recognition to fill Amanda's eyes. Or maybe it was revulsion. The two often went hand in hand where I was concerned. Mom says people just didn't *get* me. I figured that's because Dad always told them I was strange.

"Excuse me." I cleared my throat. "Could you direct me to the chief's office?" I took out my completed application from the bag on my shoulder, and her eyes popped.

"*Reece* Logan," she said with a sneer, and I jerked in surprise. Apparently, she *did* know me. She'd come to Matt's funeral with a few other kids from junior squad. Hard to believe that was four months ago. She'd hugged my dad, kissed my mom's cheek, and walked right past me. I figured that meant she'd heard all about my father's version of the accident that killed Matt—and believed it.

When she glanced over her shoulder at a group of guys in turnouts checking the equipment on Truck 3, I knew exactly what she was thinking. She probably hoped they'd pick me up and toss me out of the station for her. I saw the way her eyes scanned me from head to toe. She was cataloging. Indexing. Comparing me to Matt. When I held out my hand, she looked at it with disgust all over her face.

I swallowed hard, searched for something, *anything*, to say. "You came to the funeral. You and Gage."

She squeezed her eyes shut, and when she opened them, they were wet. "Yeah. We did."

"Thanks for that. It was…hard." I laughed once, a short uncomfortable huff of air, and then shrugged. Understatement of the century, but what the hell are you supposed to say about your brother's funeral?

"Amanda? Problem here?"

She whipped around to face the tall, thin man standing in the swath of sunlight. He took a step closer, and I recognized him. Mr. Beckett, the chem teacher from school.

Her face hardened. "Right. Hard." She picked up the rope bag she'd been packing and shoved it back into Engine 21. She slammed the compartment door, and I had the feeling she wished it were my head. I figured she didn't want to know there was someone who looked this much like Matt, sounded like Matt, walking around while Matt couldn't. When she stalked off to talk to Mr. Beckett, I knew I'd under-estimated her hatred, but I couldn't let that stop me.

"Hey!"

She whipped around. "What?"

"Chief." I waved the sheet of paper at her. "Please."

She pulled in a deep breath and ground her teeth together. "Go home."

I laughed bitterly and shook my head. Hell, hers would probably be the nicest greeting I'd ever get in this house. I stepped around her, strode to the door that led from the apparatus floor to where I figured the offices were, and prayed I'd survive this, even if it was only long enough to keep my word to my brother.

Chapter 2
Amanda

He stood with the sun shimmering at his back, and I stopped breathing.

Matt. Oh my God. Matt.

The blood rushed from my head. The gear I was packing squirted from my hands, hitting the ground with a dull thud. I watched, dizzy, as the ghost in front of my eyes stepped out of the glare and became a living thing. Not Matt. Tall, maybe even taller than Matt, same toast-brown hair, same piercing brown eyes. But where Matt's eyes used to glint with a bit of mischief, this boy's eyes held something else.

Pain.

My heart gave a long slow roll when I realized who this was.

Reece Logan. Matt's brother.

Oh crap. I shot an uneasy glance over my shoulder where the guys on Truck 3 checked their equipment, but the lieutenant wasn't with them. And then I remembered he wasn't on-shift on Wednesdays. Is that why Matt's brother was here—because he knew his father *wouldn't* be? I looked away, really wanting to avoid getting sucked into somebody else's family drama, but it was too late. He drifted closer to me, stood so close I could feel the anxiety radiating off him in waves.

Damn it, when he spoke, he even *sounded* like Matt, but without the laugh in his voice. Frowning, I looked at him again. Now that I could see him up close, I noticed his face was more angular, his lips thinner than Matt's, and there was a tiny scar running through one eyebrow. When he took out a completed application from the bag on his shoulder, my mouth unhinged. He said something about Matt's funeral, and I swear, I'd have blasted him between the eyes if Mr. Beckett hadn't picked that minute to walk in, crinkling a bag of potato chips.

He saw me talking to this boy and immediately frowned. "Amanda? Problem here?"

Crap, crap, shit. Mr. Beckett had a strict no-boys rule.

I quickly got rid of Reece and turned to my foster father. "Sorry about that."

He upended the rest of the chips into his mouth, folded up the bag, and put it in his pocket with a frown. "Who was that boy?"

I shrugged. "A new volunteer."

"Do you know him?"

Don't lie. Do not lie. No lying is another rule. "His father's a lieutenant here."

Mr. Beckett's eyebrows shot up over his glasses. "Really? He certainly didn't look twelve."

I shook my head. "He's not. He's in my grade, so he's probably sixteen."

"I wonder why he's volunteering now. What changed?"

I didn't wonder. I knew. "His brother got killed back in December."

"Ah. How tragic." Tragic—yeah, but Mr. Beckett's expression

relaxed. "But are you sure you don't know him personally? You seemed extremely upset speaking to him."

Oh, I knew Reece Logan. But I shook my head. "I never spoke to him until today." Not a lie. "I know the lieutenant, and from what he says, he and his son do not get along. I don't want that drama spilling over onto my squad."

Mr. Beckett pressed his lips into a thin line and looked down at me over the rims of his glasses. "I'm not comfortable with you continuing here if there's going to be drama."

Oh God. The blood in my veins froze. Junior squad was all I had—he couldn't take that away from me. I shook my head firmly. "There won't be. I won't let that happen."

Mr. Beckett considered that for a moment and finally smiled. "Okay. Just be sure you keep things entirely professional with that boy."

I nearly cried with relief when Mr. Beckett turned to leave.

"Oh, by the way…I came in to tell you I can't pick you up tonight. Can you get a lift?"

Yeah, from a boy. "Sure. No problem. Thanks, Mr. Beckett."

"What's on the agenda tonight?"

"Uh, we're doing PPE."

He flashed a wistful smile. "Oh, that's a fun one. Okay, have a good class. Don't let that boy's drama become yours."

Oh, count on it.

After Mr. Beckett walked back to his car, I finished checking the equipment on Engine 21.

"Man, got a minute?"

I looked up and found Neil Ernst, our instructor, standing behind me, his face tense. Immediately, I snapped up straight.

"Sure, Lieutenant. What's up?"

He waved a hand toward the parking lot, so I followed him out through the bay doors. He shoved his hands in his pockets and stared at the ground.

I started to sweat. This was bad.

"Um, yeah, so, the wife and I are moving to Florida. She's got a really good job waiting down there, and yeah. We're leaving Long Island."

I was nodding like I totally understood, but all I kept thinking was *what about us?* I took a deep breath. "What about J squad?"

Neil shrugged. "Chief's still making up his mind. He'll probably ask Steve Conner to take over for me."

I was still nodding like some lame bobblehead toy. "Okay, so congratulations. Or good luck." Or whatever.

"Yeah, thanks. Um, so I just want you to know I think you're one of the best damn cadets we've ever taught here. I hope you'll continue. When you turn seventeen, you're eligible for full volunteer status."

I knew that. I was planning to, assuming the Becketts didn't ship me back into the system. "Uh, thank you."

"I mean it, Man. You've been a great leader, a great assistant, and you really know your stuff. Whoever the chief puts in charge of J squad, I know you'll be his greatest asset."

My face burned under the praise, but it made me happy to hear. I worked my ass off for the squad, for LVFD. It was nice knowing that was appreciated. "So what about tonight's class?"

"Oh, um, yeah. So that's why I told you our plans. I can't stay tonight. We've got some hotshot real estate agent coming by tonight to appraise our place. Says she can get it sold like that." He snapped his fingers. "So I told the chief I couldn't do tonight's class. But you can. You've done PPE before—so has everybody else. Just run the practice drills, and you'll be fine."

Still nodding. "Yeah. Okay."

Neil held out his hand. "Thanks, Amanda. For everything."

I shook my instructor's hand. That was the only time I could remember him calling me Amanda. To everyone here, I was Man—short for Mandy, but a way of making me feel like one of the guys.

That had been Matt Logan's idea.

While I watched Neil Ernst walk away, my eyes got stuck on Engine 21. It had been right there. That's where I first met Matt Logan, two years ago. I'd been standing behind my foster father, trying not to shake in my secondhand shoes.

"Hey. Can I help you?" he'd asked and smiled in a way that almost melted me into a puddle.

"Hi." Mr. Beckett shook his hand. "This is Amanda, and she'd like to join the junior squad. Right, Mandy?"

I think I may have nodded or something. I know I hadn't been able to manage the powers of speech. Matt Logan was gorgeous, and I wasn't allowed to talk to boys.

Like I said—it was a foster house rule.

There were a lot of them. Don't become a statistic. (There was a ton of scary statistics about foster kids.) Don't use drugs. Don't steal. Don't lie. Don't defy. Don't skip school. I learned most of those at my first foster house. Mrs. Merodie's. I didn't last long there, because there was one really big rule I didn't know about until after.

Don't love your foster parents.

"You're in luck," Matt had said. "We're having our meeting later. Come on. I'll get you started." He'd led us upstairs to the chief's office, Mr. Beckett signed the forms, and a few minutes later, I was officially a junior squad cadet. Mr. Beckett promised he'd be back later to pick me up and left me there, having a private panic attack. What if he didn't come back? Where would I go? Who would take care of me?

"We meet here every Wednesday night and Saturday morning. Bring a notebook." Matt led me into the conference room, where three boys sat with their feet on top of the table at the front of the room. "Guys, this is Mandy. She's our newest cadet."

I remember trying not to cry when all three boys eyeballed me. They were so different. One looked like he was twenty, tall and hairy and muscular. Another looked like a fire hydrant—short, wide, no neck. And the third boy was a scrawny kid who looked young enough to still believe in Santa.

Max, the muscular one, had stood up, walked over to me, and put his hand on the wall, trapping me. My heart had started racing. He leaned in close, too close. "I'm Max. Anything you need, you tell me."

Beside me, Matt's tone suddenly went ice cold. "Max. Cut the *playa* act."

Max shot up one finger, ordering Matt to wait a minute, his eyes never leaving mine. "How old are you?"

I didn't answer. I couldn't remember. Max was standing so close, I could count the whiskers that lined his jaw, and the way he smelled…God!

"She's fourteen, Max."

White teeth flashed. "So am I, so that's perfect."

My eyes popped. He was *fourteen*? Steroids. It was the only explanation.

Suddenly, Matt was standing between us. "Off limits."

Max's lips tightened, but after a short glaring contest, he nodded and went back to his seat at the front table.

Matt led me to a seat and handed me a huge textbook.

"Logan!" Lieutenant Neil Ernst had barked from the doorway. "A word, please."

Matt headed into the hall with the lieutenant, and I tried not to shift and squirm under the stares from all those boys. A few minutes later, he was back. "Special assignment, cadets. Mandy passes all her practicals, or we all fail. Got it?"

"What? That's bull—"

"Tobay. This is a squad. She is now our sister."

Max sucked on the inside of his cheek. "Copy that."

The kid who was shaped like a hydrant had shaken his head and muttered something that sounded like, "Be easier if she was a guy." His name was Ricky, but everyone called him Bear, for obvious reasons, I suppose.

Matt angled his head. "Then start treating her that way."

A few minutes after that, Gage Garner walked in. The fact that I was a girl had no impact on him at all. He nodded, shook my hand,

and settled in to take notes. I didn't have a notebook. Matt ripped some blank pages out of his and slid them to me. "Got a pen, Man?"

I shook my head, so he took one from his pocket and slid it over.

"Can you talk?"

Startled, I blinked at him and nodded. "Yeah. Sorry. Um, thanks."

He grinned. "Oh good. I was starting to worry."

Lieutenant Neil Ernst began his lesson. It had been about fire suppression. I learned later that all of the boys, except for Kevin, the scrawny kid, had begun J squad when they were twelve. They had two years of training over me. "Don't worry, Man," Matt had said. "We'll get you up to speed fast. Right, guys?" There was a second or two of hesitation, but they all nodded. Whatever they felt about me didn't matter; they liked Matt Logan. Respected him. Listened to him.

I had been *Man* ever since. Matt made me one of the guys that day, made me part of a family, a *brotherhood*. He gave me something that was *mine*, something I could keep no matter what foster home I landed in. And now, he was dead, and everything had changed. Our lieutenant was moving away, the boy responsible for Matt's death wanted to join my squad, and Mr. Beckett wasn't sure he wanted me to stay. I realized I didn't have a damn thing.

The PA system crackled into life. "Jamison, chief's office. Jamison to the chief's office."

I hightailed back inside and upstairs and wondered how much longer I'd get to be *Man*.

Chapter 3
Reece

Get ready. I'm going to get in your face.

Halfway up the stairs that led to the station house offices, I froze.

Why did I let Alex talk me into this? What in the name of all that was holy was I doing here? Here—Lakeshore Volunteer Fire Department, where Matt and Dad had formed their exclusive little club, where I had never been welcome?

I rolled my shoulders and set my jaw. I shoved my hand into my pocket, felt for the square of paper I'd stuffed inside, and immediately felt calm.

A door slammed in the distance, jerking me back to my mission. Okay. I could do this. I walked up the stairs to the station's second floor, where I knew the offices were located. On the second floor, framed pictures lined the corridor, catching my attention. Smiling faces of guys in turnouts standing in front of shiny red trucks, newspaper clippings of honors awarded—and the losses experienced—since the Lakeshore Volunteer Fire Department was formed back in the sixties. I stopped in front of one large frame. Under the glass, a hand-painted sign commanded me to NEVER FORGET. Under that, a series of pictures stared back at me, all neatly aligned like the headstones that no doubt marked their graves. Men, way too many men, listed by the year of their death. An entire cluster of men listed for September 11, 2001.

But only one listed for December 9.

I traced Matt's name through the glass, the burn in my chest as hot as the day it formed.

"Help you, son?"

I spun and found myself facing a huge bear of a man wearing station gear—dark pants and a blue T-shirt emblazoned with the LVFD Maltese cross over the left pec. The slogan PROUD AND READY curved around the logo.

I opened my mouth, but when the man's eyes went round, I figured no introduction was needed. "Yes, sir. I'd like to join the junior squad." I held out the application form clutched in my hand.

The man took the form, held it at arm's length, and squinted at the words. With a sigh, he met my eyes. "So you're him."

My stomach dropped. "Yes, sir. I'm Reece Logan."

"And you really want to do this?"

I have to. "Yes, sir. I do."

The man thrust out a hand the size of my face. "Chief Brian Duffy. Why don't we step into my office and chat?"

I gulped once and shook the chief's hand, then followed him to the office behind the last door on the right. Two huge windows overlooked the apparatus floor. I stood and watched the crew from Engine 21 set up their bunker gear—boots inside pants—for the next alarm.

"So, Reece." Chief Duffy grabbed a pair of glasses off a desk littered in paperwork and took another look at my application.

"Just call me Logan." After a moment, I remembered to add a "Please."

Chief Duffy smiled under a bushy mustache. "Logan. Have a seat."

I sat stiffly in a straight-backed vinyl chair facing the chief's enormous desk. The chief lowered himself into a chair that groaned and protested his bulk but by some miracle held together. He just stared at me over his glasses for several minutes until I shifted uncomfortably.

"Uh, sir. I'm sixteen years old, and I realize most of the class probably started as soon as they were old enough, but I can promise you I'll work hard—"

"Why?"

I blinked. "Sorry?"

"Why now?"

I frowned and thought how best to reply. "Sir, I've always wanted to do this, but my dad and my brother—well, I wasn't…welcome then."

"Son, you really think you're welcome now?"

"Chief, I'm a strong, willing volunteer. From what the news has been saying, you don't have enough of those."

Chief Duffy's eyes went sharp when they met my eyes over the desk. "No. No, we do not. Volunteers are leaving faster than they're joining, and that is quickly becoming a problem for this house. But that doesn't mean I have to take on somebody who I am damn sure is going to upset the climate around here."

I looked down at my hands and sighed.

"Does he even know you're here, son?"

I shook my head.

"That's what I figured." Chief Duffy sighed and scrubbed a hand over the short gray hair that still covered all of his head, though I knew he was in his fifties. "What do you know about my cadets, Logan?"

I sat up straighter and looked Chief Duffy straight in the eye. "Junior squad is the future of Lakeshore, Chief. The LVFD averaged two thousand calls last year—up from previous years. But you're losing members. Even though you gained two full members from graduating cadets, you lost six members in the last fourteen months. Cadets meet twice a week and work under a supervisor, Lieutenant Neil Ernst. The squad practices fire service until age seventeen and only then are permitted on-scene. Since the squad was formed, there's been a ninety-percent conversion—"

"Okay, okay." Chief Duffy shot out a hand to cut me off. "So you've read the website. I want to know why you think you'd be a good cadet."

Because I have no other options. "Because I come from a firefighter family, Chief. Dad, brother, uncles, grandfather. It's in my genes. It's not about parades and medals and pictures in papers. It's about doing work that matters—even to the people who think their taxes are too damn high."

Chief Duffy laughed once, a sharp sound that echoed off the office walls. He studied me for a long moment, and with a nod, he reached for the phone on his desk and pressed two buttons, and then that loud voice reverberated across the entire house. "Jamison, chief's office. Jamison to the chief's office."

I cringed. Was I about to be escorted off the premises or welcomed to the brotherhood?

"Okay, Logan, we'll give this a trial run. Here are the rules. First, assuming you pass the background check, you need to know something right now. Lieutenant Ernst is out—the seventh volunteer to leave us this year. Relocating to Florida. Can you believe that crap? The junior cadet squad's new supervisor is Lieutenant John Logan. You got any issues with that?"

My stomach clenched into a tight ball. *Fuck me.* "No, sir."

"Good. Second, you step a single toe out of line, I will cut you loose, no questions asked. That means no family drama in my house. Understood?"

"Yes, sir." I swallowed hard. I could make that promise; my father was another story.

A tap on the door interrupted us. "Yes, Chief?"

"Mandy, this is Reece Logan, our newest cadet. Get him set up, will you?"

I looked up and, for a second, saw the fast burst of outrage on Amanda's face before she controlled herself. With a nod, she mumbled, "Yes, sir."

"Thank you, Chief Duffy." I shook the chief's hand.

"Better hurry, Logan. Jamison's pretty fast."

I turned and found the doorway empty.

Chapter 4
Amanda

"Hey."

Reece Logan's pissed-off voice called out to me in the stairwell. I paused on the landing, flicking him a look. "Hey, what?"

"Wait up."

I laughed at him and kept walking. Bad enough he had the guts to show his face in this house after what he did, and now he expected special treatment too? Matt was dead, Lieutenant Logan was wrecked, and it was all because Reece ruined their lives, just like Mom ruined—

Mom.

My heart slammed against my ribs when I thought of the life we used to have until she threw it all away for some loser she met in line at the Department of Motor Vehicles the year I turned seven. I swallowed hard. Okay, so Reece wasn't Dmitri, Mom's *soul mate.* But he was still the reason Matt was dead.

"There's no *waiting up* for anybody, moron. You're responsible for getting yourself where you need to be, or you get left behind," I called out over my shoulder.

He jogged to catch up to me and held up both hands. "Sorry. So where do we start?"

I led him across the apparatus floor, unlocked the door to the storeroom, and flicked on a light. I stepped aside so he could go in first, but he halted and covered his nose with a hand. It was a bit dank in here—a damp mildew odor mixed with the smell of smoke. I walked down one aisle, turned left where still more shelves and racks filled the space, grabbed two blue shirts from a box, and threw them at him. He managed to catch them before they hit the floor.

"Wear one to every meeting. That's the station uniform."

He frowned. "What about pants?"

I rolled my eyes and sneered. "You wear your own pants. Jeans, shorts, or buy a pair of uniform pants if you want." I showed him an empty open shelf. "This will be yours." I grabbed a roll of masking tape, tore off a strip, and applied it to the edge of the shelf. With a black marker, I wrote his name on the tape. "You'll get practice gear and stow it here after you master using it. For now, it stays empty."

Logan nodded. "When—"

I turned and left the storeroom. Hey, the chief said to get him set up, and that's what I did. That's all I would do. He followed me across the apparatus floor, back through the heavy steel door, and into the corridor. "Kitchen's that way." I pointed right. "Don't take food unless it's offered. It's not for us. But you can bring your own, and nobody will touch it." I strode to the left and opened another door. "Squad uses this as our classroom. We meet here Wednesdays at seven and Saturdays at nine. Bring a notebook."

"Um, today's Wednesday."

I broke into applause. "Did you figure that out all by yourself?" Wow. I thought Reece Logan was supposed to be a genius. I didn't have any classes with him, but I'd heard he was some kind of nerd, always getting perfect scores on tests.

Logan's face burned scarlet. "I mean, should I just stick around for tonight's meeting?"

I blew hair out of my eyes and shrugged. "Suit yourself. Sit anywhere." I grabbed a thick textbook off one of the shelves at the back of the room and tossed it to the table near him. It landed with a thud that echoed off the walls. "May as well start studying."

When I reached the door, he called out, "Wait."

Sighing impatiently, I turned and crossed my arms, but he didn't say anything. Instead, he crossed the room and met me at the door.

"Amanda, you don't know me. So how about you adjust the attitude, okay?"

Don't know him? I ground my teeth together. I knew Reece Logan was the younger brother of Matt Logan and the son of Lieutenant John Logan. I knew Reece Logan was the one driving the car that crashed back in December, killing Matt. I knew Reece Logan only cared about one thing—perfect grades. He was a straight-A dork with chess-club friends and zero interest in firefighting.

And now, he was standing in my squad room, and suddenly, I wanted to know *why*. Matt started junior squad when he was twelve. Reece never set foot in the building until now. So why was he here?

What the hell was he trying to prove? And just as suddenly, I decided I didn't give a crap.

I shot him a glare. "I know everything I need to know about Reece Logan." I stalked out of the room and headed back to the apparatus floor to start pulling practice gear for tonight's class.

Crap. The chief told me to get Logan set up. I should have gotten him a notebook or something. Cursing under my breath, I turned, headed back to the conference room, and walked in just as Reece, naked from the waist up, tugged one of the shirts I'd just given him over his head.

Wow.

For a chess geek, he had broad shoulders. Reece and Matt looked like twins, except for one thing. Matt was broad and muscular while Reece was kind of skinny—like Captain America before the top-secret super-soldier transformation. My heart twisted inside my chest, and the breath suddenly backed up in my lungs.

His head whipped around, his eyes wide. He quickly tugged the shirt down, but he wasn't fast enough. I saw the mark on his chest, right over his heart, and I wanted to cry and punch him at the same time.

I coughed and pretended everything was just fine. "Free tip, dude. You, um, might want to shut the door when you strip." I crossed my arms, leaning on the door frame.

Logan blushed like some middle schooler at his first dance. "Maybe I knew you were there," he said, trying to play it cool, and I bit my cheek to keep from laughing. He may have his brother's broad shoulders, but Reece Logan was still a dork who liked to play chess in shorthand.

True fact: I heard him shout "Queen, h4!" at another chess club kid while we were changing classes once. The other kid stopped dead in the center of the corridor with a look of horror on his face, so I figured that meant Reece beat him. He was always doing puzzles—crosswords, sudoku, cryptograms. During lunch periods, he usually had his head bent over a tablet or a puzzle book, pen tapping his chin.

Not that I looked or anything. It was just hard not to notice.

He stood there, looking at me like I'd just kicked his puppy or something. With a curse, I searched for something—anything—nice to say. I wasn't that good at *nice*. I felt bad about making him all embarrassed and stuff, so figured I owed him one. "Um, yeah, so nice ink." I jerked my chin at his chest. "What is it?"

"Um, it's, uh, an infinity symbol. Kind of."

"An infinity symbol. In bloodred ink?"

"It's…symbolic."

Yeah. Of the blood on his hands, no doubt. "So who did you get to ink you? You're not eighteen." As far as I knew, Reece was my age—sixteen.

"Fake ID," he admitted with an expression that pinched my heart, and I wished he'd smile again. His smile was so much like Matt's. When Matt smiled at me, I'd thought it meant he liked me, not just as a cadet or a fellow junior, but as a *girl*. I wasn't bad looking. And I noticed him staring at my chest more than once. But Matt Logan liked girls with long, flowy hair who wore heels and dresses. I didn't own a dress, I couldn't walk in heels, and I almost always wore my hair twisted into a coil to keep it out of my face when I worked.

Besides, the Becketts had that whole no-boys rule.

So I never told Matt how much I liked him. And now he's dead, and the reason why was standing in my squad class, looking at me like I just stabbed him through the heart.

He grabbed the book I tossed on the table. "Where do you suggest I start?"

I rolled my eyes and swallowed the *duh* I wanted to shout. Seriously, I thought he was a genius. "The beginning is usually good."

Reece's eyes shot to mine, and his jaw tightened. "Just so I know, how many questions per day do you answer seriously? What's the sarcasm ratio? Probably hit the daily quota by now, right?"

I glared at him for a second or two and finally took the seat next to him. The chief did say to get him all set up, so I guess I owed him a straight answer. "That *was* serious. You need to know this book backward, forward, and sideways if you expect to last in this squad."

He held up a hand. "Fine. Anything else?"

Oh yes, actually, there is. "Yeah. Why are you here? Matt's death really messed up your dad. You being here—"

"Yeah. I get it." He cut me off before I could finish. "It's family stuff. Complicated."

My eyebrows shot up. He didn't know the meaning of *complicated*. "Family stuff? Really? And yet, here you are in *our* house instead of your own."

He sighed and looked away. "He moved out."

Oh. I didn't know that. I squirmed and tugged at my shirt, pissed off that I actually felt sorry for him. "So the chief asked me to find out if you need a notebook since you're sticking around for tonight's class."

He shook his head. "I can take notes on this if I need to." He took out a tablet, and I rolled my eyes. Well, as long as he didn't start playing *2048* during our meeting, it would do.

"Great. Um, so, listen. Tonight's meeting, we're working on PPE and SCBA." I tapped the book. "I'd start there."

Reece gave me a shocked look and then smiled. "Um, yeah, sure. Okay. Thanks."

I smiled back, and his jaw fell open. I hightailed it out of there before things got weird.

Out on the apparatus floor, I waved at two of my squadmates.

"What's up, Man?"

I stared at Gage Garner, trying to figure out how to tell him. He used to be tight with Matt Logan. Ty Golowski probably wouldn't care much.

"Okay, listen. Chief okayed a new junior today."

"That's great!" Ty pumped his fist and flashed a mouth full of metal. He was our youngest and newest cadet and had been looking forward to hassling the next new guy for months now.

"No, not really. It's Reece Logan."

Gage's face went red, and he huffed out a breath through his nose—always a sign of temper for him. "Are you freakin' kidding me?"

I shook my head. "Wish I was. He showed up this afternoon and spent some time upstairs. Chief Duffy called me in, said to show him around, get him set up. He's in the conference room now."

Gage swiped a hand under his nose. "Does *he* know?" He jerked a thumb over his shoulder to where Lieutenant John Logan was bullshitting with a few of the guys on Truck 3.

I jerked. Crap! John wasn't supposed to be here on a Wednesday. And judging by the grin on his face, I was betting on no. "I'll tell him."

I adored John. He and Matt were like the station's own comedy duo, finishing each other's sentences and thinking on the same wavelength. Whenever I imagined my own dad, I pictured someone like John.

"No, wait," Gage said. "We should meet the kid first." He turned and shoved through the door and into the conference room. Reece was still in the chair where I'd left him. When he heard the squeaks of shoes on linoleum, he jumped to his feet and rubbed his hands down his legs, eyes darting from me to Gage to Ty and back again.

"Hey," he said, clearing his throat. "I'm Reece. Reece Logan."

"Yeah, I know. Um, wow. I'm Ty. Tyler Golowski."

"Hi, Ty." Reece smiled, and another chill crawled down my back. My eyes kept saying, "It's Matt," while my brain kept saying, "No way."

Noise out in the corridor made Reece take a step backward. The rest of the squad filed in. Max Tobay, doing his best lady-killer strut, Kevin Sheppard—well, Kevin just kind of bounced everywhere he went— and then Bear Acosta.

Before anybody could say a word, the squeak of wheels from the utility cart signaled this week's class was about to start. My jaw dropped when I saw the toast-brown hair, the wide shoulders, the smile just like his son's. Crap, crap, *shit*. This was going to get ugly.

Really ugly.

John Logan shoved into the room with a cart loaded up with gear. I took my seat and waited for the inevitable shit storm to rain down on us.

"Okay, gang, I'm Lieutenant John Logan, and I'm taking over for Neil. Do what I tell you, when I tell you, and we won't have a problem. As soon as I get all this gear unloaded, I want you all to gather around and just wait. Got that?"

Tyler's eyes darted anxiously from Logan to Logan, but John hadn't noticed Reece…yet. I rubbed my palms down my pants and swallowed hard, sneaking glances at Reece. He was chalk white and statue still. The tension in the room crackled, and abruptly, Reece stood up and cleared his throat.

Ty slid his chair a little farther away.

John finally registered the tension in the room, straightened up, and turned around. His eyes popped wide and then hardened the second he saw Reece. A muscle tightened in his jaw.

Reece's knees twitched, but he stood his ground and nodded once. "Dad."

That was all it took. One word. One syllable.

John's eyes—same dark eyes as Reece—shot down, took in his T-shirt, and flashed hotly. In three strides, he was in Reece's face, finger thrust toward the door. "Outside. Now."

And for the first time since I got sucked up into the foster care system, I thought maybe I was lucky.

***

When I was in first grade, a girl in my class got a special surprise one day. Her dad came home from Iraq and showed up while we were doing reading circle, still wearing his military uniform. Erin cried and hugged him, and everybody clapped. I wondered if my dad would come home like that and surprise me in school, hugging me close and twirling me around. And then, he'd see me. He'd look at me, and his eyes would get all serious, and then he'd fold me up in the biggest hug and say, *Mandy, look at you. I missed seeing you grow up.* But it would be okay, because he was home now and loved me. I'd see it in his eyes. That's what I thought a dad would be like.

But that's not how John was. There was no love in his eyes. All I saw was blame and fury. Reece saw it too. I could tell by the way he kept squaring his shoulders. What the hell was he trying to prove? Better question: why was he trying to prove it *here*? Junior squad wasn't some after-school special.

While father and son had their stupid staring contest, everybody froze in place, waiting for John's reaction. For the first time since my mom was sentenced, I was kind of happy I didn't have a family. It would *kill* me to see that look on *my* dad's face. Reece abruptly turned and walked to the door. The lieutenant followed, practically breathing fire, and slammed the door behind him.

I rushed to the door to listen, along with most of the squad.

"Lieutenant Logan!"

The chief's voice exploded from the hallway, and everybody on my side of the closed door exchanged matching *holy crap* looks—all popped eyes and open mouths.

"Brian, what the hell is this?" the lieutenant demanded.

"Lieutenant."

"Uh oh," Bear whispered.

I let out a low whistle. Chief Duffy was pissed. You could always tell by the way he bit out your rank, kind of spit it at you. The problem was John was just as pissed. *Come on, John. Don't blow this.*

"Chief." He answered rank with rank, and I breathed a little easier.

"Lieutenant Logan, Reece is your newest cadet. Do you have a problem with this?"

There was silence for a long moment.

Don't say it, John, I mentally shouted at him.

"No, sir. No problem *here*."

"Since Reece has assured me he also has no problem working with you, I am not needed here. Am I, Lieutenant?"

"No, sir."

"Logan."

Reece's softer voice asked, "Yes, sir?"

"I look forward to seeing your progress. Carry on."

Chief Duffy did not wait for a response. His heavy footsteps faded down the hall. The group of us hightailed it away from the door and back to our seats just as the door opened again. Reece took his seat, and the lieutenant closed the door, his face flushed.

"Okay," John said, his eyes drilling holes through his son. I shifted uncomfortably, but Reece didn't so much as flinch. "Okay. Everybody, this is Reece. Reece is—" He broke off abruptly with half a laugh. "Doesn't matter. Let's get started." John returned to the pile of gear on the cart and unfolded a bunker coat. "Everybody stand up, shove the tables back, and gather around."

Gage took a spot beside John. Reece stared at his father, and I felt this sudden pang of sympathy for him. John used to be so proud of Matt. I watched them but pretended I wasn't, wishing John were *my* dad. Not that I wished Matt were my brother, because—ick. I just wanted what they had. Private jokes to laugh at, stories that embarrassed each other, knowing with a single look when the other was about to blow up and backing off before he did, having someone you could always count on.

No matter what.

John and Reece faced each other, their physical resemblance so strong, they looked like clones. John's hair may be graying at the sides, but it was the same shade—the color of toasted almonds. Reece was lean and narrow where his father was broad. But he was also a good four inches taller than John. Matt would have fallen between them—taller than John, not as tall as Reece.

I had no idea who I took after. I shut my eyes and tried to remember my mom's face, but all the details were gone now. I couldn't remember her dimples or her birthmarks or the lines on her face. I asked her once if my dad knew about me. She snorted once and said he left the second he found out. Just as well. I'd rather not have a dad at all than one who looked at me the way John was looking at his kid right now.

It must have taken one hell of a lot of guts for Reece to be here, knowing the kind of reception he'd get.

Like he felt my eyes on him, Reece's gaze suddenly snapped to mine and held. I wished he wouldn't look at me like that...like the way I'd always wished Matt would look at me but never did. I shifted and squirmed, and suddenly, his face smoothed out and went blank until his dad's voice made him blink.

"Okay. Your PPE is your last line of defense between you and a fire. There are quite a few types of personal protective equipment, but today, we're going to talk about the most typical ensemble, which is...Tyler?"

"Um, structural ensemble, Lieutenant?"

"You asking or telling?"

"Um, telling."

"Correct. The structural ensemble is commonly called what, Gage?"

"Bunkers, sir."

"Bunker gear. That's right. Your PPE meets the standards established by the National Fire Protection Association. Reece, what NFPA standard covers PPE ensembles?"

All those emotions spread over Reece's face again, and I figured he knew John was purposely looking to trip him up. I wasn't sure why that bothered me so much, but it did. John crossed his arms and waited for his son to choke.

"Fifteen hundred, Lieutenant," Reece replied with a look that asked *is that all you got?*

John's grin froze, then slid off his face. He frowned and looked odd for a moment. Kind of sad, kind of pissed off, kind of hurt. Holy crap, it was the same series of emotions on Reece's face not a second earlier.

"Good guess. All right. The tones sound. People are depending on us to respond to their calls sooner, not later, so that means the faster we get rolling, the better the chances of saving people and property. You need to learn how to put on all this gear in less than two and a half minutes."

I already knew how to don PPE and started to zone out by watching Reece's face. When he didn't know anyone was watching him, his face was in constant motion. His eyes spoke as clearly as words—especially the *fuck you* glare he shot toward John. His lips went tight and flat one minute, and they curved and lifted the next. And there was this little concentration frown wrinkling his forehead, like he was trying to memorize every word his father said.

John spoke about the bunker pants and worked his way up from there, describing each piece of gear in detail. It started to worry me that Reece wasn't taking any notes. This stuff isn't like the trigonometry you learn once and then never use again. Everything we learned in squad was critical for survival—ours or somebody else's.

"Amanda."

I jerked back to the present and met John's eyes.

"Here. Time me."

I stepped forward, took the stopwatch he handed me and clicked the button. "Go."

He kicked off his shoes and stepped into the boots that had already been tucked into the pair of bunker pants, then with a leap and a tug, he had the pants up. He snapped both suspenders over his shoulders, fastened the waistband, fell down to his knees, slipped his arms into the coat, and flipped it over his head. It took about three seconds to seal the coat and loop the cuffs over his thumbs. He grabbed a protective hood, tugged that over his head, but then shoved it back so it bared his hair. Next up was the air tank. He gave the dial a few cranks, waited for the bell, slipped his arms through the straps, and tossed it over his head so it hung upside down on his back. A quick tug on the straps tightened them, and he was back on his feet, slipping the oxygen mask over his face and lifting the hood back over his hair to cover the mask's straps. He slid his hands into thick gloves and only then placed a black helmet on top of his head.

He clapped his hands twice, my signal to stop the clock.

"One minute, forty seconds, Lieutenant."

The class applauded, and John grinned. "Not my best time, but it'll do. Okay, everybody, start practicing. You need to don PPE in two and half minutes or better to pass. Everybody got that?"

I looked at Reece, wondering if he'd been able to keep up. John only described the gear; he didn't really teach us how to use it. John took off the gear and arranged it all back on the floor. Tyler went next, and I crossed my fingers. He always struggled with PPE.

"Two minutes, twenty-two seconds. Cutting it too close, Golowski. Practice."

Gage was up next. He had the best times in the squad. "Two minutes, twenty-*three* seconds. Really, Gage? You're gonna let Golowski beat you?" Gage's lips tightened into a line.

I snuck another look at Reece, impressed to find him paying close attention, asking Bear questions when Tyler and Gage had their turns.

Finally, it was his turn. When he clapped his hands twice, John failed to stop the stopwatch.

"You're not done, Peanut."

Peanut? Reece was almost a head taller than John. What was with the *Peanut* stuff?

"What did I miss?" Reece asked.

"Think about it. It'll come to you."

Christ. I shook my head. He forgot to turn on his tank. The son of a firefighter, the brother of a firefighter, and he forgot to turn on his tank? I felt bad for him, really bad, until I looked at John.

He looked happy, and that had me pressing my lips together to keep from saying things I shouldn't.

"Dad—"

John whipped around. "I believe I identified myself as Lieutenant when I walked into this room."

Reece's jaw clenched—I could see it from here—and he nodded. I could almost *hear* his decision to accept whatever challenge John lobbed at him. Reece stripped off the gear and prepared to start over.

"Restart the clock."

"Peanut, if you don't mind, we have a lot to cover today. You flunked. Why don't you quit now? You know you can't do this work."

"I can do it—"

John smiled and took a step closer. "We both know how this ends. You'll play for a week or two, get bored, and move on to—I don't know—robotics or chess club or something. So let's save everybody some time and cut straight to the end, okay, Peanut?"

"Not quitting, Dad."

The smile clicked off, and John got up in Reece's grille. "While you're in my class, you'll address me by my rank."

If John wanted to be addressed by his title, maybe he should leave obnoxious nicknames at home. But Reece never said a word. All he did was cross his arms and glare. I bit harder on my tongue to keep from butting in.

"Hey, Lieutenant? I have a question."

John's temper strained its leash but didn't snap. With a curt nod, he turned away to answer Max. If I hadn't been looking for it, I might have missed the way Reece's shoulders sagged in relief. Before I could think twice about it, I opened my mouth and leaned toward him. "Hey, Logan. You forgot to open the tank."

Reece shook his head with an eye roll. "Right. Thanks." He gave me a look that held so much gratitude, I forgot I hated him for a second.

"Don't sweat it. Everybody forgets something on the first attempt."

"Not me. I don't forget anything when I'm actually *taught* what to do."

My mouth fell open. "Boasting and showing off are the surest ways to get killed around here."

Reece hissed in a breath and squeezed his eyes shut for a second. "I'm not boasting. I have a perfect memory."

Yeah, right. "A perfect memory. You mean, like, photographic?"

He made a sound of annoyance. "Look, just show me a list of everything I need to do, and I'll teach myself."

John heard that part, strode over, and put his hands on his hips. "You got problems with how I teach?"

46

A distinct snort left Reece's mouth. "No. No problems."

John nodded, grinning. "That's what I thought." He shoved the cart out of the way and grabbed the textbook from Reece's table. "The second part of today's class is the SCBA. That stands for self-contained breathing apparatus. It can save your life—when you remember to turn on your tank," John added with a pointed glare at his son. "Open your books and start reading. I'll be back in ten."

Wait, what? John stalked out of the room. The second the door shut behind him, Bear cursed.

"Shit, I hope he doesn't make us write a report. I don't have time to write no report."

From the corner of my eye, I saw Reece pretend he didn't hear that. I could tell he did though. His shoulders sagged just a little lower.

The door opened, and Chief Duffy crooked a finger at me.

"Jamison, a word, please."

I met the chief out in the hall. John stood there, hands on his hips, mouth tight. "He gets no special treatment," John insisted with a poke of his finger toward the classroom.

The chief took off his glasses and pinched his nose. "Jamison, I want you and your cadets to work with Reece, get him up to speed."

"Chief, I don't want him getting special—"

The chief shot John a look that plainly told him to shut up. "It's *not* special treatment. It's what we'd do for any new cadet who volunteered for J squad. Isn't that right, Amanda?"

That was true. "Yes, sir."

John continued trying to make a case, but the chief had his mind made up. Logan was staying.

Gage caught my eye as soon as I reentered the room. I joined him near the bookcases in the back.

"What's up, Man?"

"Chief says to help him. Logan." My teeth clenched.

"Are you freakin' kidding me?"

"Come on, Gage. I know what he did, but it doesn't matter. Chief's not happy with John. He was outside, listening, and he says it's up to me, to *us*, to turn this around."

Gage rolled his eyes. "What exactly are we supposed to do?"

"What we're trained to. Work as a team." I lifted a shoulder. "Come on, you were here." I waved a hand around the room. "You saw what he did. The lieutenant isn't even teaching this class. He's turning it into some kind of spanking. None of us are gonna learn anything like this."

Gage sighed. "Yeah, that was kind of hard to miss. But what do you think we can do?"

"Work one-on-one with him, get him caught up to the rest of the squad."

"Wait, you mean me?"

I shook my head. "Not just you. All of us."

"What about the drill session?"

"That's at the end of the month. And that's a really good goal to shoot for."

Gage grunted in frustration. "Fine. I'll get the guys to help. Just do me a favor and don't fall for this one too."

My whole body clenched, and I gasped in a breath. I could feel my face flaming. I never should have told Gage I liked Matt Logan, never should have asked for his advice. Not that it helped. Matt never treated me like a girl. Neither had Gage. Maybe that's the real reason everyone called me *Man*.

"Really, Gage?"

Gage put up a hand and shook his head. "Just looking out for you, Man."

All of a sudden, I hated being called Man.

Chapter 5
Reece

I'm gonna make you see me. Make you hear me. Make you fucking acknowledge that everything I am is because of Matt and everything I'm not is because of you.

I kept my eyes pinned to my textbook, but I hadn't been able to concentrate on a single word. Amanda and Gage had their heads together in a whispered meeting at the back of the room. I should get my stuff together and get ready to leave. It wouldn't be long now. Christ, I knew he was pissed off, but for a minute, I'd been afraid that he'd say it—

No. Don't go there. I shuddered.

I wasn't John Logan's favorite person. I'd known that for—hell, maybe I always suspected, down deep inside, where I was afraid to look. Matt was a year older than me and Dad's favorite. Mom had albums full of pictures of Matt in tiny firefighter costumes, mimicking Dad's poses and expressions.

There weren't many photos of me.

I tried to tell myself it was because I was the second baby. That my mother was exhausted from taking care of not one but two toddlers. If either of those reasons had been true, it would have sucked, but I could have accepted them.

Eventually.

But the truth was it was entirely my fault. My mom, my grandparents—both sides—even my favorite Aunt Sue all told me that when I was a baby, I'd screamed for hours, slept very little, and needed speech therapy just to say *da-da*. By the time I'd begun school, I'd been tested for Asperger's and ADHD and didn't have any friends. Dad and Matt had gone on countless camping and hunting trips—just the two of them. Every time I'd asked to come, Dad had told me, "When you're older."

That day had never come.

Things got way better by the time I'd hit fourth grade, when a particularly attentive teacher discovered I was "brilliant."

Her word, not mine.

She claimed all those development problems were really just frustration. My brain was whipping along at warp speed, but my body couldn't keep up, so I had a lot of meltdowns and tantrums. With the right guidance and structure, I thrived. I was put into a gifted program, and I loved it. I joined the chess club where I met Alex, the first real friend I ever made. But it turned out I wasn't brilliant at all. I just tested well because I never forgot anything. My teacher said I have an eidetic memory.

But Matt really was special. I could have resented him or been jealous of him, maybe even hated him. But he wouldn't let that happen. Maybe he felt guilty. Or maybe he just really liked me. The reasons didn't matter much, but Matt used to do things with me that Dad never did, like take me to the lake and toss me a ball. Eventually, I learned to bypass Dad and just ask Matt whenever I needed something.

I shoved a hand into my pocket, took out my note, and scrawled a few more lines. I refolded the paper and squeezed my eyes shut. *God, Matt, I miss you so fucking much.*

A throat cleared, and I jerked in my seat.

"Hey, Peanut." A skinny blond kid smirked down at me, hands buried in his pockets—the same kid who'd managed to put on the entire bunker gear ensemble in one minute, fifty seconds.

"My name's Logan."

The kid's grin got wider. "Your dad calls you *Peanut*. He really hates you."

You have no idea. For as long as I could remember, Dad called me *peanut butter cup* because of my name. I never understood it. Did he name me Reece just so he could make fun of me? I said nothing as the kid's eyes raked me up and down.

"Did you really kill your own brother?"

"Back off, Kev." Max, the kid with all the muscle, came to my rescue.

Kev shot a nervous look at Max, the tall, older guy kicked back with his feet on the table. A diamond stud glittered in his ear. He looked like he was twice our age. I nodded my thanks. All I got back was a shrug.

"You're taller than your brother, but skinnier. Probably can't even lift a hose line." The skinny kid tried to rile me again, but this time in a lower voice.

"Won't know until I try."

"I can lift the two-and-a-half on my own."

"Bullshit."

I turned at the sound of another voice and watched another boy approach. Not very tall, but he was built like a bull, all shoulders and broad chest. He had dark, buzzed hair and shuffled when he walked. "Don't listen to Kevin, dude. The only thing he can lift around here are the doughnuts."

Kevin punched the wide kid's shoulder.

"I'm Ricky Acosta, but everyone calls me Bear. That's Kevin and Ty." He pointed to the kid I'd met earlier. "And that guy's Max." Bear shuffled around and jerked a thumb over his shoulder at the guy I'd figured was already a full-fledged firefighter. Tall, dark, and ripped, with a line of fuzz outlining his entire jaw, Max looked like one of the guys in the last firefighter calendar Matt brought home, pissed off he wasn't in it. It hung over the dartboard in our basement—one of the things Mom absolutely refused to get rid of.

"He's a junior? I thought he was, like, twenty-five."

Bear held up his hands with an anxious glance over his shoulder. "Shhh, don't say that too loud. It'll go straight to his head, and there's no room in there for more."

Max lifted his middle finger and went back to reading the text.

I snorted. I knew the type well. "Are those two a couple or something?" I lifted my chin toward Amanda and Gage, still whispering at the back of the room. It had been five minutes already.

Bear laughed. "No way. Man doesn't date, and Gage does whatever she needs him to do."

"She's in charge. The squad captain," Kevin added.

I looked from Bear to Kevin to Ty. "Man?"

"Amanda. We call her Man. Makes her feel like one of the guys," Ty said proudly.

So noted. "Is she really in charge?"

"It's not official or anything. Every year, we all vote which kid is the best leader. That's Amanda now."

He didn't need to tell me that Matt used to be the squad's captain. Kevin slid my book across the table and leafed through it. "So what's your deal, man? Why you here?"

I eyeballed all three guys. I stood up, slowly eased a hip to the corner of the table, and stated the obvious. "I want to be a firefighter like you guys."

"Bullshit," Bear said again. "If you wanted to be a firefighter, why didn't you start squad when you were twelve, like everybody else?"

Crossing my arms, I shook my head. "I wasn't allowed. My dad wouldn't sign the form."

Ty and Kevin exchanged shocked looks. "Your dad? Lieutenant John *I eat fire for breakfast* Logan actually said no? Why the hell would he do that?"

I ground my teeth together. Because Matt wanted to be a firefighter first. And Dad always gave Matt what he wanted. "Doesn't matter. My mom signed the damn form this year, so I'm ready to catch up."

Another loud laugh, another round of exchanged glances. "Yeah. Good luck with that." Kevin snorted. "So what's the real story with your brother's crash?"

"Shut up, Kevin." Bear nudged him, and the skinny kid almost fell. Then he glanced at the wall clock. "Five minutes left. Better start reading." He slid my book back across the table and then angled his head at me. "You got any idea what causes green fire?"

I shook my head. "No. Why?"

Bear lifted his massive shoulders. "I heard the fire marshal talking to the chief and—"

"Oh, the arson?" Kevin's eyes went wide.

"Shhh." Bear looked over his shoulder. "We're not supposed to speculate, remember?"

"What arson?" I didn't hear anything. Then again, it's not like my dad ever talked about stuff with me.

Bear glanced around again. Amanda and Gage were still talking quietly at the back of the room. Max, the tall kid, was still kicked back in his seat. "Three so far this year. All empty houses."

"How were they set?"

"Don't know. The chief won't talk about the details with us. All I know is that there was green flame at the last one. It was up on the north side of the lake, on Greenley Street."

Before I could say anything, Amanda was in front of me. Bear shuffled to his seat, taking Kevin and Ty with him.

"Hey, Logan. He'll probably look to trip you up again." She shifted her weight and looked over her shoulder at the door.

I folded my arms. "So?" What the hell did she care?

"Here's what you do. In two minutes, when he starts firing questions at us, questions that aren't in this book, you remember this. The most important thing you have to know about SCBA is how to take care of your tank. It holds maybe twenty minutes of oxygen. You check it before and after every shift. Make sure all the pieces are working and not cracked—face mask, hose, gauge. Make sure the harness straps aren't tangled and the buckles are intact. Check the test date, and make sure your cylinder is a hundred percent full. If it's not, you need to recharge it."

Jesus. I could only gape as Amanda rattled off all the SCBA maintenance tips. "Recharge it. Right. How?"

"I'll explain that when we have more time." She waved a hand. "Next, you should always make sure the cylinder and the remote pressure gauge's readings match within ten percent. Got that? Ten percent."

"Yeah, yeah, okay." I'd never needed to take notes before. So why was I suddenly wishing I'd written all of that down?

"Last one. If he asks you when you should wear SCBA, the answer is *always*, okay? Even outdoors."

"Okay. Why are you telling me this?"

"Because outdoor fires can still burn toxic."

"No. I mean why are you doing this? You made it pretty obvious you don't like me and don't want me here, and now you're helping me. Why?"

She glanced over her shoulder again. "No, I don't. But I also don't like the way John's using my class to get back at you. So don't let him, okay?"

Don't you let him. Promise me!

The scrape of her chair jolted me out of my memory. Amanda took her seat just as my father strode back into the room, glaring holes through me.

Amanda was right; Dad did fire questions at the class, his face growing redder with each answer I nailed. By the time class was over, I was smiling.

Dad wasn't.

Chapter 6
Amanda

"I'm sorry." Gage pulled the car to the curb and shifted into park. "About before. What I said about Matt."

I lifted a shoulder and just kept looking out the passenger side window. I heard Gage sigh heavily.

"Man, listen." He shifted. "I miss him. A lot. Matt was…God—"He pounded the wheel. "He was the best. But Reece *isn't* him. I keep seeing you stare at him with hope in your eyes."

My head whipped around. "You're seeing things, Gage." *Hope* was something I hadn't had since I was nine and a lawyer promised me my mom would come home soon.

Gage held up both hands, surrender style. "You gonna be okay?"

Slowly, I nodded. "He's ours now, Gage. Like it or not." And I really, really did not.

"A brother, Mandy."

I twitched. Oh, I knew he meant a member of our brotherhood. But it felt like another reminder. Like I'd ever forget Reece was Matt's brother? I flung my head back against the seat and groaned. "This sucks, Gage. Did you see the way John looked at him?"

"Did you see the way Reece looked at John?" Gage countered, shaking his head. "That kid's messed up. I just—" He broke off, biting his lip. "Forget it."

"No, what?"

He searched my eyes. "Mandy, just…just stay out of it. You always get all messed up over family stuff. It gets into your head," he said, swirling a finger next to his own.

"No, I don't." I looked away.

Gage cocked his head and smirked. "Oh really? So you're saying that the time Kevin's mom flipped out when he got hurt during class had no effect on you at all."

I blew out a loud sigh. Okay, so maybe I was a little upset when my guys had problems with their parents or something. Didn't mean it messed *me* up. "I was worried for him. She said he had to quit."

"Man, you threw up. You actually puked and don't think that has anything to do with your own mother? Denial much?"

I shot him a glare. "She had nothing to do with that."

Gage shook his head. "Really? So why haven't you gone to see her?"

I sucked in a sharp breath. "That's really none of your business." I hadn't seen my mother in a year. As far as I was concerned, I'd never see her again.

"Oh, it's my business when it clouds your judgment."

"My judgment is fine, Gage. Back off. I promised the chief I'd help Logan learn the material, not have his babies."

He rolled his eyes. "Be serious. Whatever's between Reece and John needs to stay between *them*."

"Yeah. Okay, got it." I shoved out of the car and ignored the good night he called out. On my way up the walk to the front door, I suddenly froze.

Mrs. Beckett had planted flowers all along the front yard. Spring colors, lots of blue, white, purple, and pink, sweet smells filling up my nose. I didn't know much about flowers. There was only one I recognized.

"Mandy, sweetie, hand me that trowel," Mom had said, and I skipped over to her tools, grabbed the thing with the long curved blade.

"Good girl. Now it's time to dig. See, flowers like to play in the dirt."

"Me too!"

Mom touched a finger to my nose and laughed. "I know, and so does the bathtub. Let's make a nice deep hole…that's it…perfect. Now I'll put the flower in, and you scoop some dirt all around it so it stands up." I'd scooped and patted dirt all around the white flower with its yellow face. Mom grabbed a watering can and gave it a nice shower. We worked together, planting a long row of daisies, and then Mom said it was time to go in.

"But what about this one?"

Mom smiled and handed the last daisy to me. "That's for you. You can put it in a little vase next to your bed."

I did. Two days later, it was dead.

I turned and walked into the Becketts' house. I'd been with the Becketts for a couple of years now—a record. Mrs. Beckett stayed home, and Mr. Beckett was a science teacher at my high school. I liked them both very much, and I liked Larry, another child they fostered. He was a year behind me in school. I hoped I'd get to stay here until I aged out of the system, but there were never any guarantees.

"Amanda. What's up?" Larry greeted me from the den, surrounded by scraps of paper and poster board.

"Hey," I replied. "How's it going?"

"I finished my project. Want to see?"

"Um, yeah, sure." We'd eaten a whole bushel of apples over the last month because Larry was trying to determine what makes apples turn brown, which had something to do with acids and bases, according to Mr. Beckett. Larry had treated apple slices with a bunch of different things like lemon juice to see if the rate of browning slowed down. "Very cool, Larry."

"Yeah. Mr. Beckett helped." He smoothed out a glue bubble under one of his photos. "So how did training go today?"

"Okay. We got a new cadet."

"Sweet!"

"Amanda? That you?"

"Hi, Mr. Beckett."

My foster father stood in the doorway, reading glasses perched on top of his head, which meant he was either planning next week's lessons or grading lab reports. "How was your class today?"

"Good. We got a new instructor."

Mr. Beckett winced. "Already? Who'd Chief Duffy pick?"

"John Logan."

"Hey, did you see my project, Mr. Beckett? It's done."

Mr. Beckett turned to squint at Larry's poster board and examined the research. "Nicely done, Larry. I see you took my advice and used the milk of magnesia solution too. Good man."

Ugh. I hoped we didn't eat those slices.

"Hey, Amanda." Mrs. Beckett popped her head into the room, her dark hair pulled back in a messy bun. "Dinner in five, everybody. Get cleaned up."

Larry dropped to the floor and began picking up scraps of paper.

"I'll give you a hand." I crouched, collected the marker pens, and replaced them in their case. "It looks really great, Larry. Hope you win."

Larry shot me a hopeful grin and flipped hair out of his eyes. "You think it's good enough?"

"Yeah. I really do."

He put the board carefully on a side table, scooped the trash into the bin, and headed to the kitchen.

We sat around the round oak table tucked into the corner, pretending we were a real family. The Becketts had no kids of their own. Couldn't. So they *rented*. That's how I thought of it. Except instead of *paying* rent, they *got* paid—some for me, some for Larry. We never called them Mom and Dad or even by their first names. It was all very polite, like being invited over to somebody's house, except you didn't leave for a while.

We dug into Mrs. Beckett's meatloaf, trading stories about our days. It wasn't a real family, but I was warm, I had food to eat and clothes to wear and people who wanted to hear what I had to say. People who planted flowers in the yard.

"Did that boy give you any more trouble?" Mr. Beckett asked, and Mrs. Beckett's eyebrows shot up. I quickly shook my head.

"No, not at all."

"Good."

Mrs. Beckett cleared her throat. "So, Amanda. We've had a call from your social worker. Your mother's requested a visit."

The fork froze halfway to my mouth. "No."

"Now, Amanda," Mr. Beckett began, using his best sitcom-dad voice.

"No."

"Amanda." The fake voice was gone. In its place was Rental Dad, the voice that reminded me that even without breaking a rule, I could be shipped back at any time. I shut my eyes, but it didn't help. I could see Mom's face the night she was arrested. All she cared about was *him*. She never gave me a thought, and now she suddenly wanted to see me?

I would not let that happen.

Chapter 7
Reece

I should have done this years ago. If I had, would it have helped? I don't know, and for that, I'm sorry.

"You should have been there, Alex. He was actually speechless." I wadded up the cellophane wrapper around my sandwich and tossed it to my tray.

Alex looked up from his tablet and smiled. "Told you. Here." He slid the tablet across the table. "Your move."

I move a pawn ahead two spaces and gave him back the tablet. "We learned how to put on all the clothes. They're called—"

"Turnout gear. I know."

Of course he did. I rolled my eyes. "Sorry." It was my turn again, so I moved a knight. "He didn't teach much, just kind of demonstrated, but I was able to pick it up."

"Go to YouTube, watch videos. And then read your text."

"Done. I watched a dozen videos last night when I got home and—"

A throat cleared. I looked up and found Amanda Jamison standing next to me. My throat closed up. Under the table, Alex nudged my foot, and I jerked. "Oh, um, hey."

"Hey." She jerked her chin at me, then turned to Alex. "Hi, Alex."

Wait, what? "You know each other?"

She shrugged. "Same English class."

Oh.

Amanda turned back to me. "So, listen, Logan. The squad sits over there." She jerked a thumb over her shoulder where Gage, Max, Bear, and Kevin sat. Bear waved. I waved back, wondering what the hell she expected me to do with this information.

Her hair was down today, long and smooth, tucked behind her ears. She wore no earrings. Every girl in the school had pierced ears—some wore multiple rings. She wore a pair of well-worn jeans, sneakers, and a hoodie.

So why did my heart speed up?

"Logan?"

"Uh, sorry. What?"

"I said we have a lot of work to do to get you caught up."

"We?"

"All of us. The whole squad's gonna help you. Last night...well, it was kind of a train wreck."

"Caught that, huh?"

Her lip twitched, but she didn't smile. I shifted and looked away.

"Look, we're not doing this for you," she snapped. "Squad's important. Whatever's going on between you and your dad stays home. And that means you need to step up. You have a lot to learn in a short time. Meet me after school at the track."

"After—Alex and I were—"

"After school. Alex can come too if he wants," she called out over her shoulder as she strode back to the squad table.

"Okay, then." Alex angled his head. "I guess I won't see you later." He gathered his trash and his books and stood up.

"Oh, hey, I'm sorry about this."

"No, no, it's okay. This is important. You need to go."

I stood too. "Thanks, man. Really."

Alex left through the side door. I made my way to the squad table.

"Logan! Nice of you to join us."

Join them? I must have missed that invitation. "So what are we doing after school?"

"Working out."

Bear groaned, and I just blinked at Gage. "Sorry, what?"

"Logan, firefighting is physical, and no offense, but you look like a good gust of wind might knock you down, so we're gonna help you get ripped."

"Guys, I can handle it."

Amanda snorted. "We'll see."

The bell rang, and there was no time to argue.

The afternoon's classes went by way too fast, and by 2:45, I was behind the school, at the football field, where the lacrosse team was already practicing. A shrill whistle cut the air, and I found Max standing at the top of the bleachers, Gage and Kevin were there too.

But not Amanda.

I dropped my bag on one of the benches and jogged up the aisle to meet the guys at the top. Max and Gage exchanged a look.

"Not bad, Peanut," Max said, scanning me up and down.

I froze in place. "Don't call me that."

"Cool it, Max." Gage stepped in front of Max and put his hands on his hips. Max was incredibly well-built. It was steroids, I was sure of it. But then again, Gage was kind of broad too. "How much do you think bunker gear weighs?" he asked.

I went through the list—boots, pants, coat, helmet, tank. "About fifty pounds."

"You're right. Now, add in the weight of tools like a hose or a Halligan bar and an ax, and we're talking about seventy-five pounds, give or take. You need to be able to carry that much weight without panting, or you'll suck down an oxygen tank before you make it to the fire."

Made sense. "Okay. What do you want me to do?"

"Meet us out here every day. We're gonna run the bleachers, and every day, you're gonna add more weight until you can do it with seventy-five pounds."

Jesus H. Kristofferson, they were going to kill me.

Max stood at the top of the aisle. "Ready?"

Not even a little bit. I followed behind him at an easy jog, down the steps and back up. On the second lap, I noticed Gage wasn't running. And where was the rest of the squad? Shouldn't they all be conditioning?

"Hold up." Gage put up a hand to stop us on the third circuit. "How do your lungs feel, Reece?"

"Okay…I guess."

"Tell me your address."

"One twen…twenty-two…Heatherwood Lane." I was gasping for air, pressure building around my lungs.

"You're breathing too deeply. You need to control that," Amanda said. I whipped around and found her on the bleachers behind me. "Breathe in. Hold it for three…two…one. Let go."

I followed her instructions and felt the pressure in my chest fade.

"Again," she ordered.

I jogged down the steps, concentrating on controlling my breathing as I did. I did two more circuits, and my thighs were on fire.

"How many?" she asked Gage.

"Six."

"Okay, that's good for today. Tomorrow, add five pounds. Rope next."

Oh God. I thought *good for today* meant done for the day. When she passed me on the steps and waved a hand, indicating I should follow her, I lost all hope. Amanda led me around the bleachers to a grassy section underneath them and picked up the end of a thick coil of rope tied to a cinder block.

"Take this. Run relay-style from here to there." She pointed to the gate that led to the field. "Turn around, repeat, but reverse arms."

I took the rope and took a step.

"No. Stop." She adjusted the rope so that the length of it—and its weight—was over my shoulder. "Lean down. Grip it tight. Now go."

I ran, tugging the weighted rope behind me. When I reached the gate, I turned, switched shoulders, and ran back.

"Control your breathing."

Oh Christ. I did it again, holding my breath for a few seconds before letting it out. It definitely helped. But it was a lot to think about.

"Okay, stop."

With pleasure. I dropped the rope, leaned over my knees, and wished desperately for a bottle of water to materialize in my hand, but the only things there were rope burns. "What next?" I managed to croak out.

Amanda tucked her hair behind her ears. I didn't know why, but it made my fingers itch. She didn't answer me. Instead, she just angled her head and looked me up and down the way Gage had a little while ago. "You got any weights at home?"

I thought about Matt's stuff. He had gym equipment in the basement. A bench and a set of barbells. I think there were even some dumbbells still in his room. "Yeah. Why?"

"Tomorrow, get up early and start lifting. You've got broad shoulders, but you need to build the muscles here and here," she said with a hand to my back and my arms. "Do a set of ten with light weight. Increase the reps the next day. Next week, go heavier. Got it?"

"Sure. What else?"

"Run the bleachers every day. Weights in the morning, running in the afternoon. Now, head over to the library. Bear's waiting for you."

I held back the groan and just nodded. I went back inside the gate and grabbed my bag from the low bleacher, but when I got back outside, Amanda was gone.

***

69

The next day, I woke up an hour early and did presses, rows, and curls with Matt's barbells. In the afternoon, I ran the bleachers.

I couldn't raise my hand without coming dangerously close to sobbing.

"You have to give your muscles time to heal," Alex reminded me on Friday as we walked out of the school's main entrance.

I rolled my eyes. My drill sergeants didn't believe in time off. I'd already gotten texts from Max about doing more step runs after school and from Bear about reading another topic in the textbook and even from Ty about showing me what *firefighter's irons* were. "Yeah, well, time is apparently something I don't have a lot of. Squad has this field trip coming up. Once a month, they go out to Yaphank where there's a huge training facility, and they physically practice everything they've been studying in the classroom."

"When is the next one?"

"End of the month."

Alex shook his head. "Reece, you should sit this session out and do next month's."

No.

I shouldn't.

Because that would show my dad I couldn't do the job. The whole point of this exercise was to show him he'd been wrong about me.

Beside me, Alex sighed. "But you're not going to do that, are you?"

"Alex, I can't. The whole squad is trying to help me. I can't let them down."

He put up his hand when we reached the bus stop. "Okay. Here." He opened his messenger bag and took out a bottle of water and a banana. "Eat this now. Don't stretch, but do warm-ups before you start running up the steps."

"Wait, *don't* stretch?"

"No. The reason your muscles hurt is because they're tearing. Stretching will tear them more and, in your case, will likely cause more injury than it prevents."

Okay, then. No stretching. "Thanks, Doc." I waved the banana at him and headed for the field.

"Oh, and apply ice later!" he called out before the doors slid closed.

As soon as the bus pulled away, I remembered we were supposed to see a movie tonight. With a curse, I pulled out my phone and texted Alex my apologies for forgetting.

He immediately replied.

I knew you forgot. Your failure to mention our plans indicated that. The pain that you're in is making it difficult for you to concentrate. We can adjust and try tomorrow.

With a laugh, I texted back my thanks and headed to the field, where Max was already stretching. "Hey, Logan. You ready?"

I ate my banana, swallowed some water, and nodded. "Let's do it."

I followed behind him, my quadriceps burning and trembling with every step.

"Come on, Logan, kick it up!"

I struggled to control my breathing, but it wasn't working. I was sucking air, and my legs quit. I fell, sprawled face-first, and waited for death.

"Whoa, what happened?" Max ran back down the stairs and turned me over. He wasn't even winded. I'd have cursed him if I could…you know…actually talk.

"Jesus, Logan," Amanda's voice said from somewhere outside my visual field. It hurt even to roll my eyes.

Two hands grasped mine and abruptly pulled me up to a sitting position. The world reeled for a second, then righted itself. "Gah," I might have said. It was all a blur.

Amanda peered at me and shook her head in disgust. "Guess you're cooked for the day." She tossed me my water bottle. It sailed right past my head and landed with a dull plunk somewhere to my right. Amanda shut her eyes, and Max snorted.

"Logan, have you ever done anything physical without a game controller in your hands?" Max laughed.

Huh. I wondered if walking Tucker counted. "You know…it's all about…finger strength," I said between pants.

"Logan, think you can pull the heavy rope?" Amanda asked.

Oh God. I wasn't sure my arms were still attached. I just sat there, panting. Amanda retrieved my water bottle—it had rolled down a few steps—and popped the cap. I managed to get my arm high enough to swallow some.

"We'll forget the heavy rope for today." She pulled out her cell phone, an ancient flip, and tapped out a text message. "Go meet Bear. He's gonna quiz you on fire extinguisher types."

There were *types*?

I climbed slowly to my feet and managed to make it down to

ground level without passing out. Max and Amanda laughed, and my face burned, but I didn't look back. I made it to the library, muttered a prayer of thanks that Bear chose a table on the main floor, and slowly shuffled over.

"Hey, Bear." I fell into the chair opposite his.

"Hey, Reece. You okay? You look like you're gonna puke."

"I'll be fine."

He slid over a book. "Okay, we need to know about fire suppression."

I glanced at the book. "I had no idea there were different types of fire extinguishers."

"Yeah." He pointed to the one bolted to the wall in the corner of the library. "You need to make sure you're using the right tool for the job."

I read the page he had open. The most common types were water, dry chemical, and carbon dioxide. In addition, there were categories based on the type of fire each was best suited to put out. Class A fires were ordinary things, like wood, paper, and household stuff. Class B fires were petroleum-based, like gasoline or oil and paint. Class C fires were usually electrical, like wiring or transformers. Class D fires were metal-based, like potassium or copper. Class K fires were kitchen- and restaurant-based, involving cooking greases.

"We're taught to never use a water extinguisher on a kitchen fire. Tell me why."

I considered that for a minute. "Oil and water don't mix."

"Yeah. The water extinguisher will spread the oil drops, which just spreads the fire instead of suppressing it."

Made sense.

I kept reading. The cans were color-coded and labeled for intended uses, and some could be used for more than one type of fire. We kept this up for an hour or so, with me reading the list and Bear quizzing me, and it was really working for me. Once I read something, I never forgot it.

Matt always called my eidetic memory my superpower. But Dad? Oh, he hated it. Thought it was just another thing that made me… weird. Mom—well, she kind of played the center. She encouraged me, but she also tried to downplay my ability. That was another reason I knew I had to leave. She'd been playing the center for so long, she didn't know where the edges were anymore.

Alex was the only person I knew who thought my memory thing was cool. Smart as he was, he didn't have an eidetic memory, and so, he had to study—hard—for whatever it was that interested him at the moment. But the difference between Alex and me is that he *grasped* the things he studied. Applied them. Thought about them. Expanded on them. All I could do was regurgitate what I read. But Bear's quizzes were helping me truly understand this material.

"Okay, make sure you read the next chapter. Tomorrow, we're supposed to go over fire behavior. When we get to the training facility in a few weeks, we need you to be ready."

"I will be with this stuff." I waved a hand over the book. "But the exercise? I hurt from head to toe."

Bear grinned. He was a big kid, but not exactly a poster boy for the *Insanity* workout. "I hate working out. But I do it."

I blinked. "I haven't seen you run up and down the bleachers."

"I may be a little chubby, but I'm strong."

I didn't doubt that. "What about fast? Amanda and Max, they told me you have to be fast too, because there's only about thirty minutes of air in the tanks."

"That's only half true. The tanks are *rated* for thirty minutes, but under the stress of working the fire, we're lucky to get half of that. I have a lot of stamina. I know how to conserve my tank."

Frowning, I tried to imagine holding my breath in a real fire. "How did you learn to do that?"

A slow and evil grin spread across Bear's face. "Tomorrow, I'll show you."

I climbed to my feet, relieved my wobbly legs could hold me, and held out my hand. "Thanks, Bear."

"No problem, man. See ya tomorrow." He shuffled off to the exit. I took a few minutes to reread the fire extinguisher section and headed home.

***

I was parked in back of the firehouse by eight thirty the next morning, watching sprinklers tick across a couple of lawns. I took my note out of my pocket, read what I had so far, and frowned. A car pulled in beside mine, and I quickly put the note away, watching Amanda leave the passenger seat of Mr. Beckett's car.

She didn't look happy as she strode into the station house. He followed, several paces behind. Was he her stepfather or something?

I got out of my mom's car and headed in. Amanda was already in the conference room, distributing a stack of photocopies.

"Hey," I greeted her.

She looked up, grunted, and went back to work. I watched, wondering if I was supposed to help. She looked terrible this morning. Her hair was tied up in its usual knot, and she wore her station uniform—LVFD T-shirt with a pair of black work pants—but she was pale with purple circles under her eyes.

Amanda hadn't slept.

Why? What was she worried about?

"Logan," she snapped. "Grab that stack of textbooks and hand them out."

I stepped closer. "You okay?"

Her eyes narrowed. "Back off. Put out the textbooks."

I sighed loudly and nodded. "Yeah. No problem." I did what I was ordered.

"Amanda."

The voice in the door made Amanda snap up straight. I turned and saw Mr. Beckett looking from me to her and back again.

"You're working alone with this boy?"

She shook her head. "The rest of the squad will be here in a few minutes."

He took a step inside the conference room and picked up a textbook. "I'll wait then."

Her lips got tight for a second, and then she smiled. "Sure. We're working on fire behavior today." She chattered on, cutting me off when I tried to interject, even going as far as to turn her back on me. Finally, Ty and Kevin came in, and Mr. Beckett stood up.

"Okay. Have fun. I'll be back to pick you up just before noon."

He left with a glare aimed at me, and Amanda cursed under her breath.

"What the hell was that about?" I demanded.

She shook her head. "Let it go. It's nothing to do with you."

I snorted. "Really? Seemed like it was all about me. Who is he to you, anyway?"

She sighed. "My foster dad."

Whoa. Foster dad?

"I've been living with the Becketts since I was fourteen. He has a strict no-boys rule and doesn't like the way you look at me."

I looked away and shifted my weight. "Oh, um, sorry." Jesus, how did I look at her? I shoved my hands in my pockets and kept my eyes pointed at anything but her.

"Yeah, well, that doesn't change things, okay? He wants me to quit."

"Wait, you mean give up junior squad? I thought you were the captain."

"Relax, I'm not quitting anything. But it would really help if you'd stop staring at my ass."

The breath got caught in my lungs, and my face burst into flame. "I wasn't staring at your…at your ass. I just like to watch you walk." Oh God. The words that left my mouth sounded so much better in my head than out in the real world. I snapped my teeth together, resolved to never speak again until I was thirty.

"Hey, Man. What's up?" Kevin frowned at us.

"We're good. Grab a seat," she ordered.

Bear ambled in and nodded a greeting at me. By the time my dad came in, the whole junior squad was present and accounted for.

"Good morning, cadets. Page seventy-six, please. What is the fire triangle?" Dad waited for a volunteer, and when no one spoke up, he called on Max.

"Fuel, heat, and oxygen."

"Good. What about them?"

I read about this yesterday. "They're essential elements for ignition," I answered with confidence.

"Yes, but what about them makes them essential?"

"Remove any one of those elements to stop the fire."

Dad's jaw twitched. "Yes, but you're not answering the question."

I damn well was. "They're all essential—"

"Reece, you said that already. I want you to tell me *why* they're essential."

Amanda intervened. "When the three elements are combined in the right quantities, a fire can spontaneously occur."

Dad clapped his hands. "There it is! The right quantities. That's the key here, cadets. You know what they teach you in the military? Know. Your. Enemy." He paced between the tables, pounding a fist into his palm on each word. "The military spends countless hours gathering intelligence, analyzing, predicting, knowing what the enemy is up to. Your enemy as firefighters is fire, and to beat it, you need to know it. Reece, maybe you should read page seventy-six again."

I crossed my arms and bit my tongue.

"Lieutenant, maybe you should explain the chemical process." Amanda indicated her photocopy on the table.

Dad's eyebrows shot up. "Oh, should I? I wasn't aware that I needed to hold anybody's hand."

"I didn't suggest holding hands. I suggested explaining the process so that my squad understands the chemistry that causes fire."

I stared at Amanda, astounded.

And impressed.

Really, really impressed.

I snuck a glance at my dad. His face was red, but he smiled. "Okay. Why don't *you* explain the chemical process, Captain Jamison?" He pulled out a chair and sat.

Amanda's face flushed, but she stood up and faced the class. "Your handout explains what causes combustion. The fire triangle tells you that you need something to burn—that's your fuel. You need heat at a temperature high enough to make that fuel source burn—which is called what, Reece?"

I knew this. "Its flash point temp."

She nodded and kept going. "You also need oxygen. Why?"

Gage put up his hand. "Because combustion is an oxidation process."

I knew that too. Oxidation, the same process that causes metal to rust, is what fire was—except a hell of a lot faster.

Amanda grabbed a marker and drew a simple time line on the whiteboard. "Okay. You've got oxygen, fuel, and heat at the right combo, right here." She tapped a point on the line. "This is called ignition. Then, the fire goes through a growth stage because the flame that results from ignition is now increasing what?"

"Heat," Bear called out, and she nodded.

"Right. As heat is produced and unchecked, growth accelerates. Additional fuel sources, when heated to their flash point temperatures, will ignite. At this point, superheated gases are collecting at the highest point of a room." She marked points on her time line as she spoke. "When the fire heats everything in reach, we say it's fully developed. If nothing else changes, the fuel source and oxygen source get depleted, and the fire starts the decay process and eventually loses intensity."

She stepped aside and pointed to the first point she'd marked on the time line. "These points are how fire spreads. What are they?"

"Conduction, convection, and radiation," I answered, recalling exactly when I'd read that.

"Oh, stop it already." My father stood up and blocked Amanda's diagram. "I get it. You want me to see how much Reece memorized. Very good." He applauded slowly. "Do you mind if I get back to my lesson?"

"I do mind," Amanda snapped back. "I'd appreciate it if you taught a lesson instead of asking questions you know only our oldest cadets can answer."

Holy Jesus on a Popsicle stick.

She told him off.

She'd actually talked back to John Logan and lived to tell the tale.

Damn! I wished I'd recorded this moment on my phone. I held my breath, watching my dad's nostrils flare, the tick in his jaw getting more pronounced by the second as he gritted his teeth and chained his temper. My mouth fell open when he left the room without a word. If we'd been alone, I'd have fallen to my knees and kissed Amanda's feet.

"Man, what the hell are you doing?" Gage demanded as soon as Dad shut the door.

Amanda, her hands on her hips, stared after Dad. "I'm sorry. I lost my temper. I'm just getting tired of him using this class for family crap." She turned those angry eyes on me. "And you need to stop baiting him."

What? "When did I bait him?"

"He asked you a question, and you answered. That was fine. But he kept trying to trip you up, and you were buying it. You had him, Reece. You know the material, but you kept letting him get inside you." She jabbed a finger at her head.

This was a disaster. I ached every time I moved. I'd done more studying over the last few days than I did all semester, and it was a waste of time. Dad was never going to give an inch. I slouched lower in my seat, stared at my book, and waited for class to end.

Chapter 8
Amanda

Crap, crap, shit! This class was a total train wreck. It was just like Wednesday night's class—all John was doing was asking stuff J squad already knew and Logan didn't. When was he going to *teach* us anything? He'd been a firefighter for twenty years or more. There had to be something he could teach us.

I stared at the door John just slammed. Okay, so maybe I could have handled that better. The whole squad had been working with Logan, trying to get him all caught up. Even if John couldn't find anything nice to say to his kid, he damn well should have said something to my cadets.

I cursed again. Maybe I should say something to my cadets. "Guys. Thank you. You're all doing a lot to help Reece. He's learning fast, even if the lieutenant doesn't see it. Right, Logan?" I slid him a look. He was pouting in his seat like a three-year-old.

He jolted. "Um, yeah. Yes. Thank you all. So, uh, what do we do now?" He jerked his chin toward the door.

Good question. I blew a strand of hair out of my eyes and sat down. "Okay, here's what we're not gonna do. We're not gonna wait for the lieutenant to take his head out of his ass."

Logan choked, but when I shot him a glare, he swallowed his grin.

"Let's finish the lesson." I indicated the whiteboard. "Before John stopped me, I was about to connect a few dots here. You guys know the fire triangle, and you know the basic chemical process. Let's talk about suppression." I got up, went back to the whiteboard, and picked up a marker. "Got any questions so far?" I asked, and Logan shot up a hand.

"Like a dozen."

"Okay. Shoot."

"I read about a fire tetrahedron, a shape with a fourth side. Is that extra aspect the oxidation?"

I shook my head. "Not exactly. You're close though."

"Yeah, Logan. Check it out." Max stood up, took my marker, and started adding to the diagram. "The fourth thing in that tetrahedron is the chain reaction that starts with ignition. Here. Look." He changed my triangle to a pyramid by adding perspective. "A pyramid has four walls, right? Heat, oxygen, and fuel have to combine just right to start a chain reaction we see as the flame."

I nodded, grinning. Max was explaining this really clearly. He drew a circular arrow around the pyramid.

"As soon as ignition starts, a few things are happening. At the molecular level, the fuel source that's actively burning up is creating more heat to sustain the burn."

"What's the basic principle we learn about heat in science class, Logan?" Gage asked.

"It rises?"

"Exactly. So what do you think happens with heat rising?"

Logan angled his head at the diagram and pointed to the growth phase. "The fire grows because all that heat is spreading to the room or whatever and ignites more fuel sources."

I nodded and smiled. "Keep going."

Logan grinned back. "Okay. So if the room where a fire breaks out is heating up, the fire spreads from convection, conduction, and radiation until everything in the room is—oh." His eyes popped. "Flashover?"

"That's it. Good. Now how do we prevent that?"

The frown came back, and his lips moved silently while he tried to remember. "Ventilate the room."

Bear punched his shoulder. "You got it. Giving the hot gases an escape route cools the room."

Logan studied the diagram again. A second later, I saw the light-bulb go off. "We lowered the heat." He pointed to that panel of the pyramid. "And to cut off the oxygen, we smother it—like putting out a candle with one of those snuffers."

"What about the fuel source?" I asked, but only because I knew he had this.

He smiled. "A log in a fireplace that burns up. Fire goes out."

Yeah. He had this.

"Okay. Let's take a break and then head outside for some breathing practice."

Ty and Kevin exchanged fist bumps.

"Yes!" Max cheered.

Even Gage looked perky.

At Logan's blank look, Bear just smiled. "You'll see."

***

Outside, dressed in full bunker gear, carrying a ball under my arm, I decided not to wait for the usual arguments while my squad split into teams. "Kevin, Gage, Ty, you guys play against Max, Bear, and Logan. I'll sit this one out."

"Hell." Max shot me a disgusted look but put on his mask.

"Wait. You want us to play ball? Wearing all this gear?" Logan stared at me, jaw dangling.

"Dodgeball, Logan."

"Jesus." He looked sick.

"It's a great way to learn mask breathing and tank conservation," Bear said as he put a beefy arm around Logan. He didn't look all that comforted.

We lined up in an empty section of the parking lot. I only had one ball, so we'd have to skip the opening rush. I threw the ball to Max and stood back while he chucked it over my arbitrary line. The ball bounced off the chain-link fence behind Gage's team. Logan stood in the center of his space, looking way too much like a guy trying hard to hold his breath.

I shook my head and tried not to wince when Gage hurled the ball directly at him. He pivoted out of the way. Bear took up the ball and propelled it back to the other side, hitting Gage in the leg. Gage waved his arms in protest, but I didn't say a word.

Kevin chucked a shot with a wicked curve, catching Max by surprise. He had to execute a fantastic leap to avoid getting hit. A few of the guys on Engine 21 came out to watch, calling out advice. I glanced at my watch. Five minutes in, but I could tell that Logan was sucking down air way too fast. I called for a time-out and had everybody read their tank gauges. As I expected, Logan's was lower.

"Conserve, Logan. Short breaths and hold."

He flashed me a thumbs-up and took his position. The ball was in flight when Max nudged me. "Uh oh."

I glanced at the rear doors and saw Lieutenant Logan watching the game, the chief standing beside him. Nobody told me to stop, so I didn't call our impromptu game. I turned back just as Logan tried tossing the ball. It went far wide of Kevin, his intended target, who decided to do some trash-talking.

"Conserve your air, Sheppard!" I reminded him.

Kevin chased down the ball, and my cadets managed to keep the ball in play for a few minutes. But then Logan noticed his father. He wasn't ready for Kevin's power pitch that hit him right in the face, knocking off his helmet. I glanced at Lieutenant Logan, and he took a step forward when the ball hit, but the chief pulled him back.

Kevin and Ty ran over to Logan, full of apologies. Logan shook his head, trying to clear it. I strode over and stopped Logan from removing his mask.

"Don't stop, Logan. Keep control of your breathing. Don't pull away your mask."

The low-tank warning alarm rang, and Logan's eyes filled with panic. His breathing sped up, and he kept shaking his head. "Short breaths. Do not pant," I reminded him for the thousandth time.

"He'll be sucking face in another minute." Max frowned down at Reece, whose cheeks hollowed with every breath.

"Good. I want him to feel the last breath left in the tank," the lieutenant said as he joined us. He crouched down and clamped a hand over Logan's mask as he tried to peel it off. "The low-tank alarm rings when the tank is about three-quarters empty. At the rate you've been gulping oxygen, that'll only last you a minute or two, and that's a problem. If you were working a real fire right now, you'd have gotten yourself trapped. Worse, you'd put one of us in danger, because we don't quit until everybody's out."

Logan made a choking sound, and I figured he'd hit the bottom of the tank.

With a sound of disgust, John removed the mask from Reece's face. Reece gasped loudly, sucking in air so hard, I thought his ribs would crack.

John stared hard at him and then addressed the squad. "Note the pressure levels in your gauges right now. Strip your gear off, and then bring your tanks to the filling station."

"Copy, Lieutenant," I responded.

We stripped down and stored our turnouts the way Neil Ernst had taught us. Five minutes later, the whole squad circled around John in the air cascade room.

"Okay, juniors, file in here. Everybody took note of their gauge readings, right? Great. Now refilling your oxygen tanks can be dangerous. You guys have all seen *Apollo 13*? Then you know the kind of damage that an oxygen tank can cause when it explodes.

This is a cascading air system." He indicated the large chamber behind him.

While John explained the intricacies of the system, I watched Logan watching him. The expression on his face was…awe.

Maybe.

What did I know?

John explained how to examine the tanks for cracks and defects and then showed us how to calibrate the charging station. The cascading air system held two tanks at one time, so it took a while to get all the tanks refilled. When all of them were done, John took the squad back to the conference room.

"Okay. Start calculating your average consumption rates."

Bear winced; he absolutely hated math, but he took out a sheet of paper from the notebook he'd left behind during our dodgeball game and started to work. Logan looked lost. I went over to him, about to explain the procedure for estimating tank duration, but John stopped me.

"Let him do it himself, Man. Reece is a genius, you know."

Logan let out a choking sound and stared holes through his father, but he said nothing.

I knew Logan was some kind of brainy nerd, but a genius? I wasn't convinced. "Lieutenant, we haven't taught him the formula yet."

John folded his arms and smirked. "It's basic math, Man, not rocket science. You can figure it out, can't you, Peanut?"

Again with the *Peanut* crap? Again, Logan didn't say a word. He sat back in his chair and crossed his arms while everybody else jotted down

PSI levels at the start and end of our game and then divided what was used by the duration of the game.

"Tobay, using your little dodgeball game as a baseline, how long would it take you to empty your tank?"

Max frowned at his numbers. "I did it twice, Lieutenant. I got fourteen minutes the first time and twenty-one the second time."

"Do it again. This ain't some calculus formula you'll never use in the real world. This *is* the real world, and your life depends on getting it right."

True; Lieutenant Ernst had driven that point home to us many times. But Logan still hadn't picked up a pencil. What the hell was his problem?

"Garner, how long?"

"Nineteen, Lieutenant."

"Acosta?"

"Twenty."

"Good, good. Okay, Reece. We already know how you did, but let's share with the class."

Oh crap.

"Eleven."

John's lips curled into a smirk. "Really. You're sure?" He grabbed a marker. "Why don't you come up and show the rest of the squad your math?"

Logan's eyes narrowed, but he stood up, smoothed his hair back, and faced the whiteboard. He wrote down 2216, followed by the ending pressure level, and divided by the duration of our game.

Yes! I almost punched the air. The tanks were rated at 2216 PSI. At that pressure, they held a volume of 1,270 liters, which could be consumed at a rate of 40 liters per minute to give the user about thirty-one minutes of usable tank time. But that was *unloaded* respiration. For Logan's tank to empty after only eleven minutes, that meant he used well over a hundred liters of oxygen per minute.

"Eleven minutes." John shook his head. "You won't make it past the front door."

My simmering temper boiled over. "Max, tell Reece how long it took you to improve your tank conservation skills and break the fifteen-minute barrier."

Max squirmed in his seat. "Uh, well, I'd say maybe six months."

"Bear, how about you?"

"A year."

John glared at me from the front of the conference room, but I wasn't backing off. "Okay, Man, you made your point. Happy, Peanut? You got a girl fighting for you."

Reece turned red but never said a word.

The rest of our session passed quickly, and Mr. Beckett was back by 11:45 to pick me up. When he saw Lieutenant Logan still lecturing, he turned for the apparatus floor, where one of the guys was always willing to talk firefighting with him.

"Okay, cadets, that's it for the day. Wednesday night, we'll cover rescue procedures."

My squad stood up and filed out of the room.

"Man, a minute, please."

I turned back. "What's up, Lieutenant?"

He got right into my face, leaned down, and jabbed a finger at me. "Do not ever take over my class like this again, is that clear?"

Oh my God, was he serious? I stood up straight and stared him down. "Lieutenant, you walked out of the room with no direction and no explanation. Every cadet in this room voluntarily gives up their Saturday morning to learn from a seasoned veteran. All I did was respect their time."

He stared back, and finally, his lips twitched. "The dodgeball game was brilliant. Your idea?"

"Thanks. No, it was Bear's."

"Still brilliant." John smiled, tight-lipped, and stepped back.

"I'll tell him you said so."

John nodded. "Ah, about Reece."

Here we go. I wondered when he'd get to the point.

"Reece…dabbles. He's not serious about firefighting. I appreciate everything you and the squad are doing for him, but don't invest too much time in him. He'll get bored and move on to, I don't know, model rockets or something."

Too much time…suddenly, I was a little kid again, hearing Dmitri scold my mom. *You spend all day with your daughter. Is it too much to ask that she be fed and put to bed by the time I come over so I can spend time with just you?* I snapped out of the past, and my temper flared. "Lieutenant, Reece is trying really hard. Why don't you try just as hard and see how things go?"

I turned on my heel and stalked out of the room.

Chapter 9
Reece

I'm doing this now because it matters. It always mattered, but I didn't know how much, not really, until after Matt died.

My muscles screamed and my lungs burned, but I wanted Amanda to know I was grateful to her and to the whole squad for everything they'd been doing to help me, so I hung back after I reached the main corridor to wait for her.

"Reece…dabbles," I heard Dad say. I stepped closer to the door and listened to him tell her not to waste too much time on me. But Amanda's whole body changed. With her lips pressed into a tight line, she drew herself up tall and straight and got right into Dad's face.

"Lieutenant, Reece is trying really hard. Why don't you try just as hard and see how things go?"

My jaw fell open, and I gripped the door frame to stay upright. She'd…oh my God, she hadn't just spoken back to Dad this time. She'd actually contradicted him. And never blinked.

I was still standing there, shell-shocked, when she strode out of the conference room without even looking at me. I double-timed it to catch up.

"Amanda, wait!"

I swore I heard her growl, but she didn't slow down until she reached the firehouse kitchen at the far end of the corridor. She ripped open the refrigerator door, pulled out a plastic-wrapped sandwich, and then slammed the door so hard, bottles rattled inside.

She put the sandwich on the stainless-steel counter that lined one wall and stared at it, hands gripping the edge. The room was empty except for us and the smell of stale coffee that clung to the air.

"Amanda?" I took a step closer.

She blew out a loud breath but didn't turn. "Go away."

I blinked. I couldn't leave. "You stood up to him."

"I was stupid." She snorted and rolled her eyes.

"You were amazing! I never saw anybody talk to him that—"

"I was stupid!" she shouted and pounded a fist on the counter.

No. No, not stupid. Brave.

Amazingly brave.

Braver than I was.

I shoved my hands into my pockets. The folded-up note pricked a finger, and I looked away. Amanda continued to seethe at her sandwich, so I nodded once and backed off—one step, then two.

Then I stopped.

I turned and cleared my throat. "Amanda, I'm sorry. For all of this. Being here, sticking all of you with babysitting duty when I know you hate me. And for getting you in any kind of trouble with my dad. I'm sorry, and I'm grateful to you for all of it. Especially the part where you stood up to him. I've…" *I've never been able to do that. Not once.* "I usually make things worse when I try to talk to him so I…don't."

She made a sound of disgust, and I looked away. You'd think I'd be used to that reaction by now. I could take it from Dad. And I could take it from the people at school. But not from her.

"I don't get you, Logan," she said as I turned back for the door.

I stopped and waited for her to make her point.

"You have parents. Two of them! You have a home you get to stay in no matter what. And yet, you show up *here*, get everyone all sucked up into your funnel…" She trailed off, spinning her hand in the air.

I opened my mouth, about to tell her all about the hell that was my home, but then I saw her eyes. She lifted them, and I didn't see any of that anger now. I saw something that made her look desperate.

And I realized mine weren't the only problems in the world.

"You said Mr. Beckett's your foster father," I began, and her eyebrows lifted. "What happened to your parents?"

Her lips went tight for a second. Then she nodded and scraped a chair out from under the long table in the center of the room and sat down with the sandwich, still in its plastic wrap. "It was just my mom and me. I never met my dad. It was fine when I was very little. We didn't have much, but what we had was enough. For me, at least." Her hands curled into fists. "Mom met a guy. Dmitri," she added with a roll of her eyes and a sneer of disgust. "She was crazy about him—I mean full-out, *I'd die for you* in love with him. That didn't mean shit to

Dmitri—except for one thing. He knew she'd do whatever he wanted her to do. Anything he asked."

Oh God. My chest tightened, and my stomach pitched.

"He never touched me," she said, and I swore my knees buckled. I grabbed a chair and sat opposite her. "But he didn't like me around, always in the way, always ruining his plans, always seeing right through him."

I swallowed hard, not liking the direction this was taking. "What happened?"

"He got her involved in some illegal scheme. Framed her for all of it while he got off lightly when it all went bad. She's in prison."

"Jesus." I wanted to hold her, to wipe away the purple circles under her eyes, but I couldn't. "How old were you?"

"Nine." She unwrapped the sandwich and offered me half. Neither of us ate.

"Will you see her again?"

She huffed out a laugh. "She wants me to visit. But I won't. She'll get out when I'm nineteen. Maybe I'll see her then."

Ten years? Holy shit. "I'm sorry."

She looked up at me and then away, shrugging. "Not your fault."

We both went silent, picking at sandwich halves, listening to the hum of the firehouse refrigerator and the clang of gear out on the apparatus floor.

"What color are your eyes?" I blurted when the silence grew unbearable.

She blinked up at me. "What?"

"I can't tell what color they are. Been driving me crazy."

She looked away, pulled off a tiny piece of the sandwich, and popped it into her mouth. "Hazel. They're just a light brown, really, but they look different depending on what I wear."

She was wearing her blue station uniform shirt. "They're…" I coughed and tried again. "They're really nice."

"Thanks." Amanda looked around the room and then settled back on me. "Yours are nice too."

We both took bites of our sandwich halves at the same time.

As you do when you desperately need a reason to *Shut. The Hell. Up.*

She crumpled up the plastic wrap and pitched it into the trash can by the rear door. "Listen, the only reason I told you about my mom and stuff is so that you get over it."

I frowned. Get over it? How the hell did you get over your father hating your guts and wishing you'd never been born?

She ignored me and continued making her point. "I get it. You think your dad hates you, so you joined J squad to make him love you."

I opened my mouth to deny it, but of course, she was right.

"Logan, take it from me—you can't make anyone do anything. All you can do is live your life your way, so if you're doing this—any of this—for him, tell me now."

"What if I am?" When she scowled at me, I plunged ahead. "Did *you* sign up because you actually wanted to be a firefighter or because one of your foster parents made you do it?" I didn't wait for her answer. "What about the others?" I got what she was trying to say. But I also knew most kids joined J squad because of their family.

She put up both hands. "You're right. I joined the squad two years ago because Mr. Beckett thought it would be cool—not me. And just like I'm telling you right now, somebody took me aside and asked me to decide if I wanted this for me. It wouldn't have been fair to the rest of the squad to train me only to see me quit after I broke a nail."

I thought about what she said. Who was I really doing this for? Not Dad; nothing I did was or ever would be good enough for him.

I was doing this for Matt. Because I owed him. Because he asked. Because I fucking *promised*.

"How long did it take you to make that decision?" I finally asked her.

She crossed her arms, leaned back in her chair, and angled her head. "Not long. Couple of weeks, maybe." And then she smiled, and it made me smile too. "It gets inside you." She patted her chest, right over her heart. "Now, there's nothing I want more."

Her eyes, those strange, impossibly colored eyes, suddenly went wide, and she pushed away from the table. "I gotta go."

I watched her disappear out the door to the main corridor, knowing she'd just lied to me.

There *was* something she wanted more.

But what?

The loudest sound I had ever heard shattered the air before I could think about it anymore.

The tones!

I leaped from the table and hurried to the apparatus floor, forgetting all about my jellied leg muscles. I'd never seen the trucks dispatched.

My heart pounded, and I caught up to Amanda, standing out of the way as the crews from Truck 3, Engine 21, and Rescue 17 donned turnouts and climbed aboard.

Engine 21, Truck 3, Rescue 17. Residential fire. Second alarm. 78 Juniper Court. Trapped occupants.

"Please, please let this not be another arson," one of the men muttered as he swung onto the truck.

Goose bumps rose on my arms. Trapped occupants? Arson? God. The apparatus bay doors rolled up with a rumble I could feel in my stomach. Lights and sirens on, the trucks rolled out, Chief Duffy's official car in the lead.

Nobody hesitated.

Every person on those trucks was a volunteer. A second alarm meant this fire was big and dangerous. People were trapped.

And nobody hesitated.

Dad was on Engine 21. Warmth slowly spread from the center of my chest to the rest of my body and it took me a few minutes to recognize it.

Pride.

I watched the trucks disappear down the street, only then realizing Amanda was next to me. "I'm in, Amanda. All in." I didn't stop to analyze it. The words left my mouth, and I knew in my heart that I meant it, I wanted this. Not because of Dad or Matt, but because of *me*. Laughing, I grabbed her arms and planted a smacking kiss on her lips.

She went still.

Holy shit. What did I do? I was just about to let her go when she leaned in and kissed me back.

Really kissed me.

It didn't last long. A whisper. A sip. A breath. But it damn near rocked my socks off.

She jerked out of my arms like a rubber band snapping. I was still grinning like a moron. And Amanda?

She looked like she'd been gut-shot.

"Amanda!"

Mr. Beckett's sharp voice reverberated around the empty apparatus floor. A look of pure panic crossed her face, but she managed to erase it by the time she turned to face her foster father. Without a word, she walked away.

***

By the time I got home, all I wanted to do was crawl into the shower and then bed—who cared what order?

Tucker had other ideas.

He barked and circled me and leaped up to kiss me.

Kiss me.

Jesus H. Kristofferson, I'd just kissed Amanda Jamison. I was no expert, but I was pretty sure she'd kissed me right back.

It probably meant nothing. She didn't even like me, not really. She was only helping me because the chief made her. Amanda Jamison was hot, no doubt about it. But me? I was nothing special at all. Tucker was the only one truly happy to see me. And Alex.

Amanda never smiled at me—not really. Not the way she did on that first day, when she thought I was Matt.

Oh fuck.

That explained the kiss.

The dog cried by the door, and I sighed. I fastened the leash to Tucker's collar and dragged myself out to walk him. But Tucker had a mission. He pulled and tugged on the leash, hauling me down the street. It took me half an hour to get him back in the house, where he proceeded to give me the canine side eye until I shut myself in the bathroom.

I felt a little better after I showered and popped a few ibuprofen tablets. I'd just kicked back with the remote control when a knock on the front door sent Tucker into a frenzy.

"Hey, Alex. What's up?"

He raised both eyebrows as he bent over to greet my dog. "You haven't looked at your phone."

Aw, shit. I hadn't.

I pulled it out of my pocket. Four text messages about the movie we were supposed to see. It started…hell. Half an hour ago. "Jeez, man, I am so sorry."

He shrugged and continued scratching Tucker's head. "When I didn't hear back from you, I considered seeing the movie alone, but I look forward to our spirited debates over the plot too much for that."

I winced. "Did you buy our tickets?"

He hesitated a moment and then shrugged again.

Fuck. I pulled out my wallet and handed him enough to cover his ticket and mine, to make up for my mistake. He stared at the cash for a moment and then nodded.

Alex was between jobs again. He had a hard time staying employed. He was smarter than the average bear—a lot smarter—and found it almost impossible not to improve processes at his various places of employment, or worse, tell his bosses they were doing it all wrong. Despite his genius IQ, people were surprisingly resistant to a teenager showing them how to improve kitchen efficiencies by thirty percent or how to slash costs simply by reducing the temperature in the dining room.

I wasn't working either. After Matt died, there didn't seem to be much point, since I wouldn't be here much longer.

"I'm really sorry."

Alex gave me a tight-lipped smile. "As joining the junior squad was my suggestion in the first place, it wouldn't be logical to blame you for your forgetting your other obligations."

"Logical. Uh-huh." I faked a smile because the *forgetting your other obligations* part stung a bit. "You're not an obligation, Alex."

His eyes snapped to mine and then away. He wasn't buying this, and I was way too tired to think of ways to convince him. So I opted for a change of subject. "How about some Netflix?"

To my total surprise, he shook his head. "No. You look terrible. I'll leave." But instead of heading for the door, he crouched down to Tucker's level and continued scratching my dog's head.

I sat back down, wincing at the muscle pain. "So aside from waiting for me, what did you do today?"

Alex took out his ever-present tablet, swiped the screen, and nodded. "Ah. I finished my app, submitted an idea for a research paper to Dr. Bronson, and won six chess games."

My eyes popped. "Six? Jesus, Alex, shouldn't you pace yourself or something?" The chess club was ready to vote him off their island.

He laughed. "It was great, really. I'm still experimenting with mating patterns, so I got to test my top picks."

"Which are?"

He laughed louder and shook his head. "Nice try. If I tell you, you'll read all that's printed on each and be able to defend against them."

I squirmed. "Um, sure." I wasn't sure, but I thought Alex just called me a cheater.

"So how did J squad go today?"

I settled deeper into the sofa and wondered how to answer that. I decided not to tell him about the kiss. "I'm really not sure. Aside from the usual tense moments with my dad, we played dodgeball in full turnout gear—"

"Why?"

"It helps us learn tank conservation."

"Why dodgeball, specifically?"

I shifted again. Sometimes, Alex's giant brain made him annoying. "It's one way of simulating the kind of physical exertion needed to fight a real fire."

He cocked his head and then shook it a moment later. "No, it's not. Firefighters have few, if any, reasons to throw objects. It would have been better to play tug-of-war, to mimic hose-lifting. Why not simply practice hauling people up and down ladders?"

I shut my eyes for a second. "Because we work with very limited resources. We had only a half hour to practice, so tossing around a ball was an easy impromptu exercise the entire squad could perform with minimal setup."

Alex still wasn't convinced but let the matter drop, thank God. "How did you do?"

"I ran out of air after eleven minutes."

"Is that bad?"

I nodded. "Yeah. The tanks are rated for thirty minutes, but nobody ever gets that long. But eleven was pretty bad. I have a goal to reach sixteen minutes by the end of the month."

"A five-minute gain would be a forty-five percent improvement," he said, impressed. "You have about three weeks to achieve it."

Oh God. "Yep."

Alex glanced at me and frowned. "You don't sound convinced."

I spread my arms up, winced when they screamed their protest, and let them fall. "Look at me, man. Do I look anything like the guys in Matt's calendar?"

Alex laughed and rolled his eyes. "Oh right! He was highly insult-ed he was rejected for November." I didn't laugh, and he nudged me. "You're not seriously holding yourself to that standard? Eighty percent of the LVFD would fail. Even your dad has that paunch."

I acknowledged that point. "True, but Max wouldn't. Neither would Gage." Both of them were built like ads for some sports drink.

"Reece, I have a question."

I raised my eyebrows.

"You're doing this to get your dad's attention, right? Do you really need to kill yourself in the process?"

I coughed and stood up. "Um, well, I guess I'm trying to do this right, you know? Prove to him I can be something he can be proud of. If I can't even breathe right, what chance do I have?"

Alex opened his mouth to argue and then changed his mind. He nodded gravely. "Guess I won't see you for a while. You have a mission now. A promise to keep."

I tried to untangle my thoughts. Alex was my best friend.

But I didn't tell him that my promise was no longer what was driving me.

Chapter 10
Amanda

I jolted awake, heart pounding. Crap, it was two o'clock in the morning. After the day I had, I should have slept like the dead.

It was a foster home thing…you never really slept soundly. You worried about every little sound, wondered if someone was going to sneak in and steal your stuff.

Or worse.

Mr. Beckett never said a word about the kiss. Maybe he didn't see it. I'd turned around, braced for the disappointed expression, the tone that said "Pack your bags, young lady." Instead, he'd wagged his finger. "The trucks just rolled out, and I know it's exciting, but you have work to do, don't you?"

I'd gone along with him, pretending my lips weren't branded by that kiss.

"No, it's fine. We had a great session today. Tank conservation," I'd babbled, but Mr. Beckett hadn't noticed.

"Did you hear the alarm? It's a big one."

I'd almost cried in relief. Mr. Beckett had been so jazzed about the trucks rolling, he really hadn't seen the kiss.

It was so cool. We'd climbed into his car, a little gold Nissan littered with folded-up potato chip bags, empty coffee cups, and old lesson plans, and rode over to Juniper Court. Junior cadets weren't allowed at working fire scenes. All the practice we did never involved flames. But there was no rule against driving by.

"Oh my God, it's fully involved," Mr. Beckett had said as we crawled by. We couldn't see much from the main road, but even from there, we'd been able to see the flames towering above the roofline. "Look at that, Mandy! I think they're using the deck gun."

I'd stared at the high-powered stream of water aimed at the roof, and Mr. Beckett accelerated with a sigh.

"Pretty cool, huh, Mandy?"

I'd nodded and smiled. "Yeah. Pretty cool."

I curled my hands into fists and punched my pillow. Stupid, stupid, stupid! I almost messed up everything. I left the bed Mrs. Beckett decorated with pillows in my favorite shade of blue and crept into the hall. Downstairs in the kitchen, I found Larry silhouetted in the slash of light from the open refrigerator.

"Hey, were you outside? I thought I heard the door shut."

He whipped around with a gasp. "Jesus, Amanda." He turned back to browse for leftovers and grabbed the meatloaf. The Becketts were cool about us eating their food, which was handy, since I was convinced Larry had a tapeworm or something. He grabbed some bread and a bottle of ketchup and made a sandwich. "I didn't go anywhere. I was in bed."

"Did you have a bad dream or something?"

He shook his head, and brown hair fell over his eyes. "I was hungry."

"It's two a.m., Larry. Did you get any sleep?"

He lifted his shoulders. "Yeah, a little. Want in on this?"

God, no. I shook my head, sank into a kitchen chair, and yawned.

Larry put the food away and joined me at the table. "You look zonked."

"Up early dealing with a bunch of guys in bunker gear all morning? Yeah, *zonked* pretty much covers it."

Larry smirked and took a healthy bite out of his sandwich.

I brought my knees up, curled my arms around them, and sighed. I could still smell the savory scents from that night's dinner. Mrs. Beckett cooked real food. Oh, she's not a chef or anything, but she's a hell of a lot better than that one foster house where I had to write down every bite I took.

"I like it here," Larry whispered in the dark.

I thought about that for a second. "Me too."

He took another bite and stared at his sandwich. "I got hit once for this."

"Eating?"

"No. Taking extra."

"That sucks." We had it good here. Well, as long as we never touched Mr. Beckett's potato chips. Mrs. Beckett bought individual bags of them by the carton from the warehouse store. I was kind of surprised Mr. Beckett wasn't a giant walking zit from all that grease.

"Yeah." He licked ketchup off a finger. "The Becketts are kinda normal, you know?"

I shrugged. I was pretty sure all foster families had quirks and secrets, but the Becketts were sitcom parents compared to that one home where the parents were like military commanders, always barking orders.

"My dad used to sneak out after he thought I was sleeping and come back with all this crap like computers and cell phones and cameras."

Larry's dad was in year two of a five-year sentence. The court had not been able to find his mom. I wondered if they were still looking. "Oh, Larry, I'm sorry."

Larry shook his head. "It's not your fault." He chewed quietly. "I don't miss him," he whispered.

He grabbed what was left of his sandwich and hurried back up the stairs, bare feet squeaking on the wooden floor. I thought about it for another minute and followed. I kind of missed my mom—or the life we used to have before Dmitri. But now? I hope I never see her again.

I lay in my warm bed under yards and yards of soft downy comforter and burrowed into pillows. My stomach didn't rumble—not from hunger or fear. I thought about tall boys with lean muscle and toasty-brown hair. Somewhere, in the back of my brain, just before sleep pulled me under, I was sure I heard the front door squeak open.

***

The sun woke me up late Sunday morning. I shot out of bed and hurried downstairs, biting back a curse when my foot landed on something sharp. At the foot of the stairs, there was…a tiny piece of wood and dirt. A piece of tree bark or something and some dark flecks. I bent to examine the chunk and discovered it wasn't bark—it was mulch.

Larry probably forgot to wipe his feet, and Mrs. Beckett would have a heart attack. She was a ruthless housekeeper. I headed for the kitchen, tossed the chunk of wood into the trash, and grabbed a plate.

"There's the sleepyhead," Mr. Beckett said, grinning at me over his coffee cup.

"Eggs, Amanda?" Mrs. Beckett stood by the stove, wrapped in a robe. Larry was already half-done with his breakfast.

"Yes, please." I handed her my plate.

"I was just about to come up, make sure you're not sick." Mr. Beckett said.

"Yeah, sorry about that. Didn't sleep well."

"Oh?" The smile slid off his face.

"Yeah, I heard a noise in the middle of the night. I got up but didn't notice anything weird."

His forehead creased, and then it was gone. "This is a safe place. You know you have nothing to be afraid of here, right?"

I felt a tiny pinch under my heart and smiled at the sincerity on his face. I didn't know if it was God or just dumb luck, but however I got here, I was grateful. I loved it here, but I could never tell the Becketts that, of course. After Mrs. Merodie, I was careful never to fall in love with a family again.

Of course, there are some houses you couldn't wait to leave. The last house… I shivered, remembering the creepy son who liked to sneak up on me. There was no lock on my bedroom door, so I used to hang stuff over it at night, hoping the noise would wake me if he came in.

It did.

He fell and broke his wrist and told everybody I'd invited him to my room. They believed him and kicked me out. And yet, even Creepy Kyle was better than the house before that one, where food was rationed. Oh, I didn't just like it here, I *loved* it. I loved Mrs. B's cooking, and I loved the fire service, which I wouldn't have learned about if Mr. Beckett hadn't encouraged me. I wished I could tell them both how much I loved it here and that I hoped they'd keep me until I aged out of foster care and even after that, how I wished we could stay in touch and have visits or spend holidays together.

But saying all that out loud risked losing it.

"Yes, I know. Thank you." I nodded stiffly.

Mr. Beckett reached out a hand to squeeze mine. "You never have to thank us." He poured some juice and slid it to me, and I hid my face behind the glass, hoping it concealed the tears in my eyes. "So how's your new cadet doing?"

I froze for a second. Dangerous territory! "Um, good." I shrugged. "I've got the whole squad working one-on-one with him, studying the NFPA guidelines and the textbooks."

My foster dad waved his hand. "Firefighting's not about textbooks, Amanda. It's about heart and guts." He put down his coffee cup and leaned over the table. "Did I ever tell you about Captain Ray Jenner? Toughest firefighter I ever buffed for." He shook his head and laughed once. "I couldn't have been much older than you, Larry."

Larry looked up from his plate. "What does that mean?"

"Buff? It means I was a big fan—still am. Buffs like me used to hang out at fire stations, help out. It's like volunteering, except for a particular guy."

"Like his assistant?"

Mr. Beckett laughed. "Yes, though assistant is a bit of a stretch. I was more like his personal flunky."

"Cool." Larry nodded and drained the rest of his juice.

"It was very cool. Except when you were afraid of the guy you're buffing for. Ray was a big brute of a guy—like your Chief Duffy, only mean." Mr. Beckett pointed at me. "I'm not lying when I tell you my bladder let go whenever I was close to him."

"Mark! Too much information," Mrs. Beckett said on a groan and joined us with a plate of her own.

"Sorry, Diane." He winced. "Anyway, when I was about thirteen, I was seriously in love with firefighting. I wanted to join the department, but they didn't have a junior squad where I grew up. So all I could do was hang around the firehouse and hope to see some action. I'd fetch newspapers and coffee from the corner store for the men. I ran cloths over the trucks, whatever they needed, and believe me, I was happy to do it. Except when it was Ray Jenner."

Mr. Beckett's eyes glowed with excitement and maybe a little awe. "Ray used to love scaring the tar out of me. 'Beckett!' he'd bark, and I'd quiver in my shoes. 'Go out there and sweep the front.' He'd hand me a small kitchen broom." Mr. Beckett waved a hand toward the broom that leaned against a corner. "I'd go out in front of the station and spend hours sweeping the same six leaves because they'd just blow from one end of the lot to the other. He never thanked me. Not once." Mr. Beckett kicked back in his chair, sipped more coffee, and fell deeper into the past. "The other guys always did, but not him. He thought I should thank him. So I never did. I was kind of a badass."

Larry laughed. Mr. Beckett was a tall, thin man with round wire glasses and big teeth who loved shuffling around the house in corduroy slippers. He was the polar opposite of badass.

"No, really. I was," Mr. Beckett insisted with a grin. "So I'd show up whenever I didn't have chores or homework and then end up just doing more stupid chores. All I wanted to do was hang out and be part of the brotherhood, you know? I wanted to hear the stories about charging into the pit of hell, snatching some poor victim back from its greedy claws, and beating flames down with nothing but a can and a Halligan."

I nodded. I totally understood that need. Nobody becomes a firefighter for the money. My heart pinched again—I wouldn't have this, wouldn't have my squad, my brothers, if I hadn't been placed in the Becketts' home.

"What's a Halligan?" Larry asked.

"It's kind of like a crowbar," I told him. "Except it's got a fork on one end and a blade. We use it to bust through doors and walls."

His eyes went round. "Cool."

"Oh, it was cool. It was all cool. I wanted to hear all their stories about pretty ladies who thanked the guys for saving their lives. I wanted to see the medals the mayor pinned on their chests. God, I wanted that so much," Mr. Beckett said with a slap to the table for emphasis.

"So how come you're a chemistry teacher and not a fireman?"

Mr. Beckett tightened his lips and shook his head, not looking at any of us.

"I tried. Flunked the training program."

Whoa. I never knew that.

"Anyhow, one day, I had some time, so I headed to the firehouse, but they had the purple banners hanging. I didn't know who died, only that someone did. I moved in quietly and just waited for someone to tell me what needed doing. But nobody did. The truckies, they were sitting around a table on the apparatus floor, faces white and eyes haunted. I wanted to help—I *had* to help them—so I just grabbed that dumb kitchen broom and started sweeping outside. I swept for an hour, maybe two. When I had that lot whistle clean, I went back inside the house to put away the broom. The truckies—the guys sitting around that table? They were crying. Every one of them." Mr. Beckett's eyes misted. "One by one, they shook my hand, and I knew. That's when I knew. It was Mean Ray Jenner they'd hung the banners for."

"What happened?" Larry asked quietly, sweeping hair out his eyes.

Mr. Beckett took another sip and shifted on his chair. "I don't know. Some said he got lost in the smoke and panicked. Other stories I heard said he pulled out two kids, then went back in for their parents. To this day, I don't know what really happened. Guys don't talk about it. They feel it hard. But they go back the next day and keep doing the job."

There was awe in Mr. Beckett's voice, and it made me think about John Logan. When Matt died, he felt it hard—that was obvious to all of us. But he did the job. I thought it was a sign of strength. Something to admire.

I didn't think that anymore.

Chapter 11
Reece

Matt taught me everything. I learned a few things from you too. I learned to run away when my emotions got stronger than I was.

I unlocked the front door, led my dog into the hall, and unfastened his leash. I tossed my keys on the hall table and found Mom in the kitchen, groping around for coffee.

"Don't bother." I took her hand, put a to-go cup in it, and then poured some fresh water into Tucker's bowl.

She murmured something I wasn't sure was English, took a sip, and stared at me over the cup. "You're up early," she eventually managed to say.

I shrugged. I didn't always sleep well, so this wasn't unusual. "I have stuff to do. Took Tucker for a walk and bought you a doughnut too." I opened the bag, took out a couple of doughnuts—sugar frosted for her, jelly for me—and opened a cabinet for some plates. A mug that said *World's Best Dad* stared back at me. I gave it to Dad when I was in kindergarten. They'd had some lame sale at the school. We all brought in a dollar, and that's what I'd picked out.

No surprise that he left it here when he moved out.

I dropped it into the trash and then grabbed a few plates. Mom's eyes went round and then closed in pleasure when she sniffed the doughnut I held out to her. "You're trying to make me fat, aren't you?"

"No!" Jeez, can't a guy do something nice without an ulterior motive?

Mom put down her cup and her doughnut and pulled out one of the iron stools at the long granite counter. "Reece, I have something to talk to you about."

I put my own cup down with a frown. That sounded really serious. "What?"

"Um, a nice man from my book club asked me out to Sunday brunch. And I said yes."

Sunday brunch? Lame. Probably watched too many *How I Met Your Mother* episodes.

Mom sat at the counter and angled her head, waiting for me to say something. *She's still pretty.* The thought stabbed through my brain and circled for a moment, then tanked with a thud that made me wince. When I was little, I thought my mom was the most beautiful woman on earth. Then I got older and stopped thinking of her as anything but Mom. But sitting there in her flannel pajamas, brown hair matted on one side, standing straight up on the other, and a tiny bit of powdered sugar at the corner of her mouth, still, she was *beautiful*. My heart gave a painful squeeze, and words fell out of my mouth before I could stop them.

"I love you, Mom."

Her eyes went round, then filled with love and tears. Maybe that's why I said it. To see that reaction, to know at least someone loved me back. "Thank you, Reece, but you didn't answer my question. Does it bother you?" The sugar decorating the corner of her mouth where she smiled only made her more beautiful to me.

I shook my head. "No." And that was pure truth. "Go. Have fun. You deserve it, Mom."

The little smile on her lips faded, but she nodded. "You don't think I'm being selfish? That I'm pretending?"

I blinked at her, scratched the back of my neck. "Pretending what?"

She sipped her coffee and waved her hand. "Oh, you know. Pretending everything's fine, everything's normal."

Normal. I snorted. Not exactly one of my favorite words. "Mom, I have no idea what you're talking about. But if you want to go out on this date, you should do it, no matter what anybody else says." Especially if *anybody else* was Dad.

She blew the hair out of her eyes and put down her cup. "You know this date doesn't mean I don't miss Matt, right?"

I dropped my doughnut back on the plate. "Yeah, I know. I'm sorry. I'm so sorry."

She reached over and squeezed my hand. "I never blamed you. Not once, Reece."

"I was driving, Mom. With only a permit."

She shot up straight. "So you *do* think I'm pretending."

"Again, pretending what, exactly?"

She gave me this helpless look. "That I'm over losing him." She slid off the stool, opened another cabinet, and found a treat for Tucker. He took it happily in a single bite. "That's what everybody thinks."

Everybody meaning Dad. "*Everybody's* wrong. *Everybody* can't hear you cry at night because they're not here. I am."

"You are." She pressed her fingers under her eyes for a second, then waved her hands. "Oh, Reece, I'm tired. So tired of making excuses, tired of trying to find the right balance between you and Dad. The truth is I'm glad the tension and all that anxiety is gone. I don't want him to come home. And I want you to quit the junior squad."

I drew in a sharp breath. I loved Mom, and there was so much I owed her, but this? I couldn't do it. "Mom, I get it—the tension and the anxiety and stuff. But I don't want to quit—not now. I…well, I like it."

Mom crossed the room, picked up her cup, and tried to look cheerful. "Does that mean things are going well?" She sipped more coffee.

Shrugging, I sat beside her. "Okay, I guess. Dad tolerates me because the chief said he has to. But the juniors are great. Everybody's been helping me catch up. And Amanda's been giving me books to read. You know, inside tips."

Mom's eyebrows quirked. "Amanda. Are you two—" She waved her hand.

Hell. I hid my face behind my own coffee cup and squirmed. "No, Mom."

"What's she like?"

Ask me something easy, like what's the value of pi to the sixteenth decimal. "I don't know. She's tough. Smart. And really misses Matt."

"Ah. She's the tall blond who came to Matt's funeral. I remember." She crumpled up the doughnut wrapper and then squeezed my hand. "Honey, I signed the permission form because—well, because I was angry. But maybe that was a mistake. Maybe you should just let this go. Your dad is…oh, you know how he is."

I grabbed the paper ball, flicked it across the counter, and tried to swallow my disappointment. That was Mom-speak for "Don't get your hopes up." Maybe she was right. Dad wasn't gonna change for her or for me. But I had to try before I—

"I'm going to get dressed," Mom said. "Hey, could you run to the Home Depot and pick up the paint? I'll leave the details upstairs."

"Yeah, sure."

She grabbed the paper ball and the empty cups and pitched them in the trash bin. Instead of heading for the door, she wrapped her arms around me and kissed my head. "Thanks for the treat, honey. I love you. Be safe." She ruffled my hair and left the room.

I stared after her for a long moment. Then I pulled out my note and scribbled a few more lines. I carefully refolded the note and put it back in my pocket, lowered my head, and screamed inside until Tucker dropped a saliva-slimed toy in my lap.

I picked it up with two fingers, gave it a toss, watched my dog chase after it, and sighed.

I'd trade places with him in a nanosecond.

***

After Mom left for her date, I started reading one of the firefighting books Bear gave me and lost track of time. Arson investigation, or fire forensics, was seriously interesting. I used to think that fire burned up everything in its path, including evidence, but the book suggested differently. Investigators looked at things like char patterns and depth, heat shadows, the color of the smoke, and even the crowd watching a fire for clues suggesting arson. An out-of-balance fire triangle—oxygen, fuel, and heat sources—could mean arson.

Tucker leaped on the sofa, sending my books flying.

"You want to join J squad, Tucker?"

Tucker's ears twitched, and he stared at me, big soulful eyes asking what the hell a dog had to do to get a treat around here. I scooped up the books and saw a section on fire science.

"Hey, Tucker, look." I showed him the book he'd knocked over, and he woofed. "People earn degrees in fire science—hmm."

That was an interesting idea.

I hadn't really given a lot of thought to college. I'd probably study math.

If I weren't planning to leave. But I was, so no point in making plans.

But studying math might be fun. I liked numbers. I liked asking questions that had definite answers, answers that could be unequivocally proven. Numbers were clear. Pure. Reliable and consistent, when the rest of my world was anything but.

I switched books. The next one was a collection of stories from NYFD veterans. These guys saw it all, fought it all. They had smoke headaches. Did the SCBA gear prevent those? And heart ailments— the human body was never designed to haul seventy or eighty pounds of gear up a dozen flights of steps after being in a dead sleep less than fifteen minutes earlier. I read that book cover to cover, because those guys were clear and pure and reliable, just like math. They were firefighters, and they fucking loved the job they did so much, they'd do it for free.

Volunteers. Like me.

The thought filled me up.

I wrote out a list of questions to ask the next time I saw my squadmates and outlined a plan for translating everything I read into practical application. That was going to be tough. I hadn't been near flame or smoke yet, so I had no evidence I could use to predict my behavior in those circumstances. I could mimic heavy smoke with a blindfold. But extreme heat? That one would be a challenge I could only meet with experience. Just like Amanda said—*knowing* and *doing* were two different things.

By lunchtime, I'd walked Tucker, written out a few pages of questions, closed the books, and headed out on Mom's paint run. She wanted to update the main bathroom, take down the ancient wallpaper, and just paint the room a soothing shade of green. The paper was mostly gone, except for a few stubborn sections. I looked at the samples she'd tacked to the wall and wondered who the hell named these shades. *Eel Green?* No, thanks. She'd already splashed a sample patch on the bare wall. It was sage green. I took her list and her car, drove to the Home Depot, and wandered up and down the aisles while I waited for the color mixing, grabbing brushes, rollers, a tray, and some rolls of tape. I came around a corner and bam! Smacked into somebody's cart.

"I'm sorry, I didn't—" I started to apologize but clamped my lips together when I heard a muttered curse from a familiar voice.

"What the hell are *you* doing in a Home Depot?" My dad looked at me like I'd just jumped naked out of a cake or something.

I waved a hand over my cart. "Mom wants to paint the bathroom."

He folded his arms, examining the contents of my cart. "Did you tell them it's for a bathroom? You probably didn't. Come on."

Without waiting, he swung around, strode back to the paint counter, and told the kid he needed some mildew inhibitor added to paint that he was already mixing. The kid slid me a look of annoyance but grabbed some bottles. Dad grabbed more stir sticks and tossed them into my cart.

"You got rubber bands?"

What? "I don't know. Maybe at home."

"Put rubber bands over the can, and use them to scrape the brush."

"Okay." I blinked. I must have tripped on the space-time continuum and fallen into a parallel universe.

He reached into my cart and shoved stuff around. "This is the wrong roller. This is for popcorn ceilings. Stucco. You want a smoother nap."

Oh.

He tossed the correct roller cover into the cart, threw the other into a bin of paint brushes.

"Here you go." The guy behind the counter slid my two cans of mildew-resistant paint toward me. I hefted them back into my cart.

"Is all the wallpaper off the wall?"

I shrugged. "Most of it."

He shook his head. "Not good enough. The walls have to be perfect. The better you prep, the better the results. Come on."

I followed him down another aisle, where he snagged a bottle of wallpaper remover from a shelf and put it in my cart. "Oh, you need the thing with the teeth too. I don't think we have one," he muttered.

I froze midstep. *We?* He threw something called a perforating tool into the cart and followed that up with a putty knife.

"That should do it, I think." He nodded, even managed an uncomfortable smile. "You know how to use the roller?" He picked it up and waved it in the air. "You want to make a big W on the wall, get a good spread of paint, then go back over it, fill in the spaces."

A big W. Sure. "Makes sense."

He stared at me—just stood in the middle of a Home Depot aisle and looked at me like someone had clubbed him over the head. Abruptly, he shook his head and said, "Well, I guess that's it."

"Hope so." I took out my wallet and counted the bills Mom had left for me.

There was an eye roll. I didn't know what that meant. "Here." He shoved a hundred-dollar bill at me.

I wanted to crumple it up into a ball and stuff it down his throat. But I couldn't. I'd never been able to stand up to him. I took it and slipped it into my wallet. "Thanks."

His eyebrows went up, but he said only, "No problem."

"Okay, well, see ya." I headed for the cash register line and left him staring after me.

A couple of hours later, Tucker started barking the house down seconds before the doorbell rang. I was elbow-deep in scraping wallpaper. I wiped my sticky hands on a towel, jogged down the stairs to answer it, and gaped.

"Dad. What are you doing here?"

"Wondering that myself," he muttered. "Thought I'd give you a hand with the bathroom. I did promise your mother I'd paint it but—" He trailed off, but I knew where he was going. Matt died, and the bathroom update suddenly got shuffled to the bottom of a very long list. "Problem with that?"

I snapped my mouth shut. "No, no problem. Come on up." I headed back upstairs. "I've got that goop sitting on what's left of the wallpaper."

Dad surveyed the working site I'd arranged. On the large landing at the top of the stairs that led to all the rooms on the second floor, I'd laid out a drop cloth, the cans of paint, and all the crap he'd tossed into my cart. He lifted his eyebrows but didn't say anything.

This was a joke; it had to be. He couldn't stand to be near me, and suddenly, he's buying paint, offering to redo an entire room with me? I lowered my shoulders, picked up the knife, and started scraping. I'd gotten all of the paper scraped except for the wall behind the sink and toilet.

"You made a good dent in this." Dad nodded, and my jaw dropped again. His eyes skimmed down my torso, and I had to resist the urge to squirm. But again, he didn't say anything. He just took the putty knife from my hand and started scraping paper from behind the toilet. We worked in silence—him scraping wallpaper into confetti, me picking up the scraps and shoving them into a trash bag. He showed me how to disconnect the sink so we could scrape the paper behind that too.

When the walls were clean and dry, I grabbed a few rolls of tape and taped covers over the fixtures. Dad grabbed the drop cloth and spread that over the floor. I pried the cover off the first can of paint and was about to dip in a brush when I remembered the rubber bands I'd left in the hall outside the room. I grabbed a few and stretched one over the can of paint the way he told me. I dipped in a brush, scraped the excess off against the rubber band, and painted a wide border at the top of a wall. Dad watched me with a flicker of…of something in his eyes.

"What?" I froze in my return trip to the paint can.

He jerked and shook his head. "Sorry. Didn't mean to stare. Just wondering when you got so jacked."

Jacked? *Me?* I glanced down at my body. My shirt was wet in spots from the wallpaper removal goop. That shit was gross. "I don't know. I've been working out." *Passing out* was more accurate, but I didn't tell him that.

He didn't say anything, just kept giving me that weird look. I painted another stripe.

"You got another brush? I'll start this wall."

It was my turn for a weird look. "Um, yeah, I think this was a three-pack." I indicated the staging area. A few seconds later, he was back with his own brush. We cut in the borders on all the walls. I grabbed the paint tray and tipped some paint into the well.

"You should open the other can, mix them both. Sometimes the colors are off a bit."

I nodded and opened the second can, catching another one of Dad's weird looks from the corner of my eye. "What?" I asked, annoyed.

"Sorry, Peanut. Guess I'm not used to doing stuff with you without a fight or a hundred questions," he said with half a smile.

I put the paint can down with some force. "Do you even like peanut butter cups?"

He shook his head. "Not really, why?" He tore open the plastic on the roller cover, slid it over the roller, and dipped it into the paint.

"Why do you keep calling me that?"

He stopped scraping paint off the roller long enough to frown. "I don't know. Habit, I guess. It was cute when you were little."

It wasn't cute; it was mean. It's always been mean. I took a deep breath and spoke my mind. "I hate it." I used to cry whenever he called me that, but he'd laugh and say, *Toughen up!*

My shoulders tightened, anticipating his usual response, but it never came.

"Your grandpa? He used to call me Jackie. Fucking hated that."

I almost dropped my paint brush. "Where the hell did he get *that* from?"

Dad shrugged. "I don't know who started it. I was John Junior, so I guess they called me Jack instead of John to tell us apart. He always called me Jackie whenever I did something he thought wasn't manly enough."

I stared at my dad in his work boots, jeans, and T-shirt that clung to his broad shoulders and revealed the tats he had on both biceps and wondered how the hell anybody thought he wasn't manly. My grandfather died when I was little. I didn't remember him. I knew he was an NYFD firefighter. Died of a cancer that was probably smoke-related.

"Do you—" I broke off, silently beating myself up for kicking the sleeping bear.

"What?"

"Nothing. I just wondered if you miss him."

Dad angled his head and dragged the roller over the W he'd painted. "Nah, not really. You probably think that's harsh, but my old man was a harsh guy."

Ironic much? I said nothing, just poured more paint into the tray. I snuck glances at my dad while he rolled paint onto the walls. His shoulders were tight, and there was this rhythmic twitch in his jaw.

The reason why hit me like a kick to the groin. The paint can lid slipped through my fingers and landed on the drop cloth, sticky side down. He was nervous. No, no, he was anxious—as anxious as I was. So why the hell was he here? Was that story his way of telling me he'd quit calling me candy names? Did we actually *bond* over something?

A dozen possibilities circled my brain, including a fume buzz, but I shook them off. I didn't care what his reasons were; I only cared that he was here. Maybe this was a sign. Maybe he'd move back in. We hadn't killed each other. It was a good sign.

It had to be.

When he put the roller down to stretch his back, I picked it up and carefully rolled paint in a big W pattern so he wouldn't start in on me.

We painted side by side until all the walls were covered. It didn't take long at all.

"Sage green, huh?" Dad took a step back and scanned the room. "Not bad. Where's your mother? She should check it out, make sure it meets with her approval."

"Out." *Oh shit.*

"Out where?"

"Um, well, she had a—" Holy hell. Now would be a great time to start washing the brushes. I uncovered the tub, turned on the water, and got busy.

"Reece, she had a what?" He crouched to pick up a roll of paper towels and wiped paint off his hands.

I kept my eyes pinned to the green paint circling the drain. "Um, she had a date."

He snapped up straight. "A *what*?"

I swallowed hard and turned to face him. "She had a date, Dad."

His face went red, and he shot out a hand to clutch the door frame. He stared at the painted walls, at me, and abruptly turned away. "Unbelievable. Matt's dead a couple of months, and she's out with other guys?"

My blood started to boil. "Dad. She misses Matt—"

"Bullshit!" He exploded. "If she missed her dead kid, would she be—" Abruptly, he clamped his mouth shut and wiped a hand over his red face.

I thought it over for a minute and decided I felt bad for him. It took me a minute to decide, because it shocked me that I did. "Come here. I want to show you something." I led him to Mom's room—the bedroom that used to be theirs. I unmade the side of the bed she slept on. "Look."

Dad crossed his arms. "What? It's a pillow."

"It's Matt's pillow, Dad." Underneath the pillow, I showed him the folded square of blue cloth. "This is one of his LVFD shirts. She sleeps with these. Every night. And she cries."

Dad shook his head, turned away, walked back to the bathroom, and stared at the paint drying on the walls. "She should talk to *me*. Goddamn it, she shouldn't be dating other guys."

My jaw clenched. This was so typical, blaming everybody else for the shit he caused. "You *left*. Remember?"

"Yeah." His face fell apart. He shut his eyes, and when he opened them, I swore they were wet. "I remember." He shoved past me, walked down the stairs, and slammed the door on his way out.

I stood in that bathroom, fists clenched and muscles trembling, trying to hold it all in, hold it back, but it was too much. Something deep inside me snapped, and I drove my fist through the sage-green wall.

Chapter 12
Amanda

At school Monday, I dodged slow walkers swinging backpacks and practically ran right into Reece on my way to my first period of the afternoon.

"Hey."

"Oh, hey, Amanda." He gave me one of those long, slow looks that was kind of like a slow-burning fuse.

"Meet us on the field right after school."

He blinked. "What, today?"

"Yeah, Logan. Today. What's wrong? You got a date?"

"No." He shifted his weight from one foot to the other. A slow red flush crawled up his neck. My fingers itched to follow it. "I'll see you later."

For a minute, I watched him walk away. If I were a regular kid, I'd move in on Reece Logan. He was cute—all the Logans were. But I'm not a regular kid. I'm a rental. I didn't have the luxury of a second chance when I screwed up. How many chances did parents give their real kids? What a stupid question. It didn't matter how many times *real* kids screwed up, because I wasn't anyone's real kid. Anyone who wasn't in prison, I mean. I could be returned at any time, exchanged for a younger model, and I could never afford to forget that, no matter how much I liked a boy.

Did I like Reece? Maybe I just felt sorry for him. Maybe it was just too personal for me, seeing somebody's family shredded. Reece had this look of desperation that went from quiet to full-out violent storm levels. It drove him. I knew that much from the day he walked into the LVFD. I understood that; I felt desperate too.

And that's why I was helping him.

I didn't know much about family, except for the old reruns of *The Waltons* Mrs. Merodie used to like to watch. Families are supposed to support each other, band together. Family forgives. Family always comes home. But real life was *way* different. My father wasn't home long enough to become one of my memories, my mother wouldn't get out of prison for at least three more years, and foster families traded me like a two-year-old cell phone. *Real life* meant in fourteen months, I could be homeless.

A statistic.

Technically, I had until twenty-one before I aged out of the foster care system, but the sad truth is when parents rent a kid, they want them young and cute. Eighteen-year-old wards of the state who get kicked out usually end up in group homes.

In other words, *hell*.

I wanted to turn a hose on Reece Logan for having the nerve to show his face in the house where his brother used to work. So why was I suddenly imagining what it would be like to break some rules with him? Why was he so tempting?

I made my way to Mr. Serrano's office for our weekly appointment.

"Hi, Amanda. Come on in."

"Hey."

"Your social worker wants a report. I've talked to your teachers, and every one of them has nothing but praise for you."

My eyebrows shot up. This was news. "Even Mr. Anton?" Mr. Anton was my math teacher, and math teachers were, by definition, not of my world.

Mr. Serrano laughed. "Yes, even Mr. Anton. Your grade in his class has improved." He tapped a few keys on his computer and rotated the screen so I could see my progress report. "Your grades are good, Amanda, but need to be better."

I closed my eyes and tried not to mouth off. Mr. Serrano irritated every nerve I had. He wore the same clothes every day—a pair of tan Dockers and a Lakeshore High T-shirt. Okay, so technically, I wore the same clothes too, but that was only because I didn't own any other stuff. His hair was always carefully combed to the same side, and he wore wire-framed glasses that were slightly bent so that one eyebrow always dipped under the frame and the other arched over. His desk looked like he'd just taken it out of its box. There wasn't a crumb, a scratch, or even a sticky note on it. All it held was his computer and phone.

"What's the point? I can't even afford community college."

"Amanda, you *can*. I admit scholarships are a bit of a lottery win, but you'll fill out the financial aid forms. Pell grants don't need to be repaid, and you definitely qualify. There's plenty of aid available to foster kids like you who don't want to be one of the statistics."

The dreaded statistics.

I'd heard this tired old song too many times from foster parents, my social worker, and Mr. Serrano. Homeless and pregnant before twenty, living off welfare and food stamps, couch-surfing among a small circle of dirtbag friends. Mr. Serrano's stupid statistics kept me up at night. The statistics freakin' haunted me, because once I aged out of foster care, they wouldn't just be some threat. They'd be my life.

"I also talked to Chief Duffy at the firehouse."

I opened my eyes.

"He says you're a fine firefighter with a keen eye and a strong heart."

I—um, wow. I blinked away the tears that suddenly filled my eyes. I didn't know what to say to that. That was almost gushing, and Chief Duffy did not gush.

"He thinks you'd make a fine civil servant—in the police or fire service in a town that would pay for the job."

Mr. Serrano's mention of the word *town* ignited a whole new panic sequence. I couldn't drive. I didn't have a car. I didn't have money to buy a car. How could I find a job in such a mythical town if I couldn't get there? Long Island wasn't exactly a mecca of public transportation. There was only one solution—I'd have to leave.

The thought was like a kick to the solar plexus.

Mr. Serrano clicked a few more things on his computer screen, and a second later, the local community college website appeared. "My suggestion is this." He tapped his screen.

"Nursing school?"

He nodded. "Chief Duffy mentioned that all of the volunteers are trained in life-saving skills, which tells me you already have an interest and probably an aptitude for the kind of work that might make others squeamish."

I thought about that for a minute and decided he was right. I had no issues with blood and guts, like Gage did. I smothered a snort. He nearly puked during our last motor vehicle extraction drill, and that was all staged.

"It won't be easy, but you could finish the nursing program at the community college in two years, before you age out of your current foster arrangement. With a license and two-year degree under your belt, you'll find a job fast. It won't be a glamorous high-paying job, but it sure beats slinging burgers at minimum wage. You'll be able to afford rent, though again, not something extravagant. If you land work at a university hospital, you might even receive tuition reimbursement benefits. Do you know what that means?"

I shook my head.

"It means your employer will foot some of the bill for you to continue your education and get another degree—your four-year or maybe a master's. Those credentials, of course, greatly improve your odds of getting the higher-paying jobs."

I stared at the screen, studying the course outline. It was four semesters. I'd be twenty years old and still in foster care—maybe even still with the Becketts, if I didn't step a pinky toe out of line.

"If you hate nursing, big deal. You still have a job and a degree you could always use for something else. You could save your way toward a car or a move to a city with a paid fire service. Or you could join the police department. The state police force earns the most, but a few of the counties pay well too. You'll have benefits and security, and Amanda, those are worth more than the salary." Mr. Serrano shifted his chair to look me straight in the eye. "I love teaching and love guiding students like you toward solid life plans, but the truth is I worry all the time about losing this job because of things like budget cuts and political changes that alter the state aid we receive for critical programs. You find a job in nursing or civil service, and you wouldn't have to worry—at least, not as much. Do you understand?"

Wouldn't have to worry. I wasn't sure if I knew what that felt like. It was probably something like believing in Santa Claus.

I leaned forward. "What do I have to do?"

Mr. Serrano's lips twitched. "Well, as I said, your grades are good but could be better. You did well on the PSAT but should take the ACT and SAT. You should know I talked to Mr. Beckett. He and his wife agreed to keep you until you age out."

My eyes popped at this news.

"He said that?"

"Yes, he did. He said you haven't been any trouble at all. As long as that continues, I see no reason why Mr. Beckett would change his mind."

I leaned back in my seat and closed my eyes with a sigh. The weight that rolled off my shoulders was so heavy I was kind of surprised I didn't float to the top of Mr. Serrano's office now that it wasn't holding me down.

He smiled and held up a finger. "I'm going to give you some homework. Kids complain all the time that school never prepares them for the real world, like balancing a checkbook or understanding a simple job application." He pulled open a wide drawer in the cabinet behind his desk, rifled through some files, and started pulling out brochures and flyers and stapled sets of documents. "I want you to read all this. The library has several programs you should attend. There are also some websites you should visit that provide all sorts of advice and guidance for transitioning out of foster care. And finally, there are some after-school jobs you should consider applying for. You need income, and you need to establish credit as soon as possible, so when the time comes for you to sign a lease, you'll have a credit rating and references."

A lease? Credit? Holy crap. Panic was creeping up the back of my neck again, its long bony fingers about to squeeze. But I took the stack of papers Mr. Serrano had thoughtfully put into a big manila envelope and slid it into my backpack. I'd read them. I would read every freakin' one of them.

I would *not* be one of the statistics.

And that meant I had to stay far away from Reece Logan.

***

Monday afternoon, behind the school, I watched Reece race Max up and down the bleachers, trying damn hard not to be impressed with his lightning-fast progress and failing miserably. They'd done four laps, and even Max was sucking wind, but Reece would have done more if I hadn't stopped him.

"Okay, Logan, that's enough." I waved him back down. He handed Max the five-pound hand weights and joined me at ground level, chugging half a bottle of water. "That was good. Really good. How are the leg muscles?"

"Bananas help," he panted.

"Good. What else have you done today?"

"Uh, this morning, I did some weights in my basement for about half an hour."

"Okay, let's hit the rope."

"Copy that, Captain." He grinned and hurried ahead. I grinned back before I remembered I was seriously pissed off at him.

"Wait up a minute."

He stopped, turned, and waited for me to catch up. I watched his eyes drop to my body and tried not to be happy about it, because I wasn't, damn it. Not one bit. "About the other day. After the alarm sounded."

Dark eyes stared into mine with a glint, but the jerk didn't say a word.

I sighed loudly. "Reece. The kiss."

"I remember." His voice was suddenly deep and raspy.

"Well, you need to forget it. That can't happen. Ever. Mr. Beckett was seconds away from walking in on us. If he sees that, you know what'll happen to me?"

His eyebrows lowered, and he shook his head.

"They can ship me back, Logan. Kick me out."

"Back? Back where?"

"Into the system. Maybe I'll get sent to a different foster home. Odds are it won't be in this town. But it's more likely I'll get stuck in a group home until I age out. Know anything about group homes, Logan?"

He shook his head.

"They're a tiny step up from juvie." I held up my fingers, less than an inch apart.

He swallowed hard, his eyes solemn. Okay, so I was laying it on a bit thick, but he needed to know I wasn't kidding around.

Reece took a step closer. "You really like living at the Becketts'?"

I nodded. "It's been the best so far."

"Do you miss your mom?"

"Um," I stammered, the shock of his question like a punch to the gut. And then I thought about that. Did I miss Mom? "No. Maybe. I don't know." I raised my hands, then let them fall. "Every time I think of her, all I feel is mad. And feeling mad kind of makes you forget everything else." I liked feeling mad a hell of a lot more than feeling sad. "She wants to see me."

Oh God, blurt much? I had no idea why I told him that.

"Will you go?"

"What's the point? So she can tell me what I already know?"

"What's that?"

I couldn't suppress my frustration. "Oh, how sorry she is, and she never meant to hurt me, and how things will be better when she gets out—like I'd believe a word of that."

Reece angled his head, studying me for a moment. "But what if it's true? I mean, wouldn't that change things? You'd have your family back."

My family back... There was something in his tone that made me think of Matt—something *final*. He didn't get it. But I did. My mom might not be dead, but my family wasn't something that could be repaired. "Like I said, what's the point?"

He rolled his eyes. "To know where you stand. To know somebody loves you," he elaborated.

I snorted. *Love.* "Love is a friggin' lie, Logan! Fiction. A fantasy!" I waved my hands in the air. "Love is how my mother ended up going to prison and how I ended up—" The look in his eyes pinched my heart. He pressed his lips together, looking like a kicked puppy, and suddenly, all I could think about was his lips on mine, and that made mine start tingling and—*crap*! "Logan, take my advice. You want to know where you stand? It's wherever your feet stop. Simple. And love? Do whatever you have to do to avoid it." *Crap, crap, shit.* My eyes burned, and my voice cracked, and I'd had enough. "Forget about the tug rope today. Go meet Bear."

He studied me for a minute and finally nodded, jogging off to the school's main entrance. The library would be open for only another half hour, so I hoped Bear was prepared.

Logan needed all the help he could get.

"He's really improved."

I whipped around at the sound of that deep voice and found Max standing against the fence that bordered the field. "Yeah."

"So why do you look so miserable?"

139

Sighing, I shook my head. "Ever want something you know you'll never get?"

He laughed. "Yeah. A Maserati."

My lips twitched. Max might be a conceited jerk sometimes, but he was funny. He pushed off the fence and started coiling my rope.

"What's going on, Man? You got a thing for Logan? Is that why you look like you're gonna cry?"

A thing for Logan? Holy crap.

"He…ah, hell, he gets inside my head, Max. I feel bad for him. All that crap with John?"

Max's lips tightened. "Yeah, well, maybe he wouldn't have so much crap with his dad if he hadn't taken the car without a license."

Matt's accident. "Yeah. Maybe."

Max handed me the neatly wound rope, and I slung it over my shoulder, along with my backpack. "Can I ask you something, Man?"

"Sure."

"I heard you tell him your mother wants you to visit."

I froze.

"Why don't you want to go?"

I turned and started walking. "If you heard me tell him that, you must have heard my answer too."

He caught up to me. "I did. But I don't buy the *why bother* thing. I think you're scared."

Yeah. Right.

"I'd go with you. I don't have my license, but I'd take the train with you. So you had someone you could trust."

Tears stung my eyes again. I held out my hand. "Thanks, Max."

He grinned, and it was a real smile, not one of his charm-you-out-of-your-panties grins. "No sweat."

He clasped my hand, thumbs up.

The way the guys always did it.

"So do you want to go?"

"I don't know. I kind of hate her, Max."

"Nah. You're pissed off. Might be good to get it off your incredibly nice chest." He nudged me with an elbow, dark eyes pinned to my boobs.

I rolled my eyes. "Knock it off, Tobay." I slapped his arm, but he only raised his eyebrows, silently demanding my answer. "I'll think about it, okay? I haven't seen her for ages. It's…"

"I know, Man."

A sudden thought struck. "I still won't go out with you, you know."

He shot me a look. "I didn't ask. I'm just offering to come with."

I stopped and faced him with a frown. "Okay, why?"

Max shook his head, laughing. "Because we're squadmates, girl. Two in. Two out. That's the way it works."

I studied his face and finally nodded. "Okay. If I decide to go, I'll drag your ass along with me."

"Cool." He started walking, and I watched him for a second or two. It was. It really, really was.

Chapter 13
Reece

The needle's almost in the red, Dad. Let's see how brave you are. I'll be at his altar, because I have nothing left to burn.

At school on Tuesday, Alex and I had just grabbed lunch when Gage waved us over.

"Logan! We could use your help."

At the squad's usual lunch table, Bear was in the middle of a large-scale freak-out.

"What's going on?"

"I got an F," he said with a look of horror.

I looked at him sideways. "Bear, an F isn't the end of the world."

"Yeah, it is. If I fail this class, I can't stay on the squad."

Whoa. I didn't know that. I put my tray down and grabbed a seat. "What class?"

"Bio." He folded his arms on the table and let his head fall on top.

Max raised his eyebrows over the bottle of water he'd just guzzled. "So study extra this week. No big deal."

But Bear's face just got redder. "I can't! I have to work, and we're doing knots this week in J squad."

Amanda shook her head. "Bear, we're not going to let you fail. Logan's a genius. He'll help."

I choked on my turkey sandwich. "I'm not a genius. I just memorize stuff. Alex is the genius." I looked around, but Alex wasn't there. "Where the hell did he go?" He was no longer behind me. I scanned the cafeteria and found him at our usual table. "Amanda, could you tell him to come back and eat with us?"

"Heard you saw the trucks roll on Saturday. Pretty damn cool, right?" Kevin grinned, and I smiled back. He was right. It was.

"Come on, that wasn't really the first time you saw the trucks roll out, was it?" Gage asked with a smirk.

"Actually, it was."

Gage grinned. "I've seen it probably a hundred times by now. Never gets old."

Max looked up from the hot cheerleader he'd been eyeballing. "Did you hear anything about it? The fire, I mean."

Gage shook his head. "No, why?"

"The address. Juniper Court. There's a boarded-up house on that block. Foreclosure."

Bear cursed. "You think it's another one?"

"Another what?" I cut in.

"Arson." Gage tipped back his bottle and swallowed some water. "We've had a few this year. Nobody knows who it is."

"How do you know it's arson?"

Max leaned in, dark eyes shifting around for eavesdroppers. "We don't. The guys won't talk to us about it. But we hear shit, you know?" He took another careful look around. "Like the first one, back in January. It was an empty house, windows all boarded up. Neighbors swore they saw light in the house for days but never said anything until after the place poofed."

"Yeah, and Gage was working with Steve Conner. Tell him what you found out." Bear slapped Gage's arm.

"Steve's our fire marshal. He doesn't fight fires; he investigates them after—you know, for the reports. His laptop ate a document, so he asked me to help him recover it. I saw the report. The suspect is a real pyro. They think he was practicing. Inside what was left of the structure, they found piles of ash, which they think was kindling. Best guess, oil-soaked paper arranged like fuses."

"Whoa, I read about that. Trailers, right?"

Max nodded. "Wait, it gets better. We got snow—a lot of it. Everything's quiet for weeks until most of the snow is gone. Then, another arson—this time, a boarded-up place over on Delaney. I overheard the chief talking to Steve about this one. Steve said he was sure it was the same guy, but he was escalating."

"Escalating? Like getting sicker?"

Gage shook his head. "More like more dangerous."

"How does Steve know this? Doesn't the fire burn up everything?"

"No, dude." Gage waved a hand. "That's a myth, and Steve says it's what eventually gets arsonists caught. Fire leaves a footprint through a destroyed structure. Steve can look at scorch marks and the color of flames to tell you if a fire is electrical, chemical, accidental, whatever."

"Right. Rainbow fire."

Gage laughed. "You know about that?"

I nodded. "Read it in one of the books. Gasoline burns yellow, copper burns green."

Gage's eyebrows raised. "Keep reading, dude. You'll be an expert in no time."

A groan from Bear interrupted our fun. I glanced at him, but he was frowning over a notebook. "What's tripping you up, Bear?"

"Body planes, bro. I keep messing up which one's sagittal and transverse."

"No problem. Look." I took his shoulders and turned him to face me. "All you need to remember is that the sagittal plane slices the body right down the center into a left and right side. What's the first syllable in *sagittal*?"

"Uh, sag?"

"Right. Sag, as in—" I held my hands in front of my pecs as if they were weighted down. "Just imagine that line cutting right between a pair of—"

"Saggy tits! Holy shit, man. That's genius." Bear grinned. "Your dad says you read textbooks just for fun. Is that true?"

I took another bite, chewed, and tried to ignore the burn in my gut at his words. Okay, so I *did* read textbooks for fun; I had no life to speak of, so what the hell else was there to do? The sandwich soured and knotted in my gut. A whole series of inventive ways to commit patricide danced in my mind, but I said nothing.

"I don't get it, Logan. All my parents do is nag, nag, nag me to get my grades up. Your grades are way up, and your dad still gives you shit. What the hell is up with that?"

"Because he's jealous," Amanda said quietly, sliding into Max's seat.

I jerked my eyes to hers. Jealous, huh? I thought about it, but whatever was wrong between my dad and me couldn't be distilled to a single word. The truth was my dad was a smart guy—in practical, commonsense ways. I was a smart guy in other ways, ways that filled my head with facts. I had a perfect memory, could pass tests easily, and could read books in a matter of hours, but what difference did any of that make when I had no ideas of my own? Dad knew that. I was smart, just not smart *enough*.

"So, Logan, do you think you could maybe help me pass some of my classes?"

"Some? How many?"

"I suck at bio and math. And maybe history."

"Like I said, Alex is the real genius." I looked around, but he wasn't with Amanda. He was still at our table. "Did you tell him to sit here?" I asked her, and she shook her head.

"He said he'd catch up with you later."

Oh.

Max perched on the table and laughed. "Damn, Bear, the only thing you don't suck at is gym and lunch."

"Hey, I'm good in Spanish."

"Because you speak Spanish at home, dumbass."

Bear slanted him a look. "We're Portuguese."

"Same thing."

"And I'm the dumbass?" Bear rolled his eyes.

I exchanged glances with Amanda, but she just shook her head. I couldn't take any more. "Okay, okay, I'll help you if you two promise to stop arguing like an old married couple."

Max folded his lips over his teeth and bent over at the waist. "Eh, what's that, dearie? Speak up." He cupped his ear.

The bell rang, thank God. Max took off with a grin and a wave. Bear groaned. "Quiz time. Hope I pass."

"Remember what I said."

"Sagging tits! Got it. See you later. And practice your knots!"

Amanda's eyes almost fell from her skull. "What the hell did you tell him, Logan?"

"Just a way to keep body planes straight, no big deal. Come on. I'll walk you to class." I held out my hand—a totally unconscious gesture. Until she took it. Then it became the only thing I was aware of.

Abruptly, the note in my pocket felt like a thorn. I let go of Amanda's hand to tug it out.

"What's that?" she asked, but I shook my head.

"Nothing," I said.

And the thing is that really wasn't a lie.

Not anymore.

I stuffed the paper back in my pocket, finished the rest of my classes, and spent the rest of the evening practicing knot tying.

***

Wednesday evening, I sat in the same chair I'd occupied the previous week. I had my text and even brought a notebook this time. My leg bounced under the table, and my stomach kept twisting.

I was the first one here. We were doing knots today, or so Bear said. He'd had me reading everything from Boy Scout to nautical websites. I was pretty sure I'd dream about knots.

"Hey." Amanda strode in, hung her backpack over her chair, and sat down.

I jerked at the sound of her voice, my blood pumping a little faster through my system. She was wearing her station uniform and had her hair pulled up in its usual vicious twist. It looked better when it was loose. I bet it was soft. She dropped her notebook on a table, and I jolted. What the hell was I doing, thinking about her hair? I couldn't like Amanda Jamison.

Epic fail.

"Hey." I forced my attention back to my text and kept reviewing the knots I'd practiced all afternoon. I totally understood why Bear freaked out about knots now.

"You study?" Amanda asked.

"Yeah. Practiced on some old cord Matt had in a box in the basement." Mom wouldn't let Dad toss any of it.

Her eyes filled with pain before she looked away, and I winced, hating myself for upsetting her. I quickly changed the subject. "Why do you wear your hair pulled so tight? Doesn't that hurt?"

Sure enough, she shot me a look that speared straight through me.

"Sorry, Paul Mitchell, I didn't know I was supposed to get your approval."

I held up both hands. "No, I don't mean to bust your chops. I just wondered if that was part of the uniform."

She thought about that for a moment. "I like my hair off my face when I'm working. To keep it secure, I twist it like this. We done with this topic, or would you like tips on French braids?"

I laughed once and tried not to squirm. I had only the vaguest idea of what a French braid was, but the image of my hair like that was pretty damn funny. "We're done, we're done." I threw up both hands again.

Her lips twitched. She crossed her arms and slanted me a look, and my mouth went dry. She grabbed my text and flipped it open to the knots page. "Did you go through the whole section?"

"Yeah. I practiced every knot in the book plus some from a website Bear gave me."

Her eyebrows lifted. "Good thinking." She slid her gaze to the door and lowered her voice. From the backpack she'd looped over her chair, she took out a rope bag. "Okay, listen." She tugged a few feet out of the bag, put it behind her back, and kept talking. "When Neil taught us, he used to have us practice the knots over and over until our fingers went numb. We could tie knots blindfolded."

She showed me the rope. It was tied in a perfect bowline knot.

"Your dad does a great job training a cadet here and there when they come up from the academy, but a class like this?" She shook her head and shrugged. "I don't know what he's gonna do. This week, he hasn't said anything other than *knots*." She blew out a loud sigh and sank back in her chair. "Which reminds me, I have to go copy the lesson plan. Be right back."

I turned back to my text and grabbed the rope she'd left behind. The bowline knot, according to my book, could be easily untied as long as it bears no load, but it has a tendency to loosen. I examined Amanda's work, tightened it, and tied a safety knot under it. Then I untied the whole thing, started over with a basic figure eight, set it tight, and tied another safety knot on that to finish it off.

Footsteps in the corridor snagged my attention, and I could tell immediately they weren't Amanda's. My muscles coiled, and I braced for the greeting I knew I'd get from my father. He stepped inside the room and stopped for second.

"First one here, Reece? I'm not impressed with brownnosing."

I shrugged. *Yours is the last ass I'd kiss.*

He noticed the rope, grabbed it, and inspected my knot. "Whose rope bag is this?"

"Amanda's."

He nodded once, smirking down at me. "She's got a thing for Logan boys."

The blood in my veins simmered. My fingers itched on the rope, and my muscles bunched. "Amanda's a great teacher."

"Oh, you think so?" He laughed. "She's good, Peanut, but until she, I don't know, maybe fights an actual fire, I'm the best you're gonna get."

Peanut? Christ. I looked up and glared straight through him. "We had a deal, *Jackie.*"

The laughter faded. Dad nodded. "Yeah. You're right." He angled his head, took a step back, and stared at me, stared at me like it was the first time he'd seen me. There was something in his eyes I didn't recognize. Not pride, definitely not that.

But it was something.

"What?"

Dad shook his head. "Nothing."

We stared each other down for a moment longer, and then I looked back at my text. Dad took Amanda's rope, untied my knot, and tugged a few more feet out of the bag. With ten feet of rope snaking along the floor, he grabbed the rope and bent it into a U.

"What's this?" he asked, holding up the U-shaped section.

"It's a bight."

With a twist of his hand, the U became a loop.

"This?"

"Round turn."

"And this?" He manipulated the rope into another shape.

"A loop."

He passed one end through the loop, twisted it around, and stopped halfway through a knot. "This?" He shook the part in his right hand.

"The working end."

"And this?"

"Standing."

"This?"

"Running end."

He finished the knot and tossed it to me. "Dress it."

I grinned because I knew what that meant. I examined the knot he'd tied. It was a figure eight—half-assed and loose. I worked the end back out of the loop, directed it through so that the working end was opposite the running end, tightened the knot, and finished it with a safety knot. Then I tossed it back to him.

He scanned my work and finally nodded. That was all. A nod. I ran a victory lap inside my head. *Achievement: unlocked.*

"Hey, Lieutenant."

Dad turned and greeted Gage and Ty. A second later, Amanda strode back in on those long, graceful legs. She dumped a stack of papers on the table in front of me and started passing them out.

"Lieutenant Logan, I ran off copies of today's drill."

"Yeah, thanks. Take your seat."

He picked up the top sheet from the stack, glanced at it, and tossed it down like it was shit-stained.

Crap, he was pissed at her.

I fumed, wishing I had the guts to stand up for Amanda. But then, Kevin and Bear walked in, their laughter fizzling under the heat of Dad's glare, and took seats in the center of the room. Finally, Max strode in like he owned the whole damn firehouse, stinking of tobacco. Dad crossed his arms and burned the entire group of us with a single glare.

"Anybody who can't manage to get here before I do shouldn't bother. We clear on that?"

A chorus of *Yes, Lieutenant*'s rang across the conference room. Dad pointed to Amanda's rope bag. "Get rid of that."

She quickly recoiled the rope, packed it back in the bag, and tucked the bag into her backpack.

"Tobay!"

"Yes, sir." Max sat up straighter.

"Find me utility ropes, safety ropes—but don't take any off the trucks." After Max took off, Dad zeroed in on Ty. "Golowski, you know your knots?"

"Yes, sir."

"How 'bout you, Sheppard?"

Kevin grinned. "Absolutely."

"Good man. Okay," Dad said with a clap of his hands. "Here's what we're gonna do. When Max gets back with the ropes, I want everybody to grab one and tie your favorite knot. Got that? Just tie the knot you think is best. Then I want you to tell me why."

Bear groaned.

"Problem, Acosta?"

Bear shook his head, but I could see the sweat already beading at his hairline. Max returned, threw some rope coils on the table at the front of the room, and took his seat next to Gage. The ropes were assorted types and thicknesses. I recognized one as natural fiber and one as synthetic. Okay. I could do this.

I was ready.

"Pop quiz time." Dad grinned at Bear, waiting for him to groan again. "According to the NFPA 1983, which of these ropes *cannot* be used for life safety?"

Amanda's eyes shot straight to the first coil on the left. Manila rope. The text I'd read that afternoon popped into my head.

"Anybody?" Dad prodded.

I took a look around the room, and based on the tightly clenched jaws, glares, and sweat openly dripping down Bear's neck, I concluded nobody liked my father's methods of training the junior squad. I took a deep breath and stood up, shifted two rope coils to the front of the table. "These should not be used for life-saving."

"Why not?"

"That one's manila. And this one's cotton. Natural fibers shouldn't be used for life-saving."

Dad's eye twitched, but he said nothing. I took my seat and waited for the next test, but my father sighed and pulled out a chair. He grabbed a synthetic rope, unwrapped a few feet, and started talking. "I know you guys hate knots. You'd much rather put on the gear and grab some hoses. But believe me, knot tying is probably the most important skill you can learn in fire service." He bent the rope and started tying. "When I was a cadet, I nearly killed somebody with a crappy figure eight on a bight, like this one." He held up the rope and then waved a hand at the guys. "Drag your chairs around me. Take a look." He tossed his finished knot on the table. "How much do you guys think a Halligan tool weighs?"

What? The ones I'd practiced with were about thirty inches long with a heavy metal claw, blade, and fork on the ends so firefighters could use them to pry open doors, pull down ceilings, and punch through walls or windows. What the hell that had to do with knots, I wasn't sure.

"About ten pounds," Amanda said.

Dad nodded, leaned forward, and nudged his rope. "Back when I was a cadet, I was ordered to hoist some tools up to a second floor.

The fire took out the stairs. So I tied this knot around a Halligan." He waved his hand over the rope on the table. "Guess what happened?"

Oh.

"It unraveled," Gage said.

"Damn near split my lieutenant's head open." Dad nodded, the smirk that was almost permanently etched on his lips now gone. "Do you see my mistake?"

Since when did Dad admit to making a mistake? I joined the rest of the squad and looked closer at the rope on the table, but Amanda found it first. "You reversed the direction. As soon as it was loaded with weight, the knot failed."

"And how many times do you think I tied this knot wrong after that?"

"Zero," I said before I could bite my tongue. I knew my father would have made this knot his personal mission after that incident.

"Zero." He nodded at me. He slid the rope to me. "How *should* this knot be tied?"

I swallowed once, but I took the rope, untied it, and started reshaping the knot properly, bending the first bight and then the second. I wrapped one over the other, passed it from front to back, tightened it, and tied a safety knot at the end. Dad took the knot and offered it to Max.

"Tobay, would you stand under an ax or a saw tied with this knot?"

Max slid a glance my way, then examined my work. "Yeah, I would."

"Gage?"

Gage took the rope, tugged on both ends, and shrugged without ever once looking at me. "Sure."

The knot was passed around the class until everyone had a chance to dress it, set it, and agree to stand under a tool suspended by it.

"That's how you learn knots, juniors. When your brothers and sisters are willing to stand under or be suspended by your rope work, you pass." He stood up and started passing out the rest of the ropes. "Get started. Tie your favorite. Make it worthy of the brother or sister sitting next to you."

Everybody reached for a rope and began bending and twisting. I felt a hand squeeze my shoulder. I glanced up, expecting to find Max or maybe Amanda, but it wasn't either of them.

It was Dad.

Chapter 14
Amanda

I snuck a peek at Reece just as the lieutenant squeezed his shoulder. The look on Reece's face made something deep inside me thaw and melt—and then sucked me in.

"Bathroom break, Lieutenant." I murmured and hurried out of the room. It hurt to breathe, and I had to leave the room before everybody saw me. Or saw through me.

John nodded and turned back to supervise knots. Outside in the corridor, I bent over my knees, sucked in oxygen, and tried to rebuild my shields. The restrooms were down the hall. I ducked into the ladies' room, locked myself in a stall, and cursed my freakin' heart.

Do not like this boy. Do not.

I covered my face with my hands and squeezed my eyes shut, because my heart beat its reply in a steady rhythm. *Too late. Too late. Too late.*

Happiness like a dozen birthdays, Christmas mornings, and puppies all squeezed into a single moment—that's what I saw on Reece's face, and it just about *killed* me. Not because I wasn't happy for him. It's why we were helping him, after all. But my heart wasn't supposed to flutter and my stomach wasn't supposed to flip over because of him.

He wasn't supposed to *matter*.

How did this happen? How the hell did I let this happen?

Even as the thoughts circled around inside my head, I knew the answer.

It was because he made me feel like *I* mattered.

Jeez, it was what, maybe seven years since I'd felt that way, and even then…it was just an illusion, another lie my mom told me, like Santa Claus and the Tooth Fairy. If I really did matter so much, she never would have gone along with Dmitri's stupid scheme.

Mom used to have a great job, and I went to the after-school program at my school. After work, she'd pick me up and help me do my homework. We'd watch TV and read stories before I went to bed. And then, she met him. Dmitri. God, I hated him and the way he always smelled like cigarettes and too much cologne. He didn't like me either, and suddenly, I had babysitters because Mom was out almost every night. On the weekends, Dmitri drove us all over the place, stopping here and there so he could sell whatever was in the trunk of the car. It was so boring, and at one stop, I got out of the car to go with them inside this enormous store that had a carousel horse in the window. I thought it was a toy store. Dmitri yelled at me, and Mom just did whatever he said. I went back to the car and cried in my seat for the rest of the day.

They never noticed. All they talked about was how much money they were getting.

One night when I was asleep, I suddenly heard her crying, "He loves me!" She kept screaming, "He wouldn't do that to me." I ran out of my room and found a bunch of cops in our house, handcuffs around my mother's wrists.

"Christ, she's got a kid," one of them said. And she'd suddenly stopped crying and shouting and stared at me like she'd forgotten I lived there. I still don't know what they had been up to. Only that whatever *it* was, the police had found a lot of it stashed in our house, Dmitri claiming he had no knowledge of my mother's activities.

I opened the stall and stared at myself in the mirror over the sink, wishing like hell for some kind of Teflon coating I could wear around Reece. He got what he wanted—a dad who respected him, maybe was even a little proud of him. How long would it take before he figured out he didn't need me anymore?

Nobody could know. Not even Reece. *Especially* not Reece. If the Becketts found out I was interested in a boy, they'd kick me out.

I bent over the sink and splashed some water over my face. When I reached for the towel machine, I jerked.

I wasn't alone.

"Gage, I know what—"

"You okay?" He stepped closer and took me by the shoulders. "You look like you saw a ghost."

I wish. A ghost would be a lot less scary than a group home.

I stared into Gage's eyes and tried to find my best poker face. "I'm fine."

His eyes rolled heavenward, and he laughed once. "You think I don't see the way you watch him or the way he watches you? You think I don't notice the way your pulse beats, right here, whenever you're close to him?" He ran his thumb along my neck, just under my ear, and I cursed myself. If Gage could see it, could Mr. Beckett? "I thought you had a no-boys rule."

"I do," I cut him off.

"Then what the hell are you doing out on the ledge?"

"Clinging to it with every bit of strength I have." I shoved past him, but he stopped me with a hand on my arm.

"Don't let go, Man."

I returned to the conference room and tried my hardest not to look at Reece, because Gage was right, and we both knew it. I could not let go.

"Man, you okay?" Lieutenant Logan asked, and I nodded once. I sat back in my seat and watched John lead the squad through class the way Neil used to do it—hell, maybe even better than the way Neil used to do it. Bowlines, figure eights, clove hitches, handcuffs, butterflies—he covered them all and in depth. Bear's pen was a blur across his notebook, and even Gage was nodding and listening closely. John's hands worked the ropes, patted backs, and illustrated his stories. I'd never seen him so…so *present* in the moment like this. I wondered if he had any clue it was because of Reece. I smothered a laugh. We might turn John Logan into a hell of a teacher.

"Okay, everybody untie those knots, get those ropes back into storage—"

The tones sounded, and we froze in place.

"Engine 21, Truck 3, Rescue 17, residential fire, 44 Hyacinth Road."

"Return the ropes to storage. Read the next unit. Good job, everybody," Lieutenant Logan called out as he ran to the corridor.

All of us followed and watched the volunteers in the station don turnouts and hop onto trucks before the roll-up doors were fully raised. After the bells faded, nobody wanted to leave, but technically, class was over for the week. Ty and Kevin started organizing the crews' stuff—shoes, hats, jackets—into neat piles. Bear and Max headed for the kitchen.

That left me on the apparatus floor with a dazed Reece. "That's your second response." I nudged him with a shoulder. "Still cool?"

He turned wide eyes to me. "Um, yeah." Then he flashed this wide grin, and I fell a little harder. "It—will it always be that cool?"

"Yeah," I said back with a grin. "It never gets old."

We stood on the side of the empty apparatus floor, staring at each other with goofy grins on our faces, and suddenly, everything stopped. There was nothing but Reece and me, no panic attacks in restrooms, no stupid rules to follow, no squad—all that existed was us and the heat that pulled us in. Reece stared down at me and slowly brought up a hand. He could have touched me, could have kissed me, could have gotten me in the world's worst trouble, and at that moment, I would have walked through fire to let him.

But he dropped his hand and took a step back. "Amanda. You know I'm not *him*."

Matt.

It was like someone just turned one of the hoses on me.

I took a step back this time, relieved that I could. Whatever that was, I didn't want to risk fanning it into life again. It would kill me, I was sure. "I know. I know who you are. And I know who he was.

I'm not the blue ribbon in whatever competition you still have going with him."

A storm of emotion swam in Reece's eyes, I looked away and thrust my hands in the pockets of my pants. "We should probably—"

"Hey! We're going to the diner! You two in?" Gage shouted from the door.

Reece nodded. "Yeah. Sure." He took off in that direction without a second glance at me.

I watched him go, shivering from the cold.

***

We sat around a high-top table in the diner in town, sharing an order of loaded nachos and sipping drinks—Coke for everyone except Reece. He had lemonade. Reece stuck his finger in his mouth and then winced. "Rope burns."

I laughed once and looked down at my own calloused hands. I never noticed the rough skin or the broken nails before. I wondered if boys might like to hold hands with someone whose hands were soft, like a real girl's or something.

Maybe.

What the hell did I know about girl stuff?

And then I remembered it didn't matter. No boys for me. Not until I was out of the foster care system.

I hid my hands under the table and stared out the window, trying to find something to say that wasn't about rope burns or knot tying or hose advancing. Reece looked really uncomfortable, like he was hoping a small kitchen fire would start and save him from having to talk to anybody.

Bear slurped the bottom of his glass. "So that was intense today. Hard to believe your old man ever made a mistake, you know?"

Reece shrugged, shifted. His face clouded up for a minute, but he didn't say anything. He suddenly lifted his head and asked, "Who turns seventeen first?"

"Uh, me." Max raised a finger. "My birthday's coming up soon."

Birthdays. The thought sent tears to sting the back of my eyes. When it was just Mom and me, she used to make a big deal out of my birthdays. She'd invite my friends over for cupcakes and old-fashioned games, and at the moment of my birth—six o'clock in the morning—she'd wake me up with a softly sung version of "Happy Birthday," one last cupcake she'd saved just for me, glowing with a single candle, and we'd eat it together, getting crumbs all over my bed.

"You gonna stick?" Ty asked, scooping up more nachos, and I shoved the memories back into their corner.

"Hell yeah, I'm gonna stick. I didn't work my ass off all these years just to quit when it gets good. Logan knows what I mean, right?"

Reece shifted again, his eyes darting to Max. "What?"

Max smirked. "Come on. I saw your face when those bells rang. You can't wait to be on the truck. Neither can I."

"Rig boner," Kevin announced.

Reece's eyes almost fell out of his skull. "Rig boner?"

Gage slapped the back of Kevin's head. "Jesus, dude. A little class?"

Kevin just grinned and bopped on his stool. "Like you guys never heard that before."

"Um, yeah." I scratched at my neck, which was suddenly blazing. "It's something the guys say all the time."

Reece's dark eyes locked on mine, soft and sweet, and then he flashed a grin. "That's good. I'm glad there's a name for what I felt."

"Dude." Bear put a hand on his shoulder. "Everybody feels it."

"So what about you, Logan? You gonna stick when you turn seventeen?" Max asked.

The smile froze. "Yeah. Of course."

Gage frowned and caught my eye. I shrugged. Yeah, that was weird. Yeah, I agreed; something was up. No, I didn't know what.

Max picked up on it too. "Yeah? You don't sound so sure."

"I'm sure, I'm sure." Reece waved his hands in protest.

"That's good, because everybody at this table is working hard for you." Max dropped his fork with a loud clang. "I'd hate that to be for nothing."

Reece hung his head. When he lifted it again, the smile was back. "You guys, all that you did for me, even when I know you hate me—"

"We don't hate you, Logan." Bear flung a balled-up napkin at his face.

Reece's smile faded a bit. "It's okay. A lot of people do. Kind of used to it now."

With a loud smack, I dropped both hands on the table. "Okay. Enough. Why don't you tell us what happened with your brother and why your dad is so pissed at you?"

Reece's face went white. Gage shook his head at me, and I squirmed. "Forget it. You don't have to tell us."

"No." He gulped. "You should know. You guys have been great. Really." He took a deep breath and blew it out. His voice shook. "My dad taught Matt how to drive. But not me. I asked over and over again, and he never would. So I asked—" He broke off and shut his eyes for a second. "I asked Matt to teach me. He took me out almost every day." He smiled, remembering his brother. When he spoke again, his voice sounded strangled, and I knew he was trying hard not to cry. "He was so cool. You guys knew him. He was…my best friend."

He paused and then laughed. "Everything was cool. Until it snowed."

His smile disappeared. Gage leaned forward, but Reece wouldn't look any of us in the eye.

"Matt said everybody needs to know how to drive in the snow. He took me to a parking lot, over by the mall. They hadn't gotten around to plowing one of the fields yet. A few cars were out there, turning 360s. Matt told me what to do. For an hour, we had a blast, drifting and skidding around in that snow. I was doing great—Matt said so. I practiced and practiced, and each time the car went into a skid, I was able to recover it."

Suddenly, he shoved his chair back, curled over his knees, and rocked back and forth. "Except for the last one."

"What happened?" Bear asked, and Reece shook his head.

"I wish I knew. I swear, it was the same skid I'd done a few dozen times that day. Only this one, I couldn't recover. I hit a light pole. It fell and…God! It…it crushed the top of the car." He started to breathe hard, rubbing his chest.

I wiped tears from my eyes and waited for him to go on.

"It took them twenty minutes to cut us out of the car, and I couldn't—I couldn't stop—" He clenched his hands into fists, then opened his hands and just stared at them.

They shook.

It was a long moment before he spoke again. "Matt—God! I woke up alone, and the nurses, the doctors, none of them would tell me anything. He…he died while I was asleep in my hospital bed. I broke an arm. He had a broken leg, broken ribs, broken neck."

He looked up at us then, and his eyes were heartbreak and blame. Bear sniffled and then put a hand on Reece's shoulder, gave it a squeeze. Reece jolted. It was like he forgot we were there.

"Dad didn't want to tell me. He didn't want me at the funeral. He wouldn't talk to me. Wouldn't look at me. Until I made him."

Gage's eyebrows shot up. "By joining J squad?"

Reece nodded once. "At first. But not now, not anymore. Now it's for me." He spread his hands. "And for you."

Everybody just stared at him for a minute. "Logan, we don't want payback. We're a team." Gage waved a hand around the table. "Are you telling us you're in this for the long haul?"

He nodded. "I am. Definitely."

This time, his voice held this really solid note of certainty, and there was a part of me that punched the air and shouted *Yes*! If he was planning to stick around, there was a chance, a really thin one, that he and I could be together when I was on my own, with no more rules, and I didn't know why, but I wanted that more than birthday cupcakes in bed.

I stood up, excused myself, and practically ran to the restroom for the second time this evening to hide my hopes behind a stall door. By the time I got back, only Bear and Reece were left at the table. Reece had his head down.

"Where'd everybody go?"

Bear jerked his chin at the exit. "Max had a date. Ty and Kevin got a ride with him."

"Great," I muttered. "What about you, Reece? No dates?"

"I wish." Reece sat back in his chair, wiped a hand over his mouth, and picked at a nacho chip—didn't eat it, just picked it apart. "Last winter, I fell for somebody," he began, and I felt a pinch deep in my chest.

Last winter?

"What's she like, dude?" Bear leaned in.

"She's got this, I don't know, this *style* that's hard-core strength under a layer of pure soft." He laughed once. "I can't explain it, but God, I love to watch her move."

Even though it killed me by syllables, I clung to every word he spoke.

"She didn't know I existed for a long time, and then one day, she got close enough for me to smell her. She reminds me of lemonade." He held up his glass and took a sip, shutting his eyes. "I didn't want to talk to her, didn't want her to notice me, because I would have bet money on it that she was like everybody else in my life who thought Matt was Superman or something."

Oh God. I wanted to squeeze his hand and tell him he's cool too, but I couldn't risk it.

"I imagine these scenes," he said, drawing the glass along his flushed face. "These elaborately staged moments when she'd tell me it was never Matt but *me* she wanted, and then we'd kiss and it would be so amazing, so intense, so fucking hot, it would set records."

Tears stung the back of my eyes. Oh yes, I wanted a kiss like that. I wanted *that* kiss. I looked away, disappointment crushing me from the inside out.

"Man, you okay?" Bear nudged me.

"Oh, um, sure. I gotta get back to the Becketts' house. See ya."

"Later," Bear said.

I walked away, cursing my mother and her stupid boyfriend the whole way home.

Chapter 15

Reece

You made me. But you could never be proud of me, could you? I was different. Alien. And that only made you mad.

It had been a hell of a night. I climbed up the front steps to Alex's door, knocked, and bounced impatiently until he answered.

"Hey! Did you see my text? It's working, Alex!"

He didn't smile. "Great."

I peered at him carefully. "You okay?"

"Fine. What text?"

My smile faded. "Oh, um, nothing. I thought I'd tell you how my class went."

He didn't invite me inside. "It's kind of late."

"Dude, it's barely ten o'clock." A muscle in his jaw twitched, and I frowned at him. "You're not fine. What's wrong?"

"Nothing's wrong."

"Okay." He was obviously lying, so I tried changing the subject. "We did knots tonight, and then the squad invited me to the diner with them. Alex, it was great! All that studying with Bear—it paid off. I practiced knot tying on some old clothesline I found in the basement. When Dad started class tonight, he told us a story about how he fucked up—do you believe that? My dad actually made a mistake once?"

Alex nodded and smiled with tight lips while I babbled on and on about my class and finally gave up. Obviously, he didn't want to hear about it and didn't want to talk about whatever was wrong. His eyes were flat, and the muscles in his neck were tight. Didn't need a genius to tell me Alex was pissed.

At me.

"Okay." I nodded grimly. "Whatever I did, I'm sorry."

He shook his head. "No apology needed. Like I said, I'm fine."

Fine. Sure. Okay. "See you tomorrow?"

He snorted. "Yeah. Tomorrow."

I hovered in the open doorway, a ball of nausea swelling in my gut. "Alex, please. Tell me what I did wrong."

"Nothing, Reece. You did nothing."

He closed the door in my face.

I sat down on Alex's front steps, gripped my head in my hands, and tried to figure out what I did—or didn't do. It wasn't his birthday. We didn't have plans that I forgot about. I paid him back for the movie tickets he bought. I stared at the stars and wondered why in hell somebody was always pissed off at me. I finally—finally!—got somewhere with my dad, and now my best friend doesn't want to hear about it.

Maybe I should just go now…forget about J squad.

I took out my note and started writing.

***

The days passed slowly.

Alex had graduated from avoiding and evading me to outright animosity. I still didn't have any idea what I'd done wrong and felt his absence almost as deeply as Matt's. Despite the churning in my gut, I slept like the dead every night. Must be all those hours of working out.

I was able to carry thirty pounds up and down those bleachers now. I could don personal protective gear in under two minutes. I could conserve tank oxygen for up to fifteen minutes and tie knots blindfolded.

Saturday morning, I woke with the sun. Practice day. The whole J squad had been buzzed about this for days. Once a month, the squad practiced at the county training academy in the next town. Today was that day.

I whistled for Tucker, but he twitched an ear as if to say, "Oh hell no," and burrowed deeper in his bed.

"Come on, pal. Want a treat?"

The dog stretched, pulled himself up, and padded out of my room without a single look back.

I sighed. "Jeez, you too?"

If there was anybody *not* mad at me for some reason, I'd like to meet him.

Once Tucker got some food in his belly, he was happy to go for a long walk. I took him by Alex's house, and he immediately turned up the walk, familiar with the route.

"No, boy. Alex doesn't want to see us anymore."

The dog whimpered.

"Yeah. Me too."

Back home, I headed for Matt's gym equipment in the basement, did a half-hour workout, and got ready to leave.

"You're up early," Mom said on a yawn. She padded downstairs in her pajamas, hair pulled up in a ponytail.

"I have to go to the training academy today. Can I take the car?"

She shrugged. "I guess so. I have no plans today. When are you going to fix my wall?"

I blinked at her. "Crap, I forgot. I'll do it tomorrow."

"Promise?"

"Yes. I'm sorry. I totally forgot about it."

She held out car keys. "You're not going to get hurt, right?"

"No," I said with a shake of my head. "We're not allowed to practice with real fire." I took the keys, but she didn't let go. Instead, she grabbed me in a fierce hug.

"Reece, please don't take any risks just to impress Dad."

She didn't say it. But I knew what she was thinking. It was a waste of time and effort. Didn't mean I shouldn't try. "I won't, Mom."

But I would. Of course I would.

By eight o'clock, I was parked in the lot of the training facility, a huge firefighters' playground that served the whole county. I looked around at the fake structures, the junked vehicles—all kinds of things designed to build skills.

I was early, so I sat in the car, my note spread on the center console, and jotted down another line or two, waiting for my squadmates. A knock on the window startled me out of my thoughts. Amanda stood there wearing turnout pants, and I sucked in a sharp breath. The sun did things to her hair—things that made me wish I could reach out and touch it. The suspenders on her pants emphasized her chest. With that strong, tall body, Amanda Jamison could totally pose for one of those firefighter calendars. She didn't care how she looked, and damn if that didn't make her hotter.

But looking was all I could ever do. She'd made that clear.

"You gonna stare all day or are you ready to work?"

I gulped hard and nodded. "Oh, yeah, right. Okay."

"Come on." She strode off, and for a second, I stood and watched her move. The way she walked made me want to pull up a chair. I wanted to be like her. I wanted to strut like that and have people watch me when I did.

I sighed. Yeah, right. I couldn't even talk to my own dad.

I stuffed the note back into my pocket, locked up the car, and jogged to catch up to Amanda. Across the lot, Engine 21 was parked. I'd never heard it pull in. She opened a compartment and started handing me gear. "I asked Chief Duffy for a set of turnouts for you. The helmet and the coat are pretty new, but the pants have seen better days. It's practice gear. You stick it out until you're seventeen, you'll get your own brand-new ensemble." She smiled like she really wanted that to happen.

"Cool."

"Suit up and meet us over there." She pointed west where a cluster of people in turnouts gathered by a replica of a shopping strip. "We're doing a little informal competition with the squads from Holtsville and Laurel Point. Winner gets a stupid trophy." She rolled her eyes, but something in her tone told me she wanted that win.

Badly.

"I can do this," I assured her. "I'm ready."

She nodded. "First up is hose handling. We'll go in with charged lines and fight pretend fires."

I nodded and put on the practice gear.

Two hours later, I swore I'd sweated off five pounds dragging the charged line. Hose handling was a lot harder than it looked. But now I totally understood why Amanda had me drag a weighted rope around every day. We'd spent the morning learning how to connect, charge, and advance the line. Now it was time to apply that training.

"Sweat in training so you don't bleed in battle." Dad grinned at us. "It's an old saying. You guys ready for this?"

"Copy that." Gage grinned back.

We took shifts going inside the replica of a shopping center—a *taxpayer*, Amanda called it. It was just a strip of single-level stores, empty except for a few obstacles.

"Team Two, ready!" Dad shouted.

Amanda and I took our positions, with me clutching the nozzle and her directly behind me, supporting the hose. It took two firefighters to handle a hose under pressure.

"Remember what we practiced. Keep your hands here." Amanda adjusted my grip so that the nozzle was as far from my hands as my arms would allow. "At the signal, open the nozzle. Aim high, then go low."

I didn't quite get that part. We'd been instructed to aim water high before we got inside, and then aim it *at* the fire. Combination attack, Amanda said it was called. It had something to do with maintaining a thermal balance. I'd read all about this, but so far, it was just another fact I had memorized without understanding it.

"Go!"

In tandem, we moved the hose to the front of the single-story unit. Amanda tapped my shoulder, and I opened the nozzle, almost losing my grip. The force, Jesus, the force was unbelievable. Who knew water could have so much power? The hose jackhammered in my hand.

"Too much! Close it a bit," Amanda shouted.

I pulled back on the lever, and the recoil smoothed out. Water shot from the nozzle like a cannon. We moved into the store, and I did what Amanda taught me, spraying water high and around. Our job was to advance the attack line to the back of the store. We kept the hose to our right and slowly crawled on hands and knees through the interior. Keeping my balance was damn near impossible with the hose fighting me and the equipment suffocating me, but I managed not to fall.

"Keep looking around!" Amanda ordered. "Look for flames crawling across the ceiling, buckling in supports."

Right. I learned the stream of water went wherever I looked.

Abruptly, the water cut off.

"Switch!" Dad's instructions came over our radios. Amanda took the nozzle, and I fell behind her to act as backup. The line was charged, and I took hold of it, tapping Amanda's shoulder to signal I was ready. Smoothly, she opened the nozzle—there was no kickback—and began advancing toward the rear. The stream of water hiccupped. I looked behind me to see the hose had gotten caught on the door of the building. I tapped Amanda's shoulder and jerked my thumb at the door. She nodded, and together, we followed the hose line backward, out of the building, so we could unkink it.

Outside, we were met with applause from the rest of J squad.

I peeled off my helmet and mask and wiped my face.

"Holy shit, Logan! Didn't think you'd remember not to leave your partner. I almost had a heart attack when the lieutenant looped the hose over the door." Kevin clapped me on the back.

Dad stood with lieutenants from the other stations, conferring quietly over their clipboards. I slid him a look. Of course he'd deliberately try to trip *me* up.

Dad caught my eye and snapped, "Get back in the rotation. Practice opening and closing that nozzle until you can do it with no jackhammering."

I vibrated with fury, my hands curling into fists. I wanted to hit him so badly. Instead, I just pressed my lips together while he sneered. I opened my mouth, but nothing came out. Murmurs of frustration went up among my squadmates.

"Logan." Amanda shot me a look of exasperation. "Why don't you ever stand up to him?"

You wouldn't understand. I just shook my head and walked away.

I popped the trunk on my mother's car and started unfastening all my borrowed gear. A cluster of guys were laughing as they stowed their own gear in the SUV parked across from me. I chugged water from a bottle, poured some over my sweaty head, and jerked when one of those guys called out.

"Hey, Logan." A cadet from Holtsville waved at me. He wore a station uniform with the slogan *Professionally Staffed by Volunteers* inscribed over his heart. "You're Matt Logan's brother, right?"

I nodded, wary.

"When I was twelve, I volunteered at LVFD. Your dad trained me," he said and waited a beat to see if I'd smile and call him by name and invite him to Sunday dinner or something.

I didn't.

Half the county could say they were trained by my dad. Didn't mean anything...to *me*. But to Dad? I knew the fire service forged some strong bonds. Dad claimed they were stronger than fire itself. I didn't know about that. I did know they were stronger than blood.

"Sorry to hear about your brother, man."

I snapped up straight. "Oh, um, yeah, thanks."

"All of us were damn sorry to hear about him." He waved a hand to include his group. Some of those guys jerked their chins in acknowledgment, and before I could scrape my jaw off the ground, they'd piled into the SUV and pulled away. I managed to lift a hand to wave as they drove off.

Yeah. Strong bonds.

A sudden breeze blew, and I put aside those thoughts. I shrugged out of my bunker coat. My T-shirt stuck to my back, so I peeled that off too. I rolled my shoulders and stretched out the kinks. I shoved a hand into my pocket. Phone, wallet—oh God, it was gone. I patted all my pockets, then turned them inside out—nothing.

The note was gone.

I stood there, practically hyperventilating, dimly wondering why I kept hearing my name.

"Logan! Logan!"

I blinked and found Gage jogging up to me. "Is this yours? I think it fell out of your pocket."

In his hand, he held a damp, folded square of paper. My knees buckled. "Yeah. Thanks."

"What is it?" Gage peered at me, his eyes narrowed.

I sighed. "A good-bye letter I've been working on."

Frowning, Gage stuffed his hands into his pockets. "Thought you said you were in this all the way."

"Oh, I am. I was thinking of enlisting. You know. Army. Maybe Marines."

Gage's dark eyes popped. "You're kidding me."

"Well, it's no secret my dad doesn't want me around. I figured if I… left, he and my mom might get back together." I shrugged. "Now, I'm not so sure."

Gage studied me until I squirmed. "Okay. Stow your gear, then come back to the field. They're gonna present the trophy."

Yay.

He took a step, then turned back and scratched the back of his neck. "Um, look. I know you probably have, like, real friends, but if you ever need to, like, talk or whatever—"

Oh fuck me.

"Yeah. Thanks." I cut him off before this ended in one of those awkward guy hugs.

"Okay." He took off at a jog. "Oh, um, nice ink!"

I smoothed the paper out, frowned at it, and read it over. When I was done, I closed my eyes and clutched the note to the tattoo on my chest.

"You okay?"

I jolted and spun, my breath almost choking me. Amanda stood with a hip braced on somebody's car, arms crossed over her chest, and damn if that wasn't a crime against nature. "Yeah." I carefully refolded the paper and tucked it deep into my pocket.

"Really?" She laughed once. "Doesn't look like it."

My spine snapped straight, and I put my back to her. "Let me rephrase. Nothing to you." I whipped back around when I realized she must have been standing there for a while. "How long were you watching me anyway? You got some kind of thing for my naked body?" I dropped my voice low and peered at her from under my lashes, and she snapped off the hood of the car like she'd been shot from a rifle.

"Get real." She flipped me off, her cheeks going pink, and strode away.

"Hey, come on, I was kidding." I pulled on a clean shirt and topped it with a hoodie bearing the PROUD AND READY emblem that I found in Matt's box of stuff in the basement.

I caught up to her back on the field, where the juniors were gathered around an older guy in uniform.

"Congratulations, Lakeshore Junior Squad," he said, handing a small silver trophy to Amanda, who grinned and held it high over her head like it was the freakin' Stanley Cup.

Hands slapped my back, applause rang out, and cheers of "Yeah!" echoed around the field. I smiled so hard, my facial muscles began to burn. In the chaos of cadets still in turnout gear, congratulations and high fives from a bunch of people I didn't know, I lost sight of my own crew. I scanned the area but didn't see Dad anywhere either.

That didn't bother me at all.

I shrugged and started walking to the car, a kind of heavy warmth settling in my limbs. Suddenly, the air was shattered by a loud *crack*.

"You don't know anything about me or my son, Cadet. Dismissed," my father shouted.

I whipped around, vision narrowing, blood pulsing, and found my father jabbing a finger at Amanda's face over near Engine 21. I never gave my body the command to move, never thought about it.

I just…*did*.

In a split second, I was standing between them, pinning my father to the truck by his throat.

Chapter 16
Amanda

After the training facility chief awarded us our trophy, I'd scanned the crowd, pissed off to find John Logan didn't even bother to stick around. I finally found him over near Engine 21.

I'd had enough of this bullshit.

I strode over to him. "John."

He looked up from the clipboard he carried, shifted his weight, and waited.

So I dove straight in. "Whatever's wrong between you and Reece? Fix it."

His jaw went tight. "Excuse me?"

I was too pissed off to find the right words, the right tone. "He's trying. We're all trying. Everybody's trying. Except you."

"Oh really?" John's voice held that tone it always did right before he popped. Usually, it was at Matt. Occasionally, it was at Max or Ty. But never at me.

Until now.

"Our squad—the squad you now instruct—just won this month's trophy. And you don't even bother to stick around and give your cadets a high five. Is it really so hard for you to actually give your kid a compliment?"

John spiked the clipboard to the ground, and the sound was deafening. He pulled in a lungful of breath and let it out in slow motion, like he was doing his best to control his temper, but the tension in his arms, in his shoulders, told me that plan wasn't working so well. "You don't know anything about me or my son, Cadet. Dismissed," he shouted right in my face.

I glared at him, arms crossed, and finally shook my head. *Fine.*

I turned away, just in time to avoid a seriously pissed-off Reece Logan, charging straight for his father like a bullet train. In a heartbeat, he'd shoved John up against the side of the truck, T-shirt bunched in his fist.

"Do not," he said in a low tone that sent shivers skating up my back, "ever take out your fucking problems with me on her or anybody else on this squad." Teeth clenched, neck muscles corded, breath snorting from his nostrils, Reece looked ready—and able—to tear John in half.

"Reece! It's okay. Back off." I tried to break them up, but Reece's arms were like iron bars.

"Hey, hey, cool off, guys. Let him go, Reece."

Firefighter Jimmy Haggerty shoved his way between father and son and managed to back Reece up a few steps.

John's lips curled into their usual smirk. "Not bad, Peanut. You've been lifting." He smoothed out his shirt and picked up his clipboard.

"Stop with the Peanut crap, *Jackie.*"

John's eyebrows shot up.

My mouth fell open.

Who was this guy?

"Okay, okay, enough." Jimmy led John to the truck. "Reece, why don't you guys take off? Logan, get in the truck," he said to John.

John held up his hands in surrender, still smirking, and climbed aboard without a word. Reece glared after him for a moment and then strode away.

It took me almost a full minute to close my mouth. By that time, Reece's long legs had taken him halfway across the damn lot.

"Hey, Reece! Wait up!" I didn't catch up to him until he'd reached his car.

"What?"

Tired as he was, as we all were, I was totally amazed to see the temper that still sizzled in his eyes. I never saw Reece as much of a fighter. He seemed more like a sulker.

Until now.

"What?" I echoed, grabbing his arm. "You really have to ask? What the hell was that back there? You *want* to get kicked out?"

"No." He knocked my hand away. "Why the hell do you care anyway?"

I dropped my eyes to the ground. I lifted one shoulder and said only, "I didn't like the way your dad ignored my squad because he's—"

"*Your* squad?"

"Yeah. *Mine.* J squad is all I have that's mine." They took me in, made me one of them. Was it really so selfish to want to keep it? To protect it? I caught site of the emblem on my T-shirt. PROUD AND READY. Damn it, they should be more than just words. "What your dad did isn't right. Everybody pulled together to help get you trained up. We all did great today and deserved some applause for that."

"Well, maybe you should tell *him*."

"I did." I looked away, my face burning.

He continued to seethe and then blew out a long slow breath. With it, his temper finally faded. "I'm sorry."

I didn't want him to be sorry. The truth was he didn't have anything to be sorry about. But I was hot, hungry, and too damned tired to argue over it. "Okay, I guess we all keep forgetting you're new."

Reece gave me the side eye. "Trust me, he's completely aware of that."

His words, or maybe it was the look in his eyes, squeezed my heart. I always thought families loved each other just *because*—that they didn't have to perform feats like this…this twisted audition Reece was doing for his dad. But I didn't say anything. What did I know about families?

I turned, shielded my eyes against the sun, and watched Engine 21 pull out of the parking lot.

I used to like John Logan. After Matt died, John cleaned out Matt's locker and never uttered his name again. I'd tried to talk to him about a month after the funeral. I'd asked John if we could do a memorial event for Matt, but John's mouth went thin and a hard look came into his eyes—a look that screamed hatred and fury. I'd stopped talking midsentence, the closest I'd come to one of John Logan's legendary temper displays—until today. But John just shook his head and said memorials were a damn waste of time and had no point. Anybody who could forget Matt Logan had something wrong with them, and no memorial would ever be able to fix that. I couldn't argue with that logic, so I'd dropped the subject.

That hard look in John's eyes never faded.

With Reece in our house, that look just kept getting harder, and it completely broke my heart. Reece was trying so hard.

No one had ever tried for me.

I glanced back at Reece. The look in *his* eyes never faded either. The looks—John's angry and Reece's so painfully sad—were like some kind of symbiotic life-form, each feeding the other, or feeding off the other.

I clenched my fists. *Stupid. Stubborn.* They were so damn lucky and had no freaking clue.

Chapter 17
Reece

I'm not a coward. I'm not sure what I am, but I'm not that. I used to be tired. And sad. So fucking sad. But that was a long time ago. I'd kill to feel only sad right now.

I sank against my mother's car, unable to look at Amanda.

"I'm sorry," she said softly, cutting me in half.

"No! No, Amanda, it's not your fault."

"Reece, for what it's worth, I think your dad was proud of you today. He can't stand it, but he was."

I snorted out half a laugh. "He hates me, Amanda."

Her face twisted. "No."

"Trust me." I snorted again and opened the car door for her. "I had all these issues when I was a baby. Colic. I didn't sleep. I was afraid of everybody who wasn't my mom. She says we never bonded—my dad and me." I rolled my eyes. What a stupid word. *Bond.* Because I didn't do cute shit like other babies, my dad didn't have to love me? Blood, DNA—why wasn't that enough? Isn't that how it was supposed to work?

"I was about three when I figured it out. He and Matt spent a ton of time together—camping, fishing, playing catch. I used to cry and beg to join them, but—" I shook my head. This was pointless. I sounded like I was still three, whining about everything that didn't fit my sense of fair.

I walked around the car and climbed behind the wheel, and Amanda got into the passenger seat. We sat there for a long moment, staring through the windshield at the empty parking lot. The car smelled like lemons—fresh squeezed lemonade—and my mouth watered. Suddenly, the dam burst, and words just fell out of my mouth.

"Dads are supposed to *teach* their sons, you know? They're supposed to tuck them in at night, chase away the monsters under the bed, help them become men. He never did that stuff with me, just Matt." I slammed my palm against the wheel. "I should have hated Matt, but I couldn't. He's the one who taught me how to bait a hook and tie my shoes and pitch a curve ball and even piss standing up. God! I miss him. I miss him so fucking much, it feels like it's gonna kill me."

I covered the tattoo of Matt's name burned in the skin over my heart and squeezed my eyes shut, but tears dripped from them anyway. A soft warmth spread over my hand. For a minute, I thought it was Matt. I opened my eyes and found Amanda's hand covering mine.

"You're here. And you're dealing."

No, I wasn't. Not really. The note in my pocket suddenly felt like a hot knife twisting in my gut.

"Matt was what held our family together. Now he's gone…Dad's gone. Mom didn't even argue about it." I shook my head.

She didn't get it. She just kept looking at me like I was a toddler with a boo-boo on his knee.

I cursed. "Look at me, Amanda!" I waved my hand at my face. "I have his eyes, his build. I wear the same shoe size as he does, but everything about me bugs him. He will *never* love me the way he loved Matt, and I got that a long time ago. So I'll settle for—" I broke off abruptly. I'd nearly spilled the truth, and that was a secret nobody was getting from me, even if she did smell like lemonade. "I'll settle for his respect."

She stared at me for a long moment and finally nodded. "You're getting it, Reece. You worked your ass off, getting in shape, studying. I've never seen a cadet work as hard as you. Hang in there, okay?" She ended with a smile that seared itself into my brain.

Amanda had a crooked tooth.

How had I never noticed that before? One of her bottom teeth was just a little crooked, and she even had a dimple. I would have noticed the dimple if she smiled at me like this sooner. Maybe this meant she didn't hate me.

Wow. Someone who didn't hate me. I could get used to that. I grinned back and stuck out a hand. "Deal."

She took my hand, shook it once, but didn't let go. Her pulse—or was it mine?—tripped against my fingers. The lemony air inside the car taunted me, and I wanted to pull her hair out of that tight knot and bury my face in it. I could hear her breathe, feel the heat against my face each time she did. Something was happening here, something that shouldn't, no matter how much I wanted it to. And God, I wanted it, as much as I wanted my dad to forgive me. Maybe more.

Staring into my eyes, she licked her lips, and I was lost or maybe I was found. I didn't know, I didn't care, I didn't think. I'm pretty sure the world stopped turning. My heart sped up and kept time with her pulse. A strand of hair that had escaped that tight little knot fell across her eyes, and it called to me, like the ribbon on a birthday gift, begging to be unwrapped. I tugged the band in her hair free, tossed it on the dashboard, and let her hair spill through my fingers, closing my eyes as her sweet scent filled the air. I traced the curves of her face, the dimple I'd just discovered. Amanda tilted her head, nuzzling against my palm, and sighed like I was a dream she didn't want to end. I pressed my lips to hers, and her hands gripped my arms, pulling me closer, and when her lips opened under mine, time stopped. Our tongues touched, and my stomach flipped. It was a kiss that should have broken hearts, but mine was mended. When we finally separated, I patted my chest to make sure it was still there.

It was.

"Oh God, Reece. This is impossible." She touched her lips with fingers that shook, and pride burned through me, knowing I was the one who'd made them shake—that I even could. "What are we going to do?" She hugged me tight, like she wanted to keep me, and I never wanted to be kept so badly in my whole life.

I smiled down at her, because impossible or not, I was too happy not to. "I don't know, but I promise I'll figure it out."

A cell phone buzzed, and we jumped apart like we'd been Tasered.

"It's the Becketts. Oh God, I'm late."

"I'll drive you home." I started the car, pulled out of the lot, and drove with that grin on my face all the way to her place.

Chapter 18
Amanda

Crap, crap, shit! What in the actual hell just happened? A month ago, I hated this boy, and today, I'm kissing him?

Reece shifted into gear and pulled out of the lot. I sank lower into the seat and tried to pretend everything was cool, that my heart hadn't just cracked through its armor. I knew better than this. I knew better than anyone just how badly love can mess you up. I'd whispered "Love you" when Mrs. Merodie tucked me in one night, and the social worker removed me from that foster home the next day. And Mom. Jesus, Mom was doing time because Dmitri, her jerk-off boyfriend, conned her into a scheme that got *her* caught with all the evidence while he pleaded stupidity.

Okay, he pleaded no contest, but Mom was still the one who went to prison. She was in an upstate correctional facility that I couldn't visit unless someone was willing to take me. Enough said.

I snuck a glance at Reece and wished I could kick myself. He'd been through hell today. And then I—oh God. He was smiling like he'd just won the lottery.

I jerked in my seat.

Me? A lottery prize.

I tried to remember a single time in my life when anyone had treated me like something precious. Something special. Only Mom had, and then she'd…stopped.

Since the day he walked into the firehouse, Reece looked at me like I was a real girl. I was never *Man* to him but *Amanda*. And yeah, I kind of liked the way he stared at me, breathing through his mouth, trying not to look at my chest.

Matt never looked at me that way. Or made me feel the way I was feeling—ready to say fuck the rules and statistics, ready to risk everything just to be looked at that way one more time.

I blew out a long, slow breath. "I live a few blocks off Upper Cedar Grove."

He nodded. "I know where that is." He was still smiling.

I made him smile like that.

In all these weeks, in every smile I'd seen, there was always that little bit of pain Reece couldn't completely hide. I knew Reece could single-handedly fight a fire, save the kid, the old lady, and the puppy, and John would probably just smirk and say Matt could have done it better. If I hadn't seen John treat Reece like crap myself, I wouldn't have believed it. John Logan was one of the reasons this squad felt like family for me. Matt, Gage, and all the lieutenants had rallied around me, trained me up fast. I was so afraid it would be just like foster care… always the outsider, always looking in.

Oh.

The thought slammed into my brain, like a home-run swing to the head. This was what life was like for Reece inside his own family.

Having to watch over and over when his dad did things with his brother instead of him, see the way his dad blamed him for the accident that killed Matt. Jesus, if Reece were a foster kid, there was no doubt in my mind John would have sent him back.

A tear dripped to my hand, and it pissed me off because I had to decide if that sucked more than not having a dad at all.

"Which one's yours?" He signaled and turned onto the street where the Becketts lived.

Foster home number four.

"This one." I pointed to the two-story with blue shutters. "Thanks for the ride. I'm…God…I'm sorry."

"Amanda, wait—"

I shut the door before he could say anything else and ran up the walk, already feeling the cold and loneliness settle back in my bones.

***

Safely upstairs in my room, I fell face-first onto the bed, licking my lips.

They still tasted like Reece.

Suddenly, I remembered what he said the other night at the diner, about kisses so hot, so intense, they'd set records. I wanted that kiss like I wanted my next breath. I was so friggin' jealous of the girl he described, I almost got sick.

And tonight, I *was* that girl.

Oh God! I smothered a sob with my pillow. What was I gonna do? I couldn't be with Reece, and now, I couldn't be without him. Everything was such a fucking mess.

192

A knock on my door made me bolt upright. I snagged tissues from the box next to my bed and wiped my eyes. "Yeah?"

Mrs. Beckett poked her head inside. "Hey, Amanda, we're— what's wrong?"

"Oh, nothing. Just really tired. It was a hard practice today."

Frowning, she stepped inside and sat next me on the edge of the bed, holding an envelope. "Did your squad fail?"

"No. No, we won. But Lieutenant Logan didn't even stick around for the trophy presentation."

"Oh." She nodded, like she actually understood a word I was saying.

"It's not fair. We worked our asses off, and he didn't even give us a thumbs-up."

"You're right," she said. "It's not fair. But it is what it is." She stood up and walked to the door. "We're going grocery shopping. You can use what's left of the peanut butter and jelly if you're hungry."

Can I? Can I really?

"Thanks."

"I almost forgot. This came for you today."

She tossed the envelope to the table next to my bed and shut the door. I shook my head. *It is what it is.* What the hell does that even mean, and how is it supposed to make me feel better? "Good talk," I muttered to the closed door.

I tore open the envelope she'd left. It was from the county. My social worker would pick me up Monday directly after school to transport me to the correctional facility upstate for a visit with dear old Mom. I was ordered to make myself available.

It is what it is. I crumpled up the order and pitched it across the room as hard as I could.

Chapter 19
Reece

I know you hate me. Blame me for everything you lost. But I lost more than you did that day. I lost my brother and my dad. He was both of those things to me, because you wouldn't be one.

I drove all the way home on autopilot, that insanely happy moment with Amanda determined to morph into the cold greasy ball now rolling around inside my stomach.

I shouldn't have kissed her.

From the moment I saw her at Matt's funeral, I'd imagined being with her. Holding her. Kissing her. I imagined her being with me. Wanting *me*.

And then, she'd looked at me with that trademark sneer and called me Matt, and my imagination lapsed into a coma, responding only to the occasional whiffs of sweet lemons and glimpses of her smile. When she'd offered to help me catch up to the rest of the squad, I should have been happy with that. But I wanted more. I wanted *all*.

And that was always my problem, wasn't it? Always desperate for the things I didn't have, envious of the people who had them. That would stop right here, right now. I wasn't going to cause trouble or make a scene. Amanda deserved better than that from me. I'd suck it up and focus on the job.

Keep my promise to Matt.

I walked up the path to our house, unlocked the door, and found a note from Mom: *Gone shopping with Auntie Sue*. I knew I wouldn't see them until the stores closed, so I searched the refrigerator, found a covered dish that turned out to be lasagna, and slid it into the oven. While it heated, I took Tucker out for a quick walk, then sprawled on the sofa with one of the books Bear had found for me, a compilation of fire service stories from guys on the front lines in the NYFD.

It used to piss me way the hell off when Dad, Matt, and my uncle would sit around trading stories, each one more outrageous than the last, because all I could do was listen. I had nothing to add, couldn't appreciate a word they were saying. I was a spectator, a witness to their bravery. Matt's gone, Dad's gone, and Uncle Ray hasn't been around, so there were no more stories. Strange to say, but I missed that. The house felt like it lost its soul.

Matt was the sun the rest of us orbited.

I tossed the book on the coffee table, took the note out of my pocket, and unfolded it. The words I'd written so far barely lifted the first layer of resentment I carried, but I wouldn't erase or start over or revise.

It had to be stream of consciousness.

"Promise me, Reece."

"No! Just hold on. Help's coming. People are calling 911."

"Won't matter. You need to do this, Reece. Promise me."

"Okay, okay, I promise. Just keep breathing!"

"Can't. Hurts."

"Reece?"

I blinked at my mother and tucked the note back in my pocket.

"Smells good in here. You heated the lasagna?"

"Yeah." I stood and followed her into the kitchen. "How was your day?"

She shrugged and reached for an oven mitt. "Shopping is exhausting." She slid out the pan, stuck a fork in it, and blew on a piece before popping a bite into her mouth. "Mm. Perfect. Grab some plates?"

I took two from the dishwasher, and a few minutes later, we were digging into hot and spicy lasagna.

Mom peered at me through narrowed eyes. "You're too quiet. You okay?"

I snorted out a laugh. I didn't think I'd ever been *okay*. "Yeah, fine."

Mom angled her head and finally nodded. We ate in silence for a while.

"How was your fire thing today?"

"Um, good. Our squad won a trophy."

"That's great!" She didn't ask about Dad. She knew the answer, so I figured she didn't want to beat the dead horse.

"So are you doing anything tomorrow?"

Tomorrow was what, Sunday? "Nope."

"Fix my bathroom."

I winced. "Right. Hole patching."

"And shelf hanging." She pointed to a box on the counter. "Lots of shopping today."

Another promise to keep. "Okay, okay, I'll do it as soon as I wake up."

"Thank you." She stood, grabbed both plates, and headed for the sink. "I'm going to shower off my day. Wanna watch a movie?"

A movie with my mother? *So* not how I pictured spending my evening, but okay. "Great."

She smacked my arm. "You could try for a little enthusiasm."

"Sorry." I grinned at her as she headed upstairs. I picked up the book and read another firsthand account of life in the fire service for New York City—stories that made me itch. I wasn't sure I could rush into a fire, knowing I might not come out. I wasn't sure I had what it took to pull charred children from smoldering ash, or to stand shoulder to shoulder with guys like my dad, guys who didn't give two craps about me, and trust them with my life. But then, the words I was reading started to float off their pages. I swear I could hear Matt's bravado, Dad's clipped tone, and Uncle Ray's city accent. It felt like I'd left the sidelines and jumped into the action. The more I read, the more I wanted this, wanted to do this, wanted to be this kind of man.

Maybe firefighting really was in the blood.

Uncle Ray always said, *It's not what you do, it's who you are.* As soon as I was seventeen, I could respond to real calls. That was still a ways off, and I had a lot to learn before that would happen. With Amanda and Bear and all the other juniors helping me, I had a real shot at this.

It may have started off as a way to keep my promise to Matt, but it was so much more than that now.

**

The next morning, a text from Bear woke me up. Still too brain-fogged to text back, I called him.

"Hey, Logan! You got plans?"

"Jesus, Bear. It's like the crack of dawn." I yawned.

"It's eight thirty, Logan."

"You always get up this early on a Sunday?"

"You haven't met my *avó*. She drags us all out of bed for chores and food."

"Your mom?"

"No, my grandma."

Oh right. Must be Portuguese. I sat up, scratched, stretched, and started over. "So, um, plans. I have to patch a hole in the bathroom wall. Well, I have to head to the store and buy drywall compound first."

"Oh." He sounded deflated. "Maybe after, you could help me with my homework again? I aced that bio quiz, thanks to you."

I squirmed. "Come on, all I did was teach you one mnemonic."

Bear laughed. "Hey! I can help you fix the wall, and then maybe you can help me study?"

I got of out bed and searched for clean clothes. "You know how to repair drywall?"

"In case you haven't noticed, I'm kind of big. You know how many holes I've put in walls?"

I thought about it for a minute. "Be ready by nine. Text me your address, and I'll pick you up."

Still cursing that I was awake before nine on a Sunday morning, I pulled up in front of Bear's house. He was waiting for me on the porch, wearing denim shorts that reached all the way to his knees and a huge white T-shirt with an American flag. With a wave and a grin, he shuffled down the walk, folded his girth into the front seat of my mom's car, and grinned.

Bear fastened his seat belt and slunk low in his seat, nodding in time to the song on the radio. We said nothing until we reached the local home center. We roamed up and down aisles and pulled a bucket of wall joint compound from a shelf and then found some sandpaper and drywall screws. Bear led me to the lumber section where we found some plywood furring strips and tossed one into the cart. I paid for the materials, and we were back on the road, only to come to a dead stop at the first intersection, where a minivan had been T-boned by an SUV.

"Turn right or we'll be stuck here all day." Bear pointed north to a side street.

I turned, and we were soon out of the traffic, rolling with the windows down through neighborhoods barely awake on a Sunday morning. Sprinklers ticked across lawns, and a few homeowners raked yards or trimmed hedges. The faint acrid odor of smoke wafted into the open windows. Somebody was burning leaves—illegal here.

I continued driving, and when I reached a stop sign, I saw a few people all running the same direction.

"Holy crap, dude. That house is on fire!" Bear pointed to a boarded-up house on a property whose lawn hadn't been cut in weeks. Smoke drifted out from the top, leaking from windows and the attic ridge. I pulled over, cut the engine, and got out of the car.

"Logan, man, what are you doing? We can't work a scene. It's against the rules—especially without gear."

Impatient, I waved a hand to get him moving his ass. "I know the rules." Had the damn things memorized, didn't I? "And I have gear." I popped the trunk where all of the practice gear from yesterday was still packed. The only problem was the oxygen tank was pretty much drained. "We can't just leave. What if there's somebody inside?" I kicked off my shoes and shoved my feet into the boots tucked inside bunker pants.

Bear nodded, took out his phone, and called 911. I took a breath, and my nose wrinkled at the odors. In my mind, I pictured an exact copy of the chapter in my textbook about responding to a structure fire. First, firefighters are supposed to do a size-up, an assessment of the scene, so I did a three-sixty. A crowd had started to form across the street—maybe a dozen people. I looked at the house; it was a standard, vinyl-sided two-story. There was a shed to the side of the house, near the backyard. I hoped it was empty. Fertilizer, gasoline, and other lawn care products presented huge risks to firefighters. I looked for the tallest column of smoke to tell me where the fire's source was. There were two; I couldn't tell which one was taller. Smoke was venting along the soffits too. The smoke was light, thin, and looked like it was boiling. That meant it was a fast-moving fire, but I didn't see flames.

The property was boarded up, though many of the boards were loose, allowing smoke to leak.

I grabbed my cell phone, tapped the video button, and panned the lens across the small crowd standing and pointing at the burning home. Choruses of *Oh my God!* and other prayers floated over the air. Three men ran across the street with pry bars, and I forgot about video recording so I could stop them.

"Stop! If you open that door, you'll feed the fire. Wait for the crews to arrive."

"Get out of the way, kid!" A heavy guy wearing nothing but a T-shirt and boxers knocked me aside. I chased after him, my throat tightening. Christ, the stench was bad. Melted plastic, something chemical.

"Listen to me. I'm a volunteer with the LVFD. You have to wait for the crews so they can vent the building at the top."

The heavy guy peered at me and nudged his friend. "Okay. Let's grab that ladder and get the roof opened."

Jesus H. Kristofferson on a bike, did this guy have even a single functioning neuron in his brain? I heard sirens and air horns in the distance and knew the crews from LVFD would be here in just a few more minutes. I had to hold him off that long or the crew would be dragging this guy out in a body bag.

"Fire needs oxygen to burn. You have to wait for the hoses. That's how we do this. Guys on the roof vent the fire, lure it up and away from the entrances. Guys on the ground sneak in with hoses and knock it back. You open that structure, you'll flood it with fresh fuel."

The man danced on coiled muscles, itching to be useful, to do something.

"Help me get those hydrants clear." I pointed to the motorcycle parked in front of the closest hydrant. Down the block and across the street, another hydrant was blocked by a parked car.

With a nod, the man strode off, his friends following. Together, they bodily lifted the motorcycle up and out of the way just as Truck 3 and Engine 21 turned onto the scene, Chief Duffy in his own vehicle right behind them. I didn't stop to watch what the men did with the car blocking the second hydrant.

"Fire line is right here—get those people back. I want an attack line here." The chief barked orders into his radio and waved toward the front door. Then he saw me. "Logan. Acosta. What the hell are you two doing here?"

"First on scene, Chief. We called it in," Bear reported. "Reece kept that big dude from breaking down the door."

Chief Duffy glanced at the neighbor in his boxer shorts and grunted. "Good job. Okay. Acosta, I want you down there, directing traffic off this block. Logan, you maintain crowd control. Stay put."

Whoa, he was letting us stay? "Copy, Chief."

I moved to the street in front of the burning house, spread my arms, and raised my voice. "Everybody, please step back. Keep this street clear for the apparatus and let the crew do their jobs."

The crowd—now up to about thirty spectators—surged backward. I scanned faces. Everybody looked scared, sickened, and worried, except one kid. He was sending a text message.

Glass broke, and I whipped around. The truck crew already had the roof cut and, firefighter Ken Tully had just shoved a Halligan tool through a window on the top floor. The smoke turned dark and rushed to fill the hole. Flames lashed out—orange, red, green, yellow. Jesus, the heat. I felt it from here. The crew spread out—two guys already had the hose stretched, ready for Chief Duffy's order to attack. Another pair positioned a ground ladder. I tapped the record button on my phone's camera and shot some more footage. Maybe I could update the station website, since I couldn't do anything else that was useful. I panned around the fire line, recorded the chaos on one side and precise choreography on the other. The fire shot out another arm from a rear window, and my heart rate kicked into high gear. The heat, God! It was vicious. I stepped back, trying to move the crowd with me, but the smell, holy God, it was worse than the heat.

I watched and recorded, and something scratched at the back of my brain.

This wasn't right.

I studied the burning house. The flames were wrong. The smoke patterns were wrong. The smells, everything was off. Nothing matched what I'd read.

I spun around and scanned the crowd again. Bear had the traffic direction under control, along with a neighbor who'd decided to help. A police car blocked the street across from Bear. Up and down the block, the crowd of now fifty stood and watched, their expressions horrified.

All except one.

The boy sending the text message.

He didn't watch the fire. He didn't watch the crew trying to fight it. He just kept scanning up and down the street.

The textbook said to look for the people who stand out, and hell, did he stand out. He was the only thing at this scene that matched the textbook. He wore clothes at least two sizes too big for him. He looked familiar, but I didn't know him personally. I pegged him at about twelve, maybe thirteen years old. I doubted the cell phone even belonged to him, because he pressed every letter one at a time with one finger instead of using his thumbs.

I watched him a moment longer. And then, one of our guys emerged from the black smoke. In his arms, he cradled a small bundle. My heart squeezed and stopped—just stopped.

The firefighter removed his helmet and mask. Chuck Avers gently laid his bundle on the grass where Engine 21 was parked. It was a cat. A cat and two kittens, one black and white, the other with gray stripes.

All three were unconscious.

"Reece, I need a hand." He waved me over. I ran to my car to fetch a bottle of water while Chuck opened a panel on Engine 21 and took out the pet resuscitators. I stripped down, tugged off my T-shirt, soaked it in water, and wrapped it around the kittens. Their fur was a little black from soot, but I didn't see any burns. I felt for pulses along their hind legs and found a beat that was slow but steady. A good sign.

"Got a pulse in both."

"No pulse here. Mom's gone." Chuck covered the cat's body with a towel, then handed me a tank, and we squeezed oxygen into the unconscious kittens wrapped in my wet shirt. Across the street, the crowd expressed its collective sympathy.

"He moved, Chuck. This one's coming around."

Chuck glanced at the black-and-white kitten twitching under my hand and gave it a few aggressive rubs that quickly had the tiny animal wriggling in protest. "Good, good, he's getting pink again. Nice job, Reece."

I grinned but quickly grew serious when the striped kitten didn't move.

"This one's gone," he said.

"No. No, Chuck. I felt a pulse. Give him a few more minutes."

Chuck swiped a hand over bloodshot blue eyes and sighed. "Reece, I got a fire to put out. Can you take over?"

I nodded, took the bag valve, and squeezed it rhythmically. The tuxedo kitten started licking its sibling, letting out a few tiny *mews*. It didn't take long, another minute, and the tabby twitched. A minute after that, he was blinking yellow eyes at his brother in a "What the hell happened to us?" exchange that had me grinning from ear to ear.

I tried to keep the mask over both tiny faces. Tux kept fighting the mask, but Tabs was still kind of out of it. I poured some water into the bottle cap and held it steady while the alert kitten lapped it up.

"Reece, you need help?"

I looked up to find Bear actually striding toward me, his shuffle gone. "I got this. Control the crowd, and keep an eye on that kid." I pointed out the suspicious one. "He keeps texting and looking at everything except the fire."

"Copy." He strode toward the onlookers gawking from across the street just as Tabs swatted at the mask over his face.

"Hey, little guy. Welcome back."

I unwrapped them from my wet shirt, let them totter around on their own feet for a few seconds, and stood up. A cheer went up from across the street. I scooped up both kittens. "Anybody have a box we can borrow?"

"Yeah, I do!" a woman wearing a jogging suit called out. She disappeared inside a house, then returned a few minutes later with a pet carrier and a soft blanket. I put Tux and Tabs inside.

It took the crews about an hour to knock the fire down, and the chief called the all-clear. A cheer went up from the crowd, and I grinned.

"Pretty cool," Bear whispered, and I nodded. It was. Then he slapped my arm. "Look! That kid's taking off." He jerked his chin toward the suspicious boy.

"Come on. Let's follow him—shit!" My mother's car was blocked by Engine 21 and Truck 3. I started running. "Hey! Don't move!" I hollered.

The boy froze and stared at Bear with huge frightened eyes, then at me. "I didn't do nothin'!"

"Then why are you running?"

"I gotta get home."

"In a minute." I put out my hands. "I saw you as soon as we got out of the car. You have a phone. Did you call 911?"

The boy's eyes bounced from me to Bear and back. He shook his head. "No, I, uh—"

"Who were you texting?"

"Nobody! I was just—"

"Just happened to be at the scene of a fire but didn't call the fire department."

"I was walking by and—"

"Did you see anybody leave that house?"

"No." The boy's eyes shifted, a sure sign he was lying.

"Bear, get the chief."

"Copy that." Bear took off at a jog.

"No, wait! I told you, I didn't do nothing. I didn't see anything either."

"Cadet Logan," Dad barked. "What the hell is going on here?"

I whipped around and found my dad standing there with his helmet in his hands. "Lieutenant, this kid's acting suspicious. He was one of the first spectators on-scene. He has a phone but never called 911. I think he set this fire."

Dad's face went red—well, redder than it was from exertion. He put his hands on his hips, his eyes going to slits when he saw the tattoo over my heart. "And you just what, strode up to him and *accused* him?"

"No! I was trying—"

"Logan!"

Dad and I both spun at the sound of the chief's bark.

"Lieutenant, supervise salvage."

I could hear my dad's teeth grind. "Copy." He walked away, gear jingling.

The chief turned to me. "Cadet, what were my instructions to you when I found you on-scene?"

I swallowed hard. "Crowd control, Chief."

"And why are you halfway down the block antagonizing a little boy?"

Antagonizing? Whoa, wait. "I think he set the fire."

Chief Duffy's eyebrows shot into his hairline. "Based on your *minutes* of experience, you decided, by yourself, to confront someone who may be entirely innocent of any crime?"

"Yes. I mean, no! He was acting suspicious, and I didn't want him to get away until I found out more—"

"Cadet, you don't get to decide what you want without clearing it with your lieutenant and with me. I told you to stay put." He punctuated that word with a sweeping gesture toward the crowd line. "You didn't follow that order." He turned and found Bear. "Acosta!"

Bear froze. "Sir."

"Your orders were traffic control. I don't see any traffic on this lawn."

Bear's face turned a sick shade of gray. "No. No, sir."

"Why are you way down this end of the street?"

"Cats, Chief."

"What?"

"Cats. Three of them. One didn't make it. A neighbor has the two survivors. Logan resuscitated them."

Chief Duffy took off his helmet, scrubbed a hand over his hair, and sighed. "You are dismissed. Leave the scene—"

"But Chief, what about salvage?" I asked.

He stepped closer to me. I was a little over six feet tall, and he still looked down on me. "I said you are dismissed. Go home. Expect a phone call from me later when I decide what to do about you two going freelance."

Fuck. I opened my mouth, but Bear's hand came down heavy on my shoulder and squeezed.

Hard.

"Copy, Chief." Bear nodded. He turned me around and practically towed me back to my mother's car, still blocked by Engine 21 and Truck 3.

"Bear, I—"

"Get in."

Jesus. I got behind the wheel, and he folded himself into the passenger seat and shut the door. He sat there, panting, for a moment. "*Deus.*" He let his head fall back on the seat and covered his face.

My stomach clenched and flipped. My fault. All my fault. I didn't follow orders, and now Bear's in trouble.

A tap on my window made me jerk. It was the woman who provided the cat carrier. I opened it, and she handed me a blue cloth.

"Thought you could use a shirt." I took the cloth and unfolded it. It had a Superman S. She patted my hand. "You both did a good job here today. I hope you don't get yelled at." She smiled, and my eyes burned. Damn smoke was really irritating them. Chuck Avers tapped on my hood, indicated he'd move Engine 21 so we could leave.

"Thank you, ma'am," I said and started the car. I pulled away and drove down the street. Chief Duffy and my dad were having what looked like a tense conversation. Both glared at me as I rolled by. I rolled my shoulders, straightened my spine, and looked ahead.

Time to face the firing squad.

Chapter 20
Amanda

Late Sunday morning, after I'd done the chores Mrs. Beckett assigned me, I opened the front door to head out for my run, when Larry nearly bowled me over.

"Whoa, where's the fire?" I asked with a grin.

He skidded to a stop, sweat running down his face like tears, and stared at me, jaw dangling. Without a word, he bolted up the stairs to his room.

Weird.

I shook my head and started out. The weather was perfect. Excellent running weather, really.

But…

I couldn't even fool myself with this fake happy routine. No sense trying. I stepped into the street and started a brisk walk. I'd read every word printed on the literature Mr. Serrano gave me. With each word, the rock in my belly grew a little bigger.

I lengthened my stride and poured on the speed, running full-out until my lungs wanted to explode. I jogged around a corner and jerked to a stop. Trucks from both LVFD and the next town were just pulling away from a foreclosed house, or what was left of it. I pulled out my phone and texted Gage to see if he knew what happened. He replied immediately.

2 alarms! And guess who was first on-scene? Reece and Bear.

Holy crap.

I texted back and asked him to meet me at the firehouse. I wanted to hear everything that happened at this fire and how the hell Reece and Bear managed to be anywhere near the scene. I jogged back home, showered and changed as fast as I could, and started for the stairs, but Larry was huddled on the top step, blocking my way.

"Oh. Hey, Larry."

He opened his mouth but then shut it.

"You okay?"

He lifted one shoulder, let it fall.

"Come on. You can tell me. I won't get mad, no matter what's wrong."

The muscles in his throat worked, but he still didn't say anything.

With a sigh, I squished myself onto the step beside him. "Larry, you know I'd never narc on you, right?"

"Yeah, I guess." He squeezed his eyes shut. It didn't sound like he believed me. I tried not to take that personally. Larry's been bouncing around the system for a long time and knew the rules better than I did. We were friends. More than that, we were solid—well, as solid as foster kids can let themselves get. It was hard to talk. And a lot of people think that was because we don't trust them, but that's not the problem. The problem is remembering *not* to trust. You kind of settle into the routine and get used to the people around you. If you're lucky, you can fool yourself into believing they like you, maybe even love you.

But stay in the system long enough, and you know every time there's a knock on the door, it could be your social worker there to pull you out.

So you weigh the pros and cons.

You know if you say something, just *one thing* out of line, the social workers and judges are gonna get involved, and before you can protest, you're huddled in a tiny ball in the back of a county vehicle on your way to the next home, the next group center, wondering what loser they'll assign you to next.

Because for every couple like the Becketts, there are fifty who do it only for the monthly checks.

That's what happened to me at Mrs. Merodie's place. I had my own room. Toys. Clothes. I was supposed to start school. And then, the knock on the door came, and I got buckled into the backseat of that county car and driven to someplace new.

Someplace *else*.

You never see those people again. You're not allowed to call them or visit them.

So I tried to cut Larry a little slack. Whatever was on his mind, he wanted to tell me but was afraid one of us might be gone in the morning. I knew exactly how he felt.

"Hey, can you show me how to text?"

"Um, sure." The Becketts had given us both cell phones, so they could contact us when they needed to. But they weren't exactly state of the art. I took out my ancient flip phone, showed him how to double or triple-tap keys to get the rest of the letters, and clicked send.

"I kept messing up."

I cursed silently. He must have tried to text me and couldn't. "It's okay."

The look he gave me said it *wasn't* okay, not by a long shot.

"Larry, you're not in any kind of trouble, are you?"

Another shake of his head. "I didn't do anything!" He swiped a knuckle under his nose.

"Okay. okay. Good." That was some comfort at least. But I didn't want to leave him alone. "I have to go to the fire station. Why don't you come?"

His eyes snapped open and shot to mine. "No!" He leaped up, hurried to his room, and shut the door.

I stared after him for a moment, a heavy guilt squeezing my heart. Mr. Beckett had gotten me involved with the squad but not Larry, even though he was old enough. Did that mean Larry wouldn't be here long?

Oh God!

The front door opened and closed. "Amanda? Larry? Come down and help me unpack the car."

Mr. Beckett was home. On Sunday mornings, he usually got up early and headed out to run a bunch of errands, including a run to a warehouse store for supplies to stock his man cave, which was really the garage in the back of the house.

Larry came out of his room, muttering curses. "I got this. You'd better get to the firehouse before he notices you're home."

I nodded. "Okay. I'll find you later and we'll talk."

Larry edged by me, and my nose wrinkled. I grabbed his shoulder. "Dude, have you been *smoking*?" I asked, horrified.

He wrestled free. "No!" He ran down the stairs before I could argue.

Jesus, he really had me worried now. Maybe I'd talk to Lieutenant Logan about Larry and grab the forms for him to start J squad too. Even if the Becketts sent him away, his next foster parents might let him keep up, especially if John and Chief Duffy put in good words. I knew Gage and the rest of the juniors would rally around Larry just the way everybody was doing for Reece. We'd get him trained in no time. And after we aged out of foster care, we'd still get to work together and hang out and be sort of siblings and—

Damn it.

See how easy it was to plan? I forced myself to stop. I hurried downstairs and out the back door to begin the long walk to the firehouse. When I reached the fire station, I found all our vehicles back in their bays and the crews checking and rechecking equipment, inspecting gear. I walked in just in time to overhear Ken Tully and Chuck Avers talking about the fire.

"…saw trailers on the top floor. What was left of it."

Ken whistled quietly. "Explains the separate fires. Conner's on his way to the scene."

Trailers were like kindling, strips of paper or other stuff arranged in paths to make the fire spread faster. Steve Conner was our fire marshal. If he was on his way to the scene, they suspected another arson.

I headed for the conference room, where Gage, Ty, and Kevin were already sitting.

Word travels fast.

I grabbed Gage and led him to a quiet corner. "What did you hear?" I asked.

"Okay, so near as I can tell, Bear and Reece called in the fire, and the chief said they could stay on-scene to help."

My eyebrows shot up. "Holy crap! That's insane."

Gage rocked his head side to side. "I guess. Bear was on traffic duty, and Reece got crowd control. They left those posts to help Chuck resuscitate a few cats."

I frowned. Okay, they did a good thing, but they should have cleared it first.

"And then they started chasing somebody down the block. Logan's convinced the fire was arson and thinks some kid is the firebug."

Holy crap, this was bad. Really bad. "Whoa. Are they…are they out?"

Gage shrugged. "I don't know. Lieutenant Logan is upstairs with the chief now. From what I heard, there was some backtalk, but that was between the Logans."

Oh God. That wasn't good. Failing to obey orders was grounds for getting cut from the squad.

Reece and Bear could both be kicked out.

Chapter 21
Reece

He taught me everything—how to tie my shoes, how to piss standing up. He taught me everything you never did.

"Oh man, oh man. They're gonna kick us out." Bear kept rocking in the passenger seat of my mom's car.

"No, they won't. You heard the chief, Bear. He said to stay. He said to direct traffic and control the crowd, and we did. We obeyed orders."

"We *didn't*. We never should have chased down that kid. Your dad, oh jeez, he was pissed."

Pissed? Please. That wasn't pissed; that was his low setting. I pulled the car into my driveway, parked, and cut the engine. "Bear, just relax. Let's go fix the wall and wait for them to call us, okay?" We carted the tub of drywall compound and the furring strips upstairs to the bathroom. I fetched all the other tools we needed. When I got back, he was sitting on the edge of the tub, still rocking.

"I got this, Bear. Why don't you take off? I'm sorry I got you into trouble. It's me he's pissed at, not you. I'm sure you'll be just fine."

He waved a hand and grabbed for the drywall saw. "No. No way, bro. You helped me, I help you. That was the deal." He stuck the saw into the hole I'd made with my fist and made a vertical cut down, then across and all the way around, widening the hole into an even square.

"What's next?"

"Measure the hole and cut a piece of drywall to fit it."

I grabbed the tape measure, transferred those measurements to a scrap piece, and drew pencil lines to mark them. Bear told me what to do and when to do it. I just followed the directions. We cut a piece of the furring strip, stuck it through the hole, and then screwed it to the existing wall. Then we put the patch over the hole and screwed it to the strip.

"Nice. We ready to tape now?"

"Yep." He grabbed the bucket and smeared some compound over the screws and the seams. I stretched tape over the compound, then spread more compound over the tape, covering up all the edges.

"That's it? We're done?"

"Yeah, pretty much. You have to let this set and then sand it down, maybe put on another coat. Sand it, prime it, paint it. Then you're done."

I wiped my hand on my jeans and stuck it out for him to shake. "Thanks, man. I owe you big time."

He smiled and jerked his thumb at the drying patch. "You do this or the lieutenant?"

"I did," I admitted with a wince. "But he factored in."

"I'll bet."

My cell buzzed, and a second later, so did Bear's. We exchanged anxious glances and then answered our calls.

"That was my dad," I reported after I'd ended the call.

"I got the chief himself." Bear's eyes were round and horrified. "He said to come immediately to the station."

"Yeah. Same here."

Bear swallowed hard. "Gonna kick us out, right?"

I shook my head. "No. No, Bear. We did what we were supposed to do. They can't kick us out for that. They *won't*."

We cleaned up as best we could and climbed back into my mom's car. It was a short ride, silent and anxious. It should have taken us fifteen minutes if we'd hit every light. We got there in five. Did that mean something? I tried not to think about it while I was pulling around the back. When I killed the engine, Bear didn't move. He just sat there, staring straight ahead. "Bear."

He lifted his eyes to mine.

"I'll take the heat."

His eyes went round. "No. No way. You—"

I flung up a hand and cut him off. "Come on. I've only got a few weeks in. You've been on the squad for years. Besides," I added with half a laugh. "It's not like anybody expects me to actually succeed."

"No."

"Bear—"

"I said no, bro. I ain't a coward." He shoved out of the car, slammed the door, and abandoned his trademark shuffle to stalk off. I caught up to him in the main corridor.

"Logan!"

With a foot on the steps, I looked over my shoulder at Gage and Amanda. They'd just come out of our squad room. Bear kept walking, so I shook my head.

"I messed up, Gage. We have to go talk to the chief now."

Gage blew out a sigh of annoyance and shoved his hands in his pocket. But Amanda took a step closer. "Will you tell us? After?"

"If you want." I shrugged and smiled. Bear and I continued upstairs and down the long corridor, past the smiling faces of the ghosts that filled every firehouse across the country. The chief's door was shut. Bear and I exchanged a glance.

This was it.

I knocked on the door and braced for the worst.

Chapter 22
Amanda

He smiled at me.

How could he do that when the chief and his dad were probably ready to roast him over a spit?

I watched him climb the stairs to the offices, his shoulders back, head high. Even Bear stood at attention. They walked up the stairs, ready to be kicked out—it was written on both of their faces—but they walked toward that fear.

Like firefighters.

"Amanda, where are you going?"

I followed them up the stairs, Gage hissing behind me that we weren't allowed, but I didn't care. I *had* to be there. I had to know what the chief was going to do. I had to try to stop it if I could, because like it or not, Reece was part of this house now and deserved our support.

The door clicked shut just as I reached it.

"Man," Gage said. "You have to stay cool."

"Stay cool? Seriously?"

"Looks to me like you've got a thing for Logan. How'd that work out for you last time?"

"Fuck you, Gage." I slid down the wall to the floor.

Gage cursed under his breath. "I told you not to get involved with him. Do you have any idea how messed up Logan is?" he whispered.

"And *you* do?" It wasn't messed up to want your dad's respect, and it wasn't messed up to do whatever it took to keep your family together. It was brave. I clenched my teeth together and shot him a look.

"Yeah, I do," he said. He waited a beat, but I never asked him for the details he was so obviously dying to provide. He cursed and sat next to me. "Okay, look. You know that paper he keeps in his pocket? The one he's always scribbling on when he thinks nobody's looking?"

I sucked on my cheek, patience stretched to the brink of snapping. "Yeah. What about it?"

Gage looked up and down the corridor, inched a little closer. "I got a good look at it at the training facility. It's a letter to his dad. It's full of some angry words and bad memories, but that's not all." Another glance up and down the hall.

I let my head fall back to the wall behind me and shut my eyes. "What, Gage?"

"He wrote, 'I'll be at his altar,' Mandy. He underlined *his*."

I blinked and waited for the big reveal. "So what? Just get to the damn point."

Hurt flashed over Gage's face, and then it was gone. He stood up and dusted off his jeans. "Look it up when you're not so busy." He left me there alone, and I frowned at his retreating back.

I sat there for ages. I could hear some yelling, some thumping—Chief Duffy liked to bang a fist on his desk—but no discernible words.

Finally—finally!—the door opened, and I scrambled to my feet. The chief gave me a stern look, but Bear flashed a grin and a thumbs-up. I sighed in relief.

Chief Duffy shut the door. I looked at Reece, he looked at Bear, and Bear looked at me, and suddenly, everyone was doing a silent happy dance. Bear actually lifted Reece off the floor and spun him in a circle, a huge grin splitting their faces.

"Oh my God, dude, I thought we were out. I really thought we were done. I can't believe it."

I offered Bear a fist to bump. "Come on, you guys. Let's go downstairs before the chief hears us."

We headed downstairs and out the bay door from the apparatus floor. In a corner of the parking lot, I looked around, then demanded, "Tell me everything."

Bear leaned against the wall of the firehouse. "Okay. Me and Logan were driving back from the do-it-yourself store and hit some traffic, so we took a shortcut. We saw all these people running, so we looked and saw smoke from this boarded-up place. Logan pulled over, told me to call it in, and went over to get in some old dude's face."

I turned to look at Reece. He shifted and looked away. "He was going in. I couldn't let that happen."

"How the hell could you stop him?"

He shifted again and shot me a wry grin. "Um, well, I just figured he wanted a shot at playing hero, so I pointed out the blocked hydrants. He, uh, took care of them."

"Smart." I meant that as a compliment, but Reece squirmed and turned red. I spread my hands and waited a beat. "Is that it?"

"Um, not really, no. We waited for the crew to arrive. Chief Duffy told us to stay put. He told Bear to control traffic and told me to control the crowd."

"Yeah, and Reece got excellent video on his phone. The chief thinks it will help find the guy."

I snapped up straight, eyes wide. "It's officially arson?"

"He's not saying." Reece angled his head. "Why, did you hear something?"

"I heard Ken tell Chuck he saw trailers."

Reece covered his face with both hands and rubbed hard. "No. No, that doesn't fit. He was just a kid. How would he know about trailers?"

I shot him a smirk. "How do *you* know about them, Logan?"

Reece laughed once. "Touché." He scratched his head, frowning. "Okay, so suppose he did what I did and read about trailers in some book. Shouldn't be too hard to prove, right?"

"Arson is *really* hard to prove, Reece."

His frown deepened. "Amanda, we have witnesses who can put him at the scene." He waved his hand between Bear and himself.

I thought about that for a minute. "Come on." I stood up, led the guys back up the stairs, and knocked on the door to the first office on the left.

"Yeah?"

I opened the door. "Hey, Steve, can you spare us a few minutes?"

Steve Conner, the LVFD fire marshal, stood up but stayed behind his desk. "Mandy, five minutes. I'm on my way out."

I nodded. "You know Bear Acosta. But you probably haven't met—"

"Reece Logan. Heard a lot about you."

Reece shoved his hands into his pockets and looked at the floor. Steve took off his glasses, tossed them to his desk, and held out his hand. "Pretty damn gutsy."

"What?" Reece's head snapped up at that.

"Joining squad, facing your dad."

Reece opened his mouth, shut it, and opened it again. He took Steve's hand and shook it. "Thank you, sir."

Steve waved him off and sat back down. "What can I do for you three?"

"Today's fire, Steve. Bear and Logan were on-scene and want to know how you build a case for arson."

Steve crossed his arms, considered that for a minute, and nodded. "Okay. Reece, do you know about the fire triangle?"

Reece's eyes shot to mine, and I nodded my encouragement.

"Um, yeah." He squinted and frowned the way he always did when he tried to recall something he'd read from all the other *somethings* stored forever in his brain. "Heat, fuel, oxygen sources."

Steve angled his head. "What about them?"

"Um." He squirmed and frowned some more. "Well, I know the fuel source can be any flammable substance. And I read that the heat source has to be whatever the fuel source's ignition temperature is."

Steve shot up a hand. "Okay, good enough. In arson investigation, we immediately look at those three factors, see if any of them are out of whack. Arsonists like to add fuel to fires, so we look for excessive flammable materials or accelerants. Your smarter firebugs know that adding oxygen to the fire can help it spread, so we look for punched holes. Make sense?"

Reece and Bear exchanged a glance and nodded.

"It smelled funny," Bear admitted. "It wasn't just wood burning. There was a really bad smell—something chemical."

"Yeah. And the upstairs flames were kind of green," Reece added.

"Green?" Steve leaned forward. "Copper does that. So does boric acid."

"Okay, copper is used in residential pipes, but what's boric acid used for?" Reece asked.

Steve scratched his chin and swiveled in his chair. "Boric acid's all over the place—antiseptics, some insecticides, LCD TV screens, even fireworks."

"Any of which could have been in that attic," Reece said with a sigh. "Okay. I get why this is so hard."

Steve grinned, revealing a gap between his front teeth. "We're just getting warmed up. In fact," he added as he glanced at his watch, "I have to go interview the guys who were on-scene, get their reports." He was a tall, thin guy and walked around his desk in two strides. "If you want to learn more, take a look through the NFPA guidelines."

"Yeah, thanks. Thanks a lot."

"You bet."

Two more strides, and Steve was down the hall.

"Damn." Bear winced. "Forgot to show him your video."

"Yeah, let me see it," I said and wiggled my fingers.

Reece smiled and queued up the footage. It was shaky but pretty good. Guess it paid to have a good cell phone like his. I watched the exchange between Reece and some guy who liked his nacho chips, if the stains on his T-shirt were any indicator. Reece did a good job keeping the swelling crowd back, across the street and out of the way. The recording showed a nice slow pan of the crowd, then zoomed in on a slight figure, hunching over a cell phone. He wore clothes too big for him, and his phone was clearly new, judging by the trouble he was having with his text mes—

Oh my God.

"Amanda, what's wrong? Do you know this kid?" Reece gripped my arm, and I nearly launched into orbit. I kept my eyes down, forced my face to remain neutral, but Reece—Jesus, I had to get out of here.

"What? No. I thought he looked familiar, but jeez, he could be any kid, you know?" *Shut up, Amanda, shut up, shut up.*

Reece's eyes narrowed. "He does look familiar. I definitely know him from somewhere, and you do too, don't you?"

I shoved the phone away. "Back off, Logan. I said I don't know him."

He laughed once. "You're lying. Who is this kid, Amanda? Why are you protecting him?" His dark eyes flashed, and a muscle twitched in his jaw. While I stared, willing every muscle fiber in my limbs to obey my brain and not my heart, he changed. He shut his eyes, and when he lifted them again, his fury was gone.

"Why can't you trust me?" he whispered.

Oh crap, oh shit. Reece, I could never explain it so you'd understand. A knuckle rapped on the open door to Steve's office.

John Logan stood there, hands in his pockets. He sucked in a deep breath, raked a hand over his graying hair, and shifted his weight. "Reece, I need to talk to you."

I stepped back. Hurt filled Reece's eyes for a moment, but he nodded at his father. I used that opportunity to take off but hovered out in the hall.

"What, Dad?" Reece asked.

John cleared his throat. "Ah, you did good today."

I froze outside Steve's office.

Reece didn't say anything. I couldn't see him but figured he must be staring openmouthed at his father.

"You kept your head. You prevented a civilian from losing his. You saved a few animals, and you did follow orders, up until the part where you chased that kid. Proud of you."

I inched my way back, because I had to know what was happening. Big, tough John Logan looked like a middle-school boy trying to ask a girl to his first dance. Reece stared at his father, eyes round, and then a slow smile spread across his face. I pressed both hands to my face to cover the sob that all but exploded out of me. I ran down the stairs and started the long walk home.

He did it. He managed to get the most stubborn guy I knew come around. Reece would get his family back, and I—God. I was going to lose what little I had.

Chapter 23

Reece

It's funny. I joined squad to force you to deal with me. I didn't expect it to matter this much. I didn't expect to be good at it. And I am good at it. I know that I am.

I wriggled under my dad's penetrating gaze and felt a hot flush crawl over my body. I'd waited my entire life to hear words like the ones he'd just spoken. So why wasn't I flipping cartwheels down the corridor? Instead of happiness, sixteen stored-up years of disappointment ignited like papers hoarded in a hot and dry attic. It took everything I had to tamp that down.

And then, I looked at him.

Jesus, he looked like he was in labor or something. Getting out those words had needed a push from every abdominal muscle he had. The fire in my gut went out, and I managed a laugh. "Thanks, Dad." I held out my hand, and he shook it.

"Chief Duffy said you snagged some video of the scene?"

"Yeah, we came to show Captain Conner, but he had to interview the crew." I held out my phone, cued up the video, and tapped play.

"I don't know him personally, but he's familiar. I know him from somewhere, so we should be able to find him as soon as I remember where I've seen him."

"You don't remember?" Dad looked at me sideways. "You actually can't remember? I don't get it."

My eyes snapped to his, looking for the smirk, the taunting expression in his eyes, but there wasn't any.

Okay.

I guessed a serious question deserved a serious answer, so I attempted one.

"I will. I just have to go through events."

He shook his head. "You can do that? Just go through all the events in your life like a drawer full of files?"

My entire body heated up again. "Yes, I can. I know it's not normal to you, but it is to me."

He flung up both hands. "I'm not making fun of you. I'm just trying to understand how it works."

I studied him carefully and finally nodded. "I don't know how to explain it. I just replay all the times I met people, try to match the faces. I never met this kid directly. If I had, I would already have remembered his name. But that doesn't mean I haven't *seen* him."

"School?" Dad offered after a moment, rubbing the scruff on his chin.

"Most likely. Could be a grade or two behind me or something."

Dad scowled. "Okay. Do whatever works, Reece. We've had enough of these incidents. If he's the guy, I want him caught before there's another one."

"Copy," I said.

Dad smiled—a tiny, tight-lipped quirk—and strode down the corridor. The hall was empty. Amanda was gone. I should have expected that. The only reason she was here today was because Bear and I made it to a fire scene.

But she knew something—I was sure of it.

"Hey, Dad?" I called out to him before he reached the stairs.

He turned and waited. "Yeah?"

I caught up to him and held up the phone. "I think Amanda knows who this kid is. Knows but won't say."

Dad's eyes popped and then narrowed. "Come on." He led me back inside Steve's office and shut the door. "You think she's protecting this kid? What for?"

"I have no idea. I don't know what to do. Amanda's been great and—"

"Yeah, yeah, you like her. I figured that out already. But, son, this is an arson investigation. The law comes first."

I didn't hear a word he said after *son*. The word just kind of filled up my brain like some sort of fog, slowly surrounding me. I suddenly realized it was my turn to talk. "What should I do?"

"You talk to Steve Conner and let him handle this."

"But what if I'm right? What if Amanda *does* know this kid and I get her kicked out or something?"

He gave me an impatient shake of his head. "That's not on you, Reece. It would be on her for omitting information crucial to an investigation." He frowned at me and, to my total astonishment, reached out and put a hand on my shoulder, gave me a hard squeeze. "Reece, you signed up to do a job. That's what you do. You do the job. Okay?"

Suddenly, I shot back in time to a day when I was about four years old. We were at a family picnic deal. Way too many people near me and way too many sounds. Things just got *too much* for me to manage, and suddenly, I was scared. Not some wimpy *Eep* scared; this was a full-out, heart-stopping, all-the-way-to-the-bone kind of panic that used to make me want to disconnect my eardrums from my brain. I had episodes like this frequently when I was little. This one had been *bad*. I was batshit terrified, and the only thing that would have pulled me out of it was something—or someone—familiar, like my dad. But that didn't happen. Maybe I scared him. Or maybe he just didn't know what to do for me. It was Matt who helped me. When I finally calmed down enough to notice my surroundings, it was Matt's arms holding me. He would have been no more than five. Once I was calm, I'd wanted my dad, so I ran to him, and he'd put his hand on my shoulder, bracing me.

I searched through all my memories, and this was the first time since that day that he'd repeated that gesture. With my heart racing at warp speed, I nodded and smiled. "Okay."

"Attaboy." He thumped me on the back and left to do his paperwork. Alone in Steve's office, I fell to a chair in front of the desk, my entire system fried.

I did it. My father was proud of me. *I promised you I'd do it, Matt. I made Dad proud.*

Do the job, Dad said. And the job was to prove conclusively that my suspect was guilty of arson.

And my suspect had some kind of connection to Amanda.

I stared at the open door to the fire marshal's office. I flexed the muscle that was still warm from my father's backpat. He said he was proud of me. The date and time of this moment were now fixed permanently in my mind.

But I wasn't celebrating.

Amanda was freaked out by my video. The only question left was what was I going to do about it? I glanced at the empty doorway. Dad was probably downstairs, barking at his guys. Any pride he had in my firefighting ability was because I had tons of help. Help from Amanda and everyone else on J squad.

"What should I do, Matt? Goddamn it, what the hell should I do?"

I rocked back and forth on the chair and waited for a sign from heaven. I had it, I had the one thing I always wanted and—and I left the fire marshal's office.

***

I found her, standing in a ray of sunlight, staring at the burned-out shell of the house. I pulled over to the curb across the street, killed the engine, and watched her. She didn't know I was there, not yet. If I didn't know her, I'd say she was just another curious neighbor, the kind who thanked God it wasn't her house that burned.

But I *did* know her now.

I'd worked with her for weeks, running practice drills side by side. I knew the hands hidden inside the pockets of her station pants were clenched into tight fists. I knew she itched to pry a board off a window

233

and get a glimpse of the destruction inside. I knew by the way she went white in the fire marshal's office that she knew who the boy in the video was.

Knew but said nothing.

She lived for the department; why would she lie about this kid? A chilling thought skated up my back. Was she protecting him? Was he the reason she'd joined J squad—to stay one step ahead of the fire department?

"What the hell are you doing here, Logan?" she demanded after she spotted me. She looked anxiously up and down the block, where a couple of kids shot hoops in a driveway across the street.

"We need to talk."

"What? No. You need to leave. Right now."

"Amanda, I'm not going anywhere until you tell me who this kid is." I held my phone in front of her face. She didn't even glance at it.

"Not now."

"You know him, don't you? Did you know what he was doing? Did you help him? Who is he, Mandy?"

She raised her eyes, a funny half-smile on her lips. "I think that's the first time you ever called me Mandy."

Shaking my head, I tried again. "You're trying to change the subject. Who is he?"

"He didn't do it."

"Who the fuck is he?" I took two strides closer to stand over her.

"Okay! Fine." She shot me a glare. "He's my foster brother." She admitted that with so much discomfort, I dropped my guard. We

234

stared down the quiet street for a long moment. Nice houses, green lawns. The acrid smell of smoke still filled the air.

I nodded and looked away. "I wish you'd trust me."

She dropped her head and groaned. "Let it go, Reece. I'm not a good bet."

"I'm not either. But you still helped me." I shifted so I could face her directly.

"It was the look in your eyes, I guess. Same look that's in mine."

"What look?"

"I don't know. You remind me of something from when I was little. Planting daisies." She huffed out a laugh and shook her head. "We're the same. Only difference is you can get back some of what you lost. I wanted to help." Another shrug and half a laugh. "It is what it is."

There was something in her voice—a crack, a waver—that forced me to take a closer look at her. I figured I'd see fear or panic in her eyes, but I didn't. All I saw was…defeat.

"So you weren't playing me?"

Her eyes shot to mine, and she made a choking sound. "Playing you? You think I've been, what? Covering up a string of arsons on the off chance you'd wander into the LVFD one day?"

"Okay." I waved my hand impatiently. "Not me. Us. Did you join squad so you could cover up these crimes? Jesus, Amanda." I grabbed her shoulders. "What if this kid kills somebody next time? We have to *know*."

"No! No, you don't understand." She jerked free. "It doesn't matter if he did this or not. They'll kick him out, send him back into the system. Foster kids like us, we're throwaways, and this house"—she pointed in the direction of the Beckett house—"is the best one he's had, that either of us have had. I can't mess this up. It's good here. Nobody steals our stuff, nobody hurts us—"

My blood froze when those words penetrated. "*Hurts* you?"

The defeat in Amanda's eyes turned flat and hard. "Yeah, Reece. Hurts."

I couldn't speak, couldn't wrap my mind around that. Before I could figure out my next move, Amanda flung her arms up in the air and paced away. "Stop looking at me like that! I'm still who I am."

I raised my hands. "I know. I know. I...I kind of just want to kill whoever hurt you."

Amanda snorted. That snort became a laugh, and then she was laughing so hard, she sat down on the curb, an arm wrapped around her middle. "You get points for that," she said when she could breathe again. "Nobody's ever offered to commit murder for me."

"Yeah, well, I'm a giver like that."

She laughed again, then quickly grew serious. "Reece, show me the video again. Are you sure about this?"

I tugged my phone out of my pocket and handed it to her.

"What's this?" Amanda asked, scooping up the folded-up square of paper that fell from my pocket.

My skin iced over, and my stomach knotted. I lunged for it, snatched the paper out of her hand, and shoved it deep back into my pocket before she could read a word.

"Okay. Jeez, Reece. If you don't want to tell me, just say so." She held up her hands.

Shame started a slow spread inside me, and I looked away. I was the biggest kind of hypocrite—ah, hell. I drew the paper back out of my pocket and handed it to her.

Cautiously, she unfolded it. I sat on the curb next to her and waited while she read the lines I'd scrawled so far.

"It's a letter to my dad." My heart thudded behind my ribs.

Her eyes shot up to mine. "It's…angry. And so final. Like you're saying good-bye."

I am.

"Yeah," I admitted, avoiding her gaze. "I'm…not gonna stick around."

"So you lied to us when you told us J squad mattered to you." Her eyes filled, and she quickly lowered them.

I had no answer for that. What really sucked was that it wasn't true, not now. Now, J squad *did* matter. And she'd never believe that.

"Where would you go?" she asked a long moment later.

"Military," I lied.

"We've got some time then." She sighed, relieved. "Can't enlist until you're legal. Which branch?"

"I don't know yet. Maybe Marines." It didn't matter.

"First in," she murmured. "Doesn't that scare you?"

I shrugged. I wasn't sure anything could scare me now. The worst had already happened.

"When are you giving this to your dad?"

"When it's done. I have a lot left to say, but I don't know—" I didn't bother to finish the statement. None of this mattered anymore. Not the note, not even my promise to Matt. All that mattered was J squad. I shoved the paper back in my pocket while Amanda tapped the video play button on my phone.

"So what does that line mean—'I'll be at his altar'?" she asked while we watched the guy in his underwear clear the space in front of the hydrant again.

"Oh, um." *Fuck.* The knot in my gut jerked, tightened, and half my body went numb. "It's just something Matt used to say."

She frowned and finally nodded. I let out a slow breath, and the video finished playing.

"Amanda, nobody knows about this note. Nobody but you."

A bright-red bird stopped to rest on the porch rail of the house across the street. Amanda watched him for a moment. I just watched her. I still couldn't figure out what color her eyes were. Not blue, not green, not brown. I didn't know why I was so hung up on what the hell color her eyes were, because all I saw in them at that moment was pain, and suddenly, I knew exactly what I had to do, had to say.

I cleared my throat. "Um, Amanda, I know what you said about being a foster kid and the no-boys thing. But you need to know you can trust me. With anything."

Slowly, she shook her head. "I can't. I don't know how." But she leaned in to me, put her head on my shoulder, and handed me back my phone. "Can you please not show anybody this? Don't report it, not until I'm sure."

"Of what?"

She watched the red bird spread his wings and take off. "Sure of Larry. If there's the tiniest chance he's not involved, I have to know. I can't get him in trouble just because you have video of him playing with his phone."

"Amanda, this is *arson*. We have to—"

She jumped away from me. "Oh, come on, Logan! A minute ago, you wanted to kill somebody for me. You said you'd do anything to make me happy. Were those just words, or did you really mean any of that?"

I blew out a long breath. I was here, wasn't I? I'd sat in the fire marshal's office for ten minutes wrestling with this after my dad said he was proud of me. But here I was. "I really meant it. So what do you want to do?"

"I need more. I want to follow him around, see where he goes, who he goes with, and what he does."

I clenched my teeth together. That wasn't our job or our responsibility. That was for the arson investigators to do. All we had to do was show them the video of Larry. That was it. Why was this so difficult for her? He was just some kid who happened to be staying in the same foster house as she was, and now she wanted to put herself in danger for him. I didn't get it. And I sure as hell didn't like it.

"Amanda, if anything happens to you, I'll—"

She jerked like I'd just shot her. She took my hand and squeezed it for a second. "Don't do that."

"What, care about you, about what happens to you?"

"Yes! I told you—"

"No boys. I know. But I can't change how I feel. I won't."

She shut her eyes tightly, shaking her head. "This is impossible, Reece. We can't."

A car turned up the street, and she almost jumped behind a shrub. I shoved my hands in my pockets, tracking the car until it disappeared around a curve. The note singed my fingertips, forcing me to remember my plan.

And show me exactly how to make her trust me.

"Oh fuck it."

When Amanda's eyebrows shot up, I raked both hands through my hair. "This note…the truth is I've been writing it for weeks. It started out as a promise I made to Matt. Amanda, he *knew* he was dying, and he knew my dad was going to flip the fuck out. He made me promise not to… give up, you know? So I made this plan. I was going to leave—just disappear the day I got my dad to finally show me a little love. The military was a lie. It doesn't matter where I go. I just had to be away from here."

She took a step toward me, her eyes a storm of emotion. Encouraged, I kept going.

"I never expected it to work, Amanda. I figured I'd just give it a shot, do whatever it took so I could tell myself I kept my promise to my brother and then just get the hell out. But when I joined J squad and all of you decided to help me, things changed. My whole plan changed, because for the first time in my entire fucking life, I had a shot! I had a chance to really make my dad proud. It became this legend, you know? The day John Logan compliments his son!" I waved a hand over an imaginary theater marquee.

"For weeks, that day was nothing more than a daydream. Some nebulous gray point in the future. And it just hit me. Amanda, today's *that day*." I grabbed her arms and made her look directly at me. "He told me not even an hour ago that he was proud of me. Which means I did it." I smiled broadly. "Holy shit, Amanda. I did it. I can go now." I flung my arms up in the air. "Right now. Leave, fade away like I planned. There's nothing holding me to this life anymore."

Yes, there was.

"Except one thing." I crumpled up the note and pressed it into her hands. "Take it."

She looked at the paper with wide eyes. "Why?"

"I don't need it. I'm not going anywhere. I'm staying right here until the no-boys rule is null and void."

Amanda's eyes filled, and a sad smile lifted her lips for a second, but then she shook her head. "Reece, it'll be years before that happens."

"I don't care. I'm in this, Amanda. I'm all in."

Her lips curled a little. "You told me that the other day. After the alarm."

"I meant it then, and I mean it even more now." I took a deep breath and blurted out the words she needed to hear. "I love you, Amanda." She only stared at me, dumbstruck. "Did you hear me? I said I'm in love with you. So whatever's up with Larry, I'll back off and let you do what you need to until you ask me for help."

Chapter 24
Amanda

I made it back to the Becketts' house in a fog.

I love you, he'd said. Someone loved me. The concept was freakin' impossible to understand. No one loved me, including my mother.

Maybe that's why I didn't say the words back.

No.

No, I didn't say the words back because I was a friggin' coward.

I opened the front door and found Larry watching TV in the family room. I took the opportunity to sneak upstairs into his room. His closet looked like the after shot for a one-day-only sale. The rod held only three hangers—a winter jacket in a hideous shade of green, a suit with worn elbows to go to court in, and a fleece hoodie in boring gray. I took the fleece from the closet and buried my nose in it, but all I smelled was fabric softener.

I tried the garage-sale dresser next. Larry had a few pairs of underwear—white briefs, shoved in the drawer, a few pairs of socks, and a—oh God—a condom. I closed the drawer with a grimace. I moved to the desk next. Its single center drawer held some crumpled-up notes that he'd used for math homework, I guessed.

Handheld pencil sharpener, ruler, erasers, some expired book order forms.

I blew hair out of my eyes and scanned the room. His bed was perfectly made—Mrs. Beckett insisted on it. I sat on it, gave it a little bounce, shoved my hand between the mattress and box spring to see if he had a secret stash of anything, but came up empty. I stood up and sighed in frustration. This was ridiculous—a total waste of—

My foot sent something skittering across the floor. I bent down and examined it, but it was just a piece of mulch, probably something Larry tracked in. I tossed it in the waste basket next to his desk and left his room.

Back downstairs, I decided to confront him directly. "What the hell is up with you?" I demanded, whispering.

He blinked at me. "Nothing."

"You need to tell me what happened at that fire. I know you were there. Jesus, Larry, they have you on video."

The remote fell to the floor. "Go away."

"Larry—"

The Becketts' car pulled into the driveway.

"Go away or I'll tell them you broke a rule."

I gasped. He wouldn't. That would end things for both of us, and he damn well knew it. "You won't." I took a step closer.

Car doors slammed. Feet climbed the porch steps.

"I'm trying to help you, you moron," I hissed.

He shook his head. "Don't need help. Go. Away."

Things got real tense while we stared each other down. I didn't know what happened. The day before, he was terrified about something, and now, it's no big deal? Suddenly, he let out a shout, so I ran across the room and flung myself into a chair.

"Larry? You okay?" Mr. Beckett paused in the doorway.

"Oh yeah. Fine. Saw a spider."

"Well, come help unload the groceries."

"Yes, sir."

Damn it. What the hell was he up to? God, please let Reece be wrong.

Let him be wrong.

***

The next day, Larry avoided me on the bus. He spent the whole ride talking to a classmate. I cursed silently, wondering, obsessing, *praying* he wasn't in this arson stuff up to his armpits.

What if?

The question kept hissing around my brain, etching its way into my gray matter like acid. If he'd set this fire, if he was the arsonist who had been terrorizing our area all year, could I do anything to help him?

I swallowed hard. The answer was obvious.

I watched him head for his locker, debated about cutting class to follow him, but chucked that idea the second it formed. Mr. Beckett would be informed before I got off the property.

I saw Max flirting with one of the cheerleaders and decided it was time to ask for help. "Hey."

Max shot me an annoyed look and then did a double take. "Hey, Man. What's up? You okay?"

"No, not really. I need your help."

"Done." He turned back to the cheerleader. I think her name was Candy—a senior. "I'll see you later, baby." It was a clear dismissal, and she left in a huff. "Man, seriously. You're scaring me. What's up?"

"Remember the other day? I told you my mom is demanding to see me?"

He nodded. "Yeah. I told you I'd go with you."

"What about today? Right after school?" This was our last week of regular classes. Next week, we had our final exams, and then we were free for the summer. You'd think the county would know this. "I got an official county summons. The social worker is picking me up today. If your offer's still good—"

"I'll meet you by the bus stop when the bell rings."

I blew out a breath. "Thanks, Max."

"No problem." He put a strong, solid arm around me. "Now why don't you tell me what's really bugging you? Is it Logan?"

I immediately shook my head. "No. Yeah. Jesus, I don't know!"

Max's eyebrows lowered. "Tell me what he did."

"No, no, nothing." I leaned against a locker and nibbled my fingernails. "Max, it's Larry. Could you…maybe keep an eye on him?"

"Little dude? Sure, I guess. Is he hanging with the wrong crew?"

"I don't know."

"Okay. I'll talk to Gage and the other guys, and we'll keep eyes on him."

"No!" I blurted, and embarrassment burned through me. "Gage and Kevin or Ty, fine. But not Bear and not Logan."

"Why not?"

I blew hair out of my eyes. "I…I…oh crap, Max. Larry's the suspect on the video Bear and Reece shot at the fire scene."

Max let out a low whistle. "And you don't think they can stay objective. Okay. I get that. Now tell me why you didn't ask Logan to go with you today."

"Because I fucked up!" I hit the locker behind me with a palm. "I let him in, Max. He's too close and I get— well, he makes me all fuzzy."

Max's lip curled into a smirk. "I think you do the same thing to him, Man."

I stared at Max, jaw dangling. "Jesus, this is bad. Really, really bad."

Max shrugged. "Doesn't have to be. You like him, he likes you. Sounds pretty good to me."

"He loves me, Max." I whispered it like it was a horrible sin. "He said he loves me. If Mr. Beckett finds out, I'm gone, Max."

His smirk changed into a full-out grin. "Aha! That's why you asked *me* to come. He knows my legendary reputation as a chick magnet. Knows you'd never be seriously involved with me."

That was true. I didn't see any reason to emphasize it. The bell rang, and I headed for the stairs.

"Don't worry about a thing, Man. We got your back," Max called after me.

Yeah, they did.

But for how much longer?

Chapter 25
Reece

I have friends. That must shock you. The guys like me—they like that I'm smart, that I ask annoying questions. And there's Amanda, who maybe likes me a lot.

Monday morning, I took Tucker for a walk before school. Three blocks away, he turned up the path to Alex's front door.

"No, Tuck. Not today." The dog whined and lowered his head. "Come on." Tucker barked—two sharp *woof*s. "Quiet, Tucker." I tugged the leash, but the dog refused to obey.

The front door opened, and Alex stood there, hair standing on end. He glared at me and crossed his arms over a Batman T-shirt. He opened his mouth. "It's…the crack o'dawn. Why?"

I bit back a grin; Alex's perfect enunciation and grammar took longer to wake up than the rest of him. I shrugged. "Tucker wanted to say hello."

Alex's eyes darted to my dog. He cursed and stepped out onto the porch, crouching low. I let go of the leash, and Tucker scrambled up to him, desperate for pats on the head and scratches behind his ears. "Why are you really here?"

"Thought you were smart." I sighed loudly and walked closer to him. "I miss you, you dickhead."

Alex's eyes narrowed. "Yeah, right. Let me guess; you got kicked out, so now you have time for me."

"No," I corrected, trying to stay patient. "In fact, I, um…well, I did it. I got my dad to say he was proud of me." I spread my arms. "I still can't believe it."

Sprinklers clicked on across the street, and Tucker's ears twitched at the sound of another dog barking off in the distance. I turned back to my best friend, and he was staring at me. Only his eyes showed something I'd never seen in them in all the years I'd known Alex Boyle.

Confusion.

"So you got what you always wanted. And now you can leave. Did you come to drop off Tucker? Say good-bye? Gloat?"

I blinked the sudden moisture from my eyes and coughed once. "Uh, none of the above. I came to say thank you."

"Thank you," Alex repeated, his voice flat.

This was so odd, like parallel-universe-odd. Alex Boyle, speechless and confused.

"Yes. It was your idea that I join J squad. Not sure why you wanted to kill me," I quipped, happy to see a twitch in his lips. "But I survived. All the working out, all the studying—I don't think I ever really appreciated how demanding firefighting is."

"You look…broader," he said, eyes skimming my torso.

Nodding, I flexed. "I can haul thirty pounds up a flight of steps. I can suit up in full PPE in two minutes, five seconds. And I can apologize to my best friend for hurting his feelings."

Alex turned and watched the sprinklers shoot water in arcs over the lawn across the street, his throat working. "You didn't…er…well, I wasn't exactly…oh frak."

I wouldn't do it. No, no, no, I would not do it. But the urge was too strong, and I burst out laughing. A moment later, Alex was laughing too.

"I really am sorry, Alex."

He waved a hand. "Forget it. I may have overreacted. The truth is I was jealous."

"Of me?" On what planet would anybody be jealous of me?

"Ever since fourth grade, I always thought of you as something of a…well, a sidekick."

My mouth fell open, but I let him finish.

"Now, you're the superhero and I…" He trailed off, embarrassed.

"Dude, if I'm any kind of hero at all, it's because of you. You're like my Q. My Nick Fury. My—"

Laughing, he cut me off. "I get it, Reece."

"So we're good?"

"Yeah. We're good."

Tucker barked and tugged on his leash. "Oh right. Probably should get him home and fed before school. I'll see you later?"

Alex nodded. "Affirmative."

I grinned. "Sweet."

"Hey, Reece." Alex called me back when I reached the street. "What about your plan?"

"I'm not leaving. Not now."

"I don't understand. You were going to leave after you fulfilled your promise to Matt. You promised him you wouldn't leave until you squared things with your dad. You did that. So what changed?"

"It's kind of a long story. Tell you at lunch!"

**

The morning went by fast.

I caught up to Amanda in the cafeteria. "Did you find anything?"

She jerked around and shut her eyes. "Logan. Jeez, you're like a dog with a bone."

I angled my head. "Do you expect me to apologize for that?"

She shook her head. "No, no. You're right. This is important. And to answer your question, I talked to Larry yesterday." Amanda grabbed a cellophane-wrapped sandwich and put it on her tray. "Well, tried to talk to him. He's hiding something, Reece. But I still don't know what."

"Amanda, we have to report it."

"Not yet, Reece. I need more time. I have to be one hundred percent sure."

I sighed and slid my lunch tray to the cashier. "I was afraid you'd say that."

She put her tray down on the table the squad always shared, looked carefully around, and grabbed my arm. "I know what I'm asking you. I know what's at risk. And that's why I have to *know*." She sat, unwrapped her sandwich, and looked up at me. "Aren't you eating?"

"Yeah. With Alex. We have some things to talk about."

Amanda glanced at Alex, sitting over his tablet at our usual table, and clapped a hand over her mouth. "Oh my God. You guys haven't been hanging out since...since you started J squad." She shut her eyes. "I am so sorry."

"Whoa, Amanda, it's not your fault."

"No, Reece. He's, like, your best friend. And I never noticed."

I studied her carefully. She was taking this way too hard. "It was his idea. To join J squad, I mean."

Amanda looked down at her untouched lunch. Goddamnit. I knew that look, recognized it from when she told me about her mother practically abandoning her for some asshole.

"Amanda, don't."

Her eyes snapped to mine, wide with surprise. "Don't what?"

"It's my fault. Not yours. I straightened things out this morning. We're fine."

She was shaking her head before I finished the thought. "I should have noticed, Reece. I mean, you—" She kept shaking her head, and I got this bad feeling deep in my gut.

"You *didn't*, and that's exactly what I wanted. I didn't want to talk about it. I didn't want it to get in the way of my squad work. I didn't want you to think I was distracted or, you know...weak."

She shoved her tray back, and the bad feeling spread to my throat.

"Mandy, please. Please don't do this." Because I knew what was coming.

"You should go. Alex is waiting for you." Her voice cracked.

"Amanda. No."

"Reece, we *can't*. I can't. Please. Just go." Her eyes swept across the cafeteria, always looking out for Mr. Beckett.

"Hey, guys." Ty dropped his tray beside Amanda's, a straw clamped between his teeth. He looked cautiously from Amanda to me. "What's up?"

Amanda only shook her head, staring at me with stormy eyes that had their own gravitational pull. I wanted to climb over the table, sweep the trays out of my way, and kiss her until she couldn't remember her name. I loved this girl! Why didn't she understand that? The note, the plan, the promise—I'd amended all of it for her. Didn't she get that I'd do anything?

I gasped when the full meaning of those words hit me like a bucket of ice water. *I'd do anything*. And the only thing she wanted right now was for me to walk away.

I took a step away and then another, and even though every cell in my body screamed *don't move*, I gave Amanda what she needed.

It was the hardest thing I'd ever done.

***

"What was that all about?" Alex asked when I finally made it to the table.

I sank into my seat and stared at my tray, numb.

"Oh." Alex's eyes popped. "You guys are together."

I shot him a look and took a bite out of my sandwich, but it settled like lead shot in my gut.

"Talk." Alex patted the table.

I sighed loudly. "You know Amanda's a foster kid, right?"

"Yes. She lives with Mr. Beckett, the chemistry teacher."

"There are rules. A lot of them."

Alex nodded. "Ah. Let me guess. These rules involve dating?"

I rocked my head side to side. "Yeah, more or less." Disgusted, I shoved my tray back. "They said no boys, so—"

"And if they didn't have that rule, would you have a chance?"

My face burst into flame. "Um, yeah, I think so. We, um…kissed."

Alex leaned forward. "Wow. A lot happened."

And yet, nothing did. Or will. I folded my arms on the table and dropped my head down. "Alex, that's not all. The other day, there was a fire. I was there."

"I thought cadets weren't allowed on-scene?"

"We're not. But I was driving right by it with Bear. We called it in, and the chief let us stay. I did crowd control, and Bear did traffic. We followed orders, did everything by the book. The book says to watch the crowd, look for people behaving strangely. I shot some video of a kid I suspect of setting that fire."

Alex's brain must have been firing at warp speed. He nodded, following my story. "And that's what earned your dad's pat on the back."

"Right. Here's the problem. The kid I suspect? He's Amanda's foster brother, and I am so fucked."

253

"Oh frak."

I laughed once. "My dad said I need to show the video to the fire marshal so he can get the arson investigation going. But—"

The bell rang, so Alex and I stowed our trays and headed to class. "I'll wait for you at dismissal," he promised. "Tell me the rest then."

I nodded and quickly scarfed down a few bites of my lunch while Alex took off. The main corridor was almost empty by the time I made my way to my first afternoon class, AP bio lab. The science labs were all located on the first floor, east of the main corridor. I turned down the hall and saw Amanda's foster brother disappear into a dark lab.

The chemistry lab.

He was in tenth grade. The tenth grade doesn't take chemistry. So why was Larry Ecker sneaking into the lab? I took out the phone none of us were supposed to have at school and shot more video through the window of the closed door. Larry was at the back of the room, inside a large closet. I could see was the backpack he wore but not what he was doing. The late bell rang, but I needed to know—

"Mr. Logan, have you forgotten which room you're supposed to be in?"

I whipped around and found Mrs. Roth, my Spanish teacher, standing at the end of the hall. I kept the phone hidden and just nodded. "Sorry. Thought I saw something."

She took out the dreaded pink pad and clicked a pen. My heart fell. She checked off a few boxes, scrawled my name across the top, and tore off the detention slip. "See you at dismissal, Mr. Logan."

Chapter 26
Amanda

"So, uh, you and Reece." Max leaned forward to wink and elbow me from the backseat of the social worker's car.

"Shut up, Max." I turned to look out the passenger window.

"Oh, come on, Man. I'm just messing with you."

"Who's Reece, Amanda?" Mrs. DeSantis asked from behind the wheel. She was a pretty lady, not that old, with long, dark hair she wore parted to the side and tucked behind her ears.

I hated her.

"Another guy in our squad."

"Ah. So are you excited to see your mom?"

I swirled my finger in the air. "Yay."

Max snorted out a laugh. We didn't say much for the rest of the trip. I fell asleep when we hit traffic and didn't wake until we turned off I-84 a couple of hours later. I jolted to full consciousness in half a second, heart pounding and stomach threatening a rebellion.

"Good morning. You were really out," Mrs. DeSantis said, waiting for traffic to clear for a left turn.

I shrugged. No point in restating the obvious. By the time Mrs. DeSantis pulled into the Fishkill Correctional Facility gate, my heart was trying to break out of my rib cage. We got out of the car and walked to the door, with me trailing farther and farther behind.

Max grabbed my arm. "So, Man, what's the deal? You look kind of green."

Made sense. I was about to throw up. I also had to pee. The day was beautiful—almost summertime. And I started to shiver. Mrs. DeSantis signed us in. I hovered near the door, trying to keep it together.

Max tugged on one of his earrings. "Okay, look. You're a firefighter, Man. One of the bravest. You can do this."

Oh crap! I couldn't. I really couldn't. I was a fraud—a total lie. I wasn't brave. I hadn't even fought in an actual fire. I was a pretend-er—a pretend kid to pretend parents pretending to be a firefighter in a pretend squad. I looked back at the door and wondered how long it would take me to walk back to the Becketts' house.

"Spill, Jamison. What's up?"

I clutched Max's arms. "What if it's true? What if she tells me—"

Max shook his head. "Tells you what?"

"Follow me, please." The guard indicated a door, and we followed him through it, down a long corridor to a room with a bunch of tables arranged in a grid.

My mother sat at one of those tables, wearing an orange uniform. Her hair was pulled into a ponytail, and she wore no makeup. She smiled when she saw me, lines around her eyes and mouth I didn't remember seeing before. "Mandy. Oh my God, look how gorgeous you are. You are so grown up."

"Yeah, well, that's what kids do."

Her smile dimmed, but she waved a hand at the chair opposite hers. "Sit, sit. Tell me what's new."

What's new? Seriously? Okay, fine. I sat down. "I'm in a new foster home. I'm captain of the junior squad at the Lakeshore Volunteer Fire Department. I kissed a boy and then told him to go away. Oh, and I might be concealing an arsonist—still working on that." I waited a beat. "So that's pretty much it. Bye."

A hand suddenly gripped my arm. "Mandy, wait." The guard didn't like that. He walked over and gave Mom the side eye, and she let go. "Oh, honey. I'm so sorry."

Pain ripped through me when her words sucked out my soul, and I squeezed my eyes shut. Sorry? Sorry didn't even come close to scratching the surface.

"Amanda, look at me."

I lifted my eyes and glared straight through her.

"Honey, I know you hate me, and I'm sorry. I made some mistakes—"

A laugh bubbled out of me all on its own. It wasn't funny, and trust me, I wasn't the least bit amused. But that was the biggest understatement in history. "Mistakes," I echoed. "I remember the first time Dmitri came over to our place. He was pissed off that I was there. *You didn't tell me you had a kid*, he said. Remember that?"

She didn't answer. Because she remembered it too.

257

"And you just smiled brightly and shrugged and assured him that your little Mandy was an angel. You made dinner, and all during the meal, Dmitri pretended I wasn't there. He never said a single word to me. As soon as dinner was over, he asked you what time my bedtime was, and next thing I knew, I was tucked into my bed while it was still light outside. That was the first time you put him before me."

"No." Her mouth went tight, making more lines show up. "No, baby. I was trying to protect you. Things were still new, and I didn't want you to get attached—"

"Oh please. In case you haven't noticed, I'm too old for fairy tales. You know, I heard you fucking him that night. God, you were so desperate."

Her eyes—my eyes—watered, but she soldiered on, changing the subject. "Tell me about the boy you kissed. Why did you send him away?"

"Because the Becketts have a strict no-boys rule. If I break their rules, I go back into the system, and I don't want that to happen, because I really love living there."

Mom jerked like I'd just stabbed her in the heart. Some tiny part of me pumped a fist and cheered.

"Do you like him?" she asked quietly.

Did I? I picked at a nick in the table and thought about that for a moment. "I do, but it's more than just like. I might, maybe, love him."

"You're not sure?"

I blinked at the stupidity of that question. "How could I be sure? It's not like I was ever exposed to love."

"I never stopped loving you, baby. Ever."

"Yeah, right," I said with a sneer. "You dumped me with babysitters. You left me sitting in cars for hours on end while you dug yourself in deeper with Dmitri, and then *you left me*." My voice rose with every word until I was shouting by the end of the sentence. The guard watched but didn't intervene. Mrs. DeSantis and Max stood by the door. Max caught my eye and flashed a thumbs-up.

"I loved him, Amanda. Was I supposed to be alone for the rest of my life just because I had you?"

"No, Mom, but you were supposed to love me too. And you didn't."

She pressed her hands to her mouth and squeezed her eyes shut. "I know I made mistakes. I let him con me, baby. But I love you! You're my baby girl, and I want us to be a family again. I'm getting out soon, and when I do, I want us to go somewhere. Anywhere. We'll start over. Just you and me. No boys."

My face went hot. More rules? When was anyone going to ask what *I* wanted? Was I not allowed to want things just because I was sixteen, just because I was a foster child? This was bullshit. I stood up, my chair scraping the floor. "I don't want that." I turned and took a step.

"Amanda!"

"Do me a favor. Don't insist on any more visits. And don't call me when you get out."

Mom's lip trembled. "Mandy, baby, please. I love you."

"Mom, if you love me even a tiny bit, you'll leave me alone and let me live my own life."

I walked to the door and waited for the guard to let us out, absolutely determined not to let the sound of my mother's sobs make me crack.

I had to be strong. I had to be brave. I would not end up like her. I damn well would never allow my own life to get fucked up because of some guy.

No matter how much I loved him.

***

Back in Mrs. DeSantis's car, I sat in the backseat, my head on Max's shoulder. He may treat girls like crap, but I wasn't a girl. I was *Man*, and he was my squad brother.

Mrs. DeSantis was quiet on the long drive home. We hit a ton of traffic, and the rumbling in our bellies finally convinced Mrs. D to pull off at one of the rest stop fast-food chains along the route. I didn't think I could eat, but strangely, I felt good after telling my mom off.

"Girl, you were *fierce*," Max said again as we slid into a booth.

"Yeah, well, I had a reputation for bravery to uphold," I said and popped a french fry into my mouth. Mrs. DeSantis sat at her own booth, across from us, tapping away on a tablet. Probably submitting case notes on my breakdown.

Max angled a look at Mrs. DeSantis and quietly asked, "So you think you're in love with Logan?"

I lifted a shoulder. "Yeah. Maybe. I have no idea."

He pulled in a deep breath. "Man, for what it's worth, that boy is batshit crazy for you."

A soft warmth spread over my body, and I squirmed. "Oh, he is not."

"Hand to God," Max said and held up his right hand. "He watches you. And it's not weird, not like he's stalking you. It's because he can't help himself. You're like his sun."

"His sun," I repeated, liking the sound of that way too much. I sat with a burger in front of my lips for a full minute and finally thought of something to say. "He was gonna leave. And now he says he's staying. For me. So…whatever."

Max's eyes snapped to mine. "Leave? What the hell are you talking about?"

I waved a hand. "Squad was just a way to keep some promise he made to Matt to get John's respect. He got it. John gave him a big old pat on the back."

"So we just wasted our time training him. That is seriously fucked up." Max shoved back on his side of the booth, frowning at his food.

"No, not really. Like I said, now he plans to stay. I think Logan really likes firefighting and J squad."

Max shook his head. "He lied to us. All this time, he lied."

"No, he didn't lie. He changed his mind." And then I remembered the note he'd given me. "Look. He even gave me his good-bye note. Said he doesn't need it anymore."

Max took the crumpled paper and smoothed it out on the table beside his meal. As he read, his eyebrows crept closer and closer until he finally looked up at me, horrified.

"Holy hell, Man, do you know what this is?" He didn't wait for an answer. "This is a suicide note."

I choked on the soda I'd just sipped. "What? What are you talking about?"

Max rotated the paper and pointed to a line about halfway down the page. "*I'll be at his altar.* You don't recognize that?" When I shook my head, Max grabbed his iPhone, tapped the screen, and then shoved the phone at me. "Here."

On his phone, he'd pulled up Google. I read the screen, and my mouth completely dried up. Oh crap. Oh shit, this was bad. Reece copied lines from Kurt Cobain's suicide note. I wasn't a Nirvana fan, barely even knew who Kurt Cobain was. The only thing I did know is that he killed himself. I never would have connected this but—*shit!* Gage had. And didn't bother to spell it out for me.

Jesus Christ, what should we do? "What do I do, Max?" I pressed a hand to my chest, where my heart kicked like a stubborn mule every time I thought of Reece dead. "He gave me the note because he said he didn't need it anymore. He said I'm the only one who knows about it." What if that wasn't true? What if Reece was actually planning... Oh God!

No.

No, I just could not let that happen.

"What about that kid Alex?"

I thought about that for a minute. Alex and Reece were best friends. They were in the chess club. They ate lunch together all the time. Well...they used to.

"If you're right and he really is serious about J squad, that means Logan's one of us, Man. A brother. And we have to protect him."

Max held out his hand, and I clasped it—a promise made.

Chapter 27
Reece

You want to know why I'm writing you this? Because Matt made me promise—he made me fucking vow not to let you break me down.

I had to serve my detention. And after detention, I still had to study with Bear. At least I was spared the running of the bleachers. Max was with Amanda, and Gage was MIA. Alex found some studying to do while Bear schooled me on fire suppression techniques. After that, I spent forty minutes quizzing him for the biology final. He was jazzed about the way I taught him to remember the cranial nerves—sung to the tune of "The Twelve Days of Christmas." It always helped Matt. By the time we were done for the day, it was after six.

We put away the books, and I grabbed Alex on the way out. I didn't have the car today, so we started walking—Bear, Alex, and me.

"Alex, you getting sick or something? You're really sweaty." He also looked pale and kind of anxious while he played with his phone.

"I'm fine."

I looked at him carefully. He was fine before I found Bear, but he sure wasn't fine now. I hoped he wasn't pissed off at me again. Bear and I talked about the fire as we walked, and Alex continued his sweaty, anxious silence. By the time we reached the firehouse, I thought I might explode. We headed upstairs to the second level and found Steve Conner's office empty.

"He's here. Look." Bear pointed to a cup of coffee that steamed beside the computer.

I frowned. This was so damn hard; waiting wasn't making it any easier.

Raised voices got our attention. "Oh, come on! This is bullshit," my dad shouted.

I exchanged glances with Bear and Alex.

The chief spoke. "Lieutenant, this is serious."

"Oh please. It's typical Reece behavior we've been dealing with since he was born. Just ignore it."

What behavior? They were talking about me? I left Steve Conner's office with my face burning, only to find the chief and my dad talking to Amanda and Max. "Excuse me," I interrupted. "What behavior are you all discussing?" And why the hell wasn't I part of that discussion?

Chief Duffy turned, his face a study in concern. Amanda gasped and looked about ready to burst into tears. Dad looked pissed off—nothing unusual there.

"Cadet, why don't we take this into my office?"

Dad flung up his hands. "Brian, believe me, this is just a cry for attention."

"My office. Now." Chief Duffy pointed one of those thick fingers toward the open door, and like trained pets, we all marched. The chief circled his desk and sat down in the leather chair. Dad took the same guest chair I'd used on my first day. The rest of us remained standing.

Everyone looked at me. I squirmed, uncomfortable being the specimen under the microscope.

"Son, why were you in Steve Conner's office?"

I straightened my shoulders and tried not to fidget. "Waiting for him, sir. I wanted to talk to him about Saturday's fire and my suspicions."

"Excuse me?" Dad glared at me. "I told you to report to Steve Conner the day of the fire. Are you telling me you haven't done that yet?"

Oh fuck. I looked at Amanda, but she shook her head, silently pleading with me to stay quiet.

I must be the world's biggest ass. I was the hero for about a day. For one full day, I was the son my dad never acknowledged. I'd made him proud. And then I made a choice for a girl who couldn't—or maybe wouldn't—be with me.

And I was about to do it again. "Um, no, Lieutenant."

"No! What the hell do you mean no? Jesus Christ, Reece! This isn't some alternate reality game you and Alex play. This is real life. You have evidence that could indicate arson, and you didn't report it? If it were up to me, I'd kick you off this squad right now."

A big fist crashed to a desk. "Lieutenant, it's *not* up to you." Chief Duffy took back control. He shuffled papers on his desk and picked up a creased piece of white paper that had been folded and unfolded a few too many times and now looked—

Looked like the note in my pocket. I shoved my hand into my pocket, but it was empty. Blood pounded in my ears, and spots danced in my eyes. God. Oh Jesus, I was gonna be sick. I was gonna hurl all over the chief's desk. Chief Duffy must have caught on.

"Okay, everybody out. I want a moment alone with my cadet."

I'd given Amanda my note. I told her I didn't need it anymore, not since I'd met her.

And now it was on the chief's desk.

"He's *my* son!"

Oh my God! *Really?* I shut my eyes and shrugged. "Let them stay. Let them all stay." Like it even mattered now.

"Jamison brought this to my attention."

I sent her a glare I hoped sliced all the way through her stone-cold heart. She flinched but quickly masked it with a shift of her weight.

"Given the, ah, you know, distance between you and your father"— Chief Duffy rolled his hand in the air and slid a look toward Dad, who didn't so much as wince—"she brought it to me because she's concerned it might be a, um, well, a suicide note."

The word hung in the air, suspended in time. I just sat there, trying to figure out why I couldn't feel my extremities. There was nothing, nothing but numbness and some random thoughts circling my brain. I never should have let her read it, never should have listened to her, trusted her. She was the only one I'd—even Alex didn't know. Oh God. Oh my God, that was why he looked so ill.

She'd texted him. It must have been his idea to tell the chief. Or Dad. Or both.

I swallowed hard, and a bitterness in the back of my throat penetrated all the numbness. Was it the taste of disappointment? Betrayal? The answer came to me, and I almost laughed out loud at the irony. This was what it tasted like to lose hope.

The minute I named it, the pain began—a full-out attack on every receptor in my body. I knew if I looked, I'd find a gaping wound, because now, it burned. Oh Jesus, it burned. I had to leave, had to run, had to be far, far from here before I lost it. *Damn it, Matt. Goddamn it, why did you leave me?* The pulsing, pounding, *roaring* in my ears demanded action, but there wasn't one. There was nothing I could do to escape—except for one thing.

Deny.

"I'm sorry," I began, absolutely dumbfounded my voice worked. "I'm so sorry Amanda felt it necessary to worry you for no reason."

My dad flipped his palm up in a what-did-I-tell-you gesture. Chief Duffy's eyes narrowed.

"Son, are you telling me this is *not* a suicide note?"

I pressed one hand over my heart. "Chief, I promise, it's not a suicide note. But it is a good-bye note."

Dad's eyes snapped up and then away.

"What you called distance between my dad and me goes a lot deeper than that, and honestly, I'm sick of it. I am who I am, and that pisses him off for a whole bunch of dumbass reasons he's just gonna have to deal with by himself, because I quit."

"You quit? What does that mean?" Chief Duffy leaned forward, my note still grasped in his hand.

"It means I'm leaving. I don't want anything from him. I don't want to see him. I don't even want his name."

Dad made a *whoosh* sound like he'd been sucker punched that pinched my heart, but I didn't—couldn't—stop.

"I want to start over, find people who appreciate me and love me. I thought—" Abruptly I clamped my lips together with another glare toward Amanda. It didn't matter what I thought. It was pretty damn obvious I was wrong on every level.

The chief narrowed his eyes. "And what about your mom?"

I flinched. "My mother"—I tried to find the right words—"loves us both. *I'm* taking her out of the middle." My dad couldn't look at me.

"Reece, we're worried about you. Nobody here wants you to leave."

"No, sir, you're right. They usually wish I wasn't here in the first place."

Chief Duffy frowned and leaned back in his chair. "I don't understand. Why did you volunteer if you'd already decided to leave?"

"It was my brother's idea, sir. His dying wish."

Dad's chair hit Chief Duffy's desk as he jumped to his feet. Amanda and the chief both leaped up too, but it wasn't in time. Dad grabbed a fistful of my T-shirt, cocked back his arm, and ground out between clenched teeth, "He shouldn't be dead! Goddamn it, you—"

I never thought it. I never gave my hand the command to hit.

Suddenly, my dad was sprawled on the floor, a fountain of blood dripping from his nose. I glanced down at my hand, surprised to find it still there—and throbbing.

"Reece!" Amanda screamed. "Oh my God, Lieutenant, are you okay?"

"No, goddamn it, I'm not okay." Dad covered his nose and tilted his head back.

"Logan, ah, Christ. Didn't I warn you not to bring family drama into my house?"

I ignored them both and just glared at my father. "You think I don't know you blame me for Matt's death? You think I don't care that Matt is gone? This is why I wanted to go!"

"You should have—"

"That's enough!" Chief Duffy shouted. "Cadet, you're suspended. One week. Leave immediately. Do not return until class starts the night of the second week, is that understood? And Lieutenant, you'll shut your mouth right now or you'll join him. Clear?"

I shut my eyes, turned, and left the chief's office without a backward glance.

They were traitors. All of them.

***

I stopped thinking.

Off-line.

Autopilot.

Made it home. Ignored Mom. Ignored Tucker.

Upstairs in my room, I locked the door and then slid down the back of it, all the way to the floor.

Stayed there.

Don't swallow, don't swallow. It burned—oh fuck! Pain in my throat, jagged edges over the white-hot blaze.

She showed them my note. She showed them—showed *him*—and now it was gone. My entire plan. Everything I did, for nothing. I wasn't done. Goddamn it, I wasn't done. There was no point to any of it now.

No fucking point.

I uncurled the hand clenched in a fist, and it was there, right there, in my palm. When had I unlocked the box, picked it up? I didn't remember.

"Reece? Reece, open this door." Mom pounded on my locked door.

I stared at my hand, but it shook and blurred. I hid it, the key to my escape, back in its box, locked it, slid it under my bed, and opened the door. Mom shoved into my room, the dog on her heels.

"Hey, Mom."

Mom's face was white as a sheet, and the white-hot blaze in my throat got impossibly hotter. "Hey? That's all you—" Abruptly, she bit back the rest of her question and started over. "Reece. Your father called. What's this business about a *suicide note?*"

"He called you?" I verified, sneering. "What for? It's what he wants." It was the wrong thing to say, totally wrong.

Mom's face went gray, and she grabbed me and pulled me toward her, gripping me the way I held Matt when he slowly bled out, gripping me so tight, it would have hurt if I wasn't so numb.

"No! No, don't say that. Don't ever say that!" She pulled away far enough to shake me. "He doesn't want you dead, Reece. Never that."

"Then what, Mom? He sure as hell doesn't want me as a son."

"*I* do." She shook me again, hard enough to rattle my teeth. "Do you hear me? I do."

I looked at her, really looked at her, and she looked so, so…I don't know, *old*. When had that happened? Mom was the most beautiful woman in the world. Now, there were lines on her face, gray in her hair, and fear in her eyes, the darkest fear I'd ever seen.

And he'd put it there, not me, *him*. I hated him for that. I'd hate him for the rest of my life. I'd hate them both—Dad and Amanda. God, oh God.

Sobs ripped out of my lungs like some alien creature leaving its host—loud, gasping rattles that echoed off the walls of my room. I tried to hold on, clutching Mom, Tucker pawing at me, but some tiny bit of black in me grew and eclipsed everything that I was and swallowed me whole, alive and screaming.

"Reece, honey, breathe. Breathe now. That's it." Mom's voice sounded like it was broadcast from the moon over cheap radios. Dimly, I felt her hand on my head, on my back. *Stroke, pat, stroke.* "Reece, I want you to come with me. Right now. Get up. Hold Tucker's leash. Walk downstairs with me. Get in the car. Will you do that?"

I lifted my head. It felt like it had its own gravity. Mom's eyes were red from crying, and what was left of my heart shattered into pieces. I nodded, and she helped me to my feet. I took the leash. When did she clip it on? My limbs felt leaden. With her help, I made it down the stairs and into the backseat, where I closed my eyes.

When I opened them again, I was in a hospital room, my hands strapped to the bed.

Chapter 28
Amanda

Reece wasn't in school the day after he decked his dad.

Or the day after that. It was Wednesday now. Nobody really noticed he was gone, except for Bear and Max. At our lunch table that day, Bear broke the silence. "We should visit. Make sure he's okay, you know?" The bell rang before anybody agreed.

I grabbed my tray and dumped what was left into the trash, and Gage grabbed my elbow. "What happened to Logan, Man?"

I didn't meet his eyes.

"Tick tock, Mandy."

"Okay, okay." I threw my hands out and nearly smacked a sophomore on his way out of the cafeteria. "Sorry," I called after him. "I showed Reece's note to the chief. And to the lieutenant."

Gage's eyes nearly exploded from his face. "You…oh my God. You didn't."

"I did." And I hated myself ever since Reece looked at me with those dark eyes of his, burning with betrayal.

"Why? Why the hell would you do that?"

Because I didn't want to lose him.

The truth struck me right in the solar plexus. *Idiot!* I was so stupid. I'd tried so hard to keep Reece from getting too close because I knew this would happen. He'd leave me; that's what everybody did. The dad I never met, my mom, Mrs. Merodie… Every. Single. One. Left me. But Reece? He was different. Had been different right from the start. But this wasn't just leaving.

It was *going*.

Forever.

And even though I knew I had no right, I just couldn't let that happen.

My heart hurt, and tears burned in my throat, but I swallowed all that down and flicked a glance at Gage. He was staring at me pretty much the way Reece had, and I erupted. "Oh, come on, Gage! You were the one who told me about the stupid letter in the first place. You said Reece had issues. You Googled that one line and showed me, remember?"

"So you showed it to the one person who pretty much created the situation in the first place?" Gage shook his head. "Way to go, Man. You probably ruined what was left of that guy's life."

I froze while my stomach fell to the ground and I tried to remember how to breathe. "Well, thank you for all the support." I shoved through the cafeteria doors, but Gage was right behind me. "You don't even like him, so what the hell is your problem?"

"Oh, don't even pretend you did this because of me. You did this for yourself, and you still haven't said why."

"I just told you! What if it really was a suicide note?"

"If you thought it was, you should have showed it to someone who gives a shit about him, not someone who moved out of the fucking house to get away from him."

The late bell rang, and Gage took off at a run, his words echoing in the hall.

***

After school, I walked to the station house and headed up to the chief's office, but he wasn't on-shift.

"Hey, Amanda. What are you doing here?"

I turned, saw Steve Conner standing in the door to his office, and shrugged. "Looking for the chief."

"He's due in tonight."

"Good." I nodded. "That's, uh, good."

Steve angled his head. "Anything I can help you with?"

Shrugging, I turned for the stairs. "No. I wanted to talk to him about Reece."

Steve sucked in a sharp breath. "Yeah, too bad about Reece. I liked that kid. Hope they let him out soon."

I froze. *Let him out of what?* "What?" I turned back. "Let him out?"

"The hospital. John called his wife, and she took him to the hospital. For his own protection."

I pressed my hands to my gaping mouth.

Jesus! What did I do?

I turned and ran down the stairs, out the main exit, and skidded to a stop when I saw Lieutenant Logan sitting in his car on the street, a purple bruise under one eye. "What did you do?" I demanded as I stalked over and leaned into the open window. "What the hell did you do to Reece?"

John shifted tired eyes toward me, then took another drag on the cigarette he pinched between his thumb and fingers. He looked away and shrugged. "What had to be done."

"You put him in a hospital?"

He cut me with another tired look. "Was I supposed to let the stupid kid die?"

I straightened up. "*The stupid kid.* That's what you call your own son?"

He sucked in more smoke, then sighed it out. "Look, Amanda, I did what I had to do. Let it be, okay?"

"No. No, I will not. You treat him like he's some pile of crap you stepped in. He's *your* kid. Doesn't that matter? Doesn't it mean something to you that the only son you have left hates you so much he's thinking of killing himself?"

A fire sparked in John's tired eyes, and he shoved out of the car, forcing me back a few steps. "Does it—of course it means something! I didn't want this."

I folded my arms and glared. "Oh. You didn't want this. Funny how you can say that after you did everything you could to humiliate him. To hurt him. To punish him for what happened to Matt."

John dropped the cigarette, crushed it viciously with his heel, and laughed without humor. "What happened to Matt was my fault, Amanda. I know Reece thinks I blame him, but I don't and I never did. I'm the one to blame." He thumped his chest. "I should have been there. I should have—" He broke off, shook his head, and covered his face with his hands.

"Been a better dad?"

Another laugh. "I tried. I tried so hard." He dropped his hands and stared at me like he only just then noticed I was there. "You know what? I got things to do. Find someone else to play with."

He strode into the station house while I stared at the butt that smoldered on the ground, trying hard not to feel like I was the one stepped on and ground out.

***

By Saturday morning, I wanted to run away.

I still hadn't heard anything from or about Reece. Bear hadn't gotten any text messages. Neither had Alex. Gage thought I was evil, and even John Logan hated me. Mrs. Beckett woke me to start the chores for the weekend. Stripping beds, laundry, shopping. When we got home, I wanted to go for a run to clear my head.

How did everything get so screwed up? I just wanted to help him, that's all. It was supposed to be a cakewalk, because Reece has both of his parents.

I didn't, so there was no hope for me.

Oh God, maybe it wasn't him I was trying to help at all.

I moved to my window and stared outside. I liked to think I had no ulterior motives—subconscious or not—but it was time to face the ugly truth. There was some sick and twisted part of me living vicariously through Reece. I covered my face, ran my hands over my hair, and blew out a long, slow breath.

That's when I saw Larry sneaking around the garage.

The garage was at the rear of the Becketts' property, a huge separate structure big enough for three cars, but it was never used for that. It was Mr. Beckett's man cave or workshop or something. I wasn't entirely sure, since we'd been warned repeatedly to stay out of it. He had the usual stuff in there—lawn mower, snowblower, rakes, and all the other gear you needed to keep up a house—so I didn't see just what was so private about it.

Mr. Beckett was digging a hole at the rear fence for some shrub he was planting. Larry pushed the wheelbarrow into the garage, poked his head out, and seemed satisfied that Mr. Beckett wasn't watching him. He grabbed a jug of weed killer, shoved it deep under the crap in the wheelbarrow, and headed for the path that led to the front of the house.

I quickly tiptoed to Larry's room, which faced the front of the house. Mr. Beckett had a small mountain of mulch delivered that now sat in the driveway. But instead of shoveling mulch into the wheelbarrow, Larry took another careful look around, unearthed the jug, and stuffed it at the bottom of the trash can he would drag out to the curb tomorrow night. I tiptoed back to the window in my room. Mr. Beckett was still digging, and there was Larry, showing no sign of the secret mission he'd just executed.

I sank down to the bed, rubbing my stomach where guilt tried to burn a hole. I had to go retrieve that plastic jug.

Whatever was in it wasn't weed killer.

Which meant...

Reece was right.

Chapter 29
Reece

He was scared, Dad. I could see the wild terror in his eyes, feel it in the way he clutched my hands. He didn't want to go. He didn't want to die. He didn't want to leave me. Me, Dad. Not you. Me.

I twitched in my bed and glanced at the clock for the thousandth time.

"Reece?"

I shifted my gaze back to Dr. Lewis and tried not to stare at the coffee stain on his tie. "No."

"No, what?" he prodded.

"No, I don't plan to do myself harm. No, I don't think I need hospitalization, intervention, or medication. And no, I don't believe I'm a worthless human being."

Dr. Lewis tried not to sigh, but I knew he wanted to. He'd been pressing me all day to confide in him. I didn't know why the hell Amanda showed that note to the chief or my dad. How was this helping me? The only thing it did was scare the crap out of Mom and convince my dad he was right—and land me in this room.

I wanted out of this place so badly, I ached.

Dr. Lewis pulled a pen from the pocket of his lab coat and clicked it. He scrawled something on the chart hidden inside one of those metal covers. "Why did you write, *I'll be at his altar*? You did write this, right? *I'll be at his altar until there's nothing left to burn*?"

I resisted the powerful urge to slam the fucking metal cover on his fingers. "Because I wanted him to know, to grasp in his tight-assed, macho head, that he can't hurt me anymore. I'm not waiting around for him to figure out he's not winning any Dad of the Year awards from me. I joined the junior squad to impress him and reconnect with him and make him see me. The LVFD was his altar—his and Matt's. All that mattered. I stayed because it's mine now."

And that was pure truth.

"And what about this—*I'd kill to feel only sad right now*. What did you mean?"

Exactly what I wrote. Jesus, dude. How many years of school did this guy have to take for this shit? "I was sad when I was little. The constant rejection. The connection he had with Matt but not me. It was there. But after Matt died, it was more than just sad. Sad is too small a word to cover what hurts."

"Does it hurt bad enough to end it?"

I laughed. "Still no, Doc. But nice try."

I was pretty sure I saw a twitch in his lip, but he controlled it.

"Reece, do you understand why your parents were upset by this note?"

Oh yes. Yes, I did. "No," I said with a shrug.

"Are you a Nirvana fan?"

Shit. "Who?"

"Nirvana."

"Never heard of him."

"It's a band, actually. Their lead singer was Kurt Cobain. Ever hear of him?"

"Yeah, he was with that Love chick."

"Courtney Love. That's right. He wrote that same line in his suicide note."

I nodded and shrugged. "Huh. Guess I must have heard that somewhere."

Dr. Lewis wasn't buying what I was selling. "You guess?"

"I can't name a single Nirvana song, Dr. Lewis. I don't think I could pick out a picture of Kurt Cobain. But I know the name, know the story." A bead of sweat rolled down my back between my shoulder blades. I slouched lower in my bed and shut my eyes, desperate to be rid of the pimple on my ass that was Dr. Lewis.

The metal cover snapped shut. I opened my eyes to see Dr. Lewis put the pen back in his pocket and stand up. "Okay, Reece. I'll sign the discharge papers. You can go home, but I want to see you three times a week in my office."

My eyes swept around the room, and if I'd found a single sharp object, I'd have shoved it through this guy's throat. I almost laughed. If they found out I was homicidal, what would they do to me then?

Finally, the doctor left, and I let out a long sigh.

"Thought he'd never leave."

I jerked at the sound of that voice, stunned to find my dad at the door. Damn it, there's got to be something sharp in this room. "What the hell do you want?" I sat up and crossed my arms.

Dad stepped inside and shut the door. "Wanted to see how you're doing."

"Oh, just fine. Some of the other patients are starting a chess club and invited me to play."

Dad sighed. "Smart ass."

I jerked at that. I was *never* a smart ass. I was never able to talk to him, let alone mouth off to him…until now.

He walked around my bed, dragged the chair closer, and sat. I shot a glance at my IV. Normal saline. Just my luck. They'd given me some excellent drugs earlier.

The silence between us grew uncomfortable. Impatient, I cocked my head and waited for him to tell me what the hell he was doing here, but he just sat, staring at me.

I stared back. We sat there, him staring at me staring at him, for five minutes, maybe ten, until I cracked. I burst out laughing. I laughed so hard, I couldn't breathe, and when I finally caught a breath, I gasped out, "Jesus, if I'd known a suicide scare would get you to notice me, I might have actually tried it a long time ago."

Suddenly, two hands fisted around the ridiculous gown I had to wear, and Dad almost lifted me off the bed. "Don't say that. Don't you ever say it—don't even *think* it, you hear me?" He gave me such a shake, I stopped laughing and looked at him.

Really looked at him.

His eyes were wild. There were lines around them, around his mouth too. Those lines were stark white at the moment. There was a black-and-blue mark under his eye—a mark I'd put there. His eyes bulged, and in them, I saw something I would have bet he'd never felt, never even believed in.

I saw horror.

But why? What was he afraid of? Certainly not the thought of my death. Hell, he'd probably wished it had been me instead of Matt a hundred times.

"Okay. Sorry. Bad joke."

His hands, still holding me, twitched. "No joke at all, son."

Son.

That's twice now. I scanned every memory, looking for a single instance before I joined the squad, but couldn't find it. The terror he felt lay like an open book in his eyes and in the twitch I could feel through his hands. Maybe I'm cruel, maybe I'm a selfish bastard, maybe I really needed all this therapy that Dr. Lewis wanted to shove down my throat, but it made me happy that I scared him. Not happy in a spiteful way, but happy in a real, down to the bone feeling of joy.

I pushed his hands away but smiled when he looked at his hands like he suddenly wanted to cut them off. "Sorry I scared you. I was just...surprised, I guess."

His face had turned a sick gray color, so I grabbed the water cup from the table next to my bed and thrust it toward him. He gulped some down, coughed, and managed a grin. "This may be the first time since you were born that you didn't scream when I touched you."

What? My jaw dropped, and it was my turn for the wide eyes. "What do you mean?"

"Oh, Reece." He laughed once and sipped again. "You were a strange baby. Cute as hell, but afraid of every damn thing. Including me. *Especially* me. You'd scream if anybody except Mom and Matt went near you. Me? You looked at me like I was Freddy fucking Krueger."

"Come on," I said and squirmed. Jesus, what kind of kid was afraid of his dad?

"I'm serious." He dragged a hand over his face. "I couldn't wait for you to be born. Another boy." He shook his head with a proud grin. "Matt was great, and I had all these...these plans for camping trips and baseball games for all of us." He shrugged and lost the grin. "But when we brought you home from the hospital, you screamed every time I held you. Your mom said you'd grow out of it. But you never did. So I stopped holding you. When you were a toddler and fussy with your teeth or if you'd gotten hurt, I made things worse if I tried to soothe you. You screamed yourself unconscious once. Scared the shit out of your mother. Your poor mom was exhausted, trying to take care of you and your brother, and all the screaming and crying you did around me—well, I was your father. My job is to take care of you, to give you what you needed—no matter what it was. And what you needed was for me to keep away." His voice cracked, and his eyes scrunched up.

I stared at him, feeling like crap. He'd done it *for* me.

"What was wrong with me?" Aunt Sue had always said I was a difficult baby.

He laughed again and dropped his arm. "I don't know. I wouldn't let your mom find out. I didn't want you slapped with some label just so people could treat you differently." He sat up, stared at the cup for a moment, then turned it around and around. "Except I ended up doing that myself. Exactly that."

"But I did grow out of it, didn't I?"

He slid a look toward me, typical smirk in place. "Yeah. You did. That didn't mean I stopped being afraid. How could I take you fishing or camping without your mom? What if you got hurt? What if you had a nightmare? What if you gave me the Freddy Krueger look again? I couldn't risk it, couldn't stand that I did that to you. So…"

"You stayed away."

He lifted his shoulders, still not looking at me. "When you got older—and weirder," he added with a laugh that was a slash of a blade, "well, it was hard to connect. You didn't like sports like Matt."

"Yes, I did. Still do."

His head snapped around at that. "Really? What's your favorite?"

"Baseball."

"Yanks or Mets?"

"Mets." Duh.

"Huh," he said and laughed. It was a real laugh, not one of those sad ones. "I never knew that."

"That's because—" I broke off, left the bitter thought unsaid. "Never mind." He nodded, and I figured he knew what I was gonna say.

"When Matt wanted to join J squad, I thought it would be good for both of you—split you up, let you each do your own things—and it was. You made some friends who were more like you."

My jaw clenched. "More like me. What the hell does that mean?" *Difficult? Weird? Afraid of every damn thing? What?*

He held up his hands. "Smart. I know you won't believe this, Reece, but when that teacher you had back in, what, third grade, fourth grade? When she told us you were brilliant, I was never so damn proud in my life."

My face burned, and there was a tug in my chest—a weird clench that took me a minute, a full minute, to recognize as love.

"I scared the hell out of you when you were a baby, and I sure as hell couldn't teach you anything that would *engage* that busy brain of yours." He made air quotes to emphasize the word I knew was my teacher's. "I stayed out of your way. I guess I got good at staying away."

Yeah. Guess so. "And then you left for good."

He flinched, liked I'd kicked him in the stomach. "Yeah. I—oh God." He folded over his middle. "It was *my* fault, Reece. Mine, not yours, and I just couldn't face that, I couldn't. You remind me so much of him. You look like twins, you sound alike, you even do that thing with your lips he used to do." He squeezed his eyes shut for a minute, and when he opened them, they were wet. "It hurt, God, it hurt to lose him."

Oh. Of course it hurt. He was Matt's father. Of course.

"I know I hurt you, I know it, and I'm sorrier than I can tell you, because you're right—what you said in that note—I was never a father to you. It hurt so goddamn much to look at you and see the evidence of just how colossally I fucked things up." He swiped a hand under his nose and wiped his eyes, and I cracked inside.

My father was *crying*.

He didn't even cry at Matt's funeral. He got pissed off and stayed that way for months. What should I do? Was I supposed to hug him and say *no sweat*, do one of those awkward bro hugs, and go grab a beer? I thought about that for a long moment and finally concluded what's past is past. It couldn't be changed. It couldn't bring back my brother. Dad made the gesture. He broke years of silence and dropped all his tough, manly shit for me.

I cleared my throat and tried to talk around the giant lump in my throat. "Dad, there's something you should know." I broke off when my voice cracked. I swallowed and tried again. "I'm not really smart. I just take tests well."

He gave me the yeah-right look. "Reece, I was there. Your IQ is off the charts."

"No." I waved a hand. "I'm serious. I am not a genius. I'm not brilliant like Alex. I take tests well because I never forget anything I'm taught." I waited a beat, but he still wasn't getting it. "I memorize shit, Dad. That's all I can do. I'm a human computer, which means I'm only as good as the programming."

He stared at me, eyes crinkling. "What happened on June 2 the year you were ten?"

I searched through memories and grinned. "Disney World. Got lost during the parade. When you guys found me, like hours later—"

"It was not *hours* later. More like one hour."

I grinned. "When you guys found me *one* hour later, Mom was crying and hugging me, and you said, 'Come on, leave the boy alone. He just wanted to hang out with the pretty princess.'"

"Remember which one?"

"Cinderella."

"Smart kid, even then." He swallowed more of my water, then put the cup back on the table. "I'm sorry, so sorry you thought I hated you all this time. I love you. I love you, Reece."

Before I could react, before I could sink into those words and just let them kind of sink in, he was back to tough. He left the bed and stalked around the room. "What the hell were you thinking with this note shit? When Amanda showed us that piece of paper, I thought it was no big deal, just another stunt. And then I found out you used a line from some rock star's suicide note. I thought we were gonna find you in a pool of blood somewhere. Your mother needed sedatives to fall asleep, according to the brunch date." He sneered and held his hand up a few inches over his head.

Ah. He was pissed off the guy was taller than him.

"Not a suicide note."

Dad stopped prowling the room and waved two fingers under his eyes. "Look at me. Look at me and swear on Matt's grave."

I did. "It wasn't a suicide note."

It was. But just like that, it suddenly wasn't. Maybe it never was.

"So what the hell was it?"

"It was a good-bye note."

"You were gonna leave and go where, exactly?" He spread out his hands and lifted his eyebrows.

I thought about coming clean and telling him the truth, but I...I just couldn't do it. I grabbed the lie I'd been telling for so long and expanded it. "I was going to enlist. Not sure which branch yet. I like the idea of flying. But not submarines. So the Navy is a tough decision for me."

"The Navy. Baby Jesus on a bun, are you freaking kidding me?"

"No."

"Then why did you join J squad?"

I pulled up my knees. "Matt. Matt made me swear. Made me promise not to let you push me out of your life."

"When? He never regained—" His face froze when the answer dawned on him. "Jesus. Oh God. How long, Reece? How long?"

"Twenty minutes, I think." I wrapped my arms around my body, trying not to lose it. "He was pinned, Dad. Could barely breathe. He grabbed my hand, held it so tight, begged me not to let you go." I held up my right hand. To this day, it still tingled from my brother's grip. "He knew. I don't know how, but he knew he was dying, and it was my fault, and he wouldn't let go. He wouldn't let go until I fucking promised him." I looked up, looked into my dad's face, his lips trembling, his eyes wet. "I did. I didn't want to at first, because I knew what would happen if I did. I kept saying no, but he begged, and he was in so much pain. God! Dad, it was my fault, so I promised I would do what he wanted. He smiled. He smiled, and that was it—he held my hand until he lost consciousness, and I'm sorry, I'm so fucking sorry." Tears fell out of my eyes and plopped onto my arms.

Arms grabbed me, the strong arms I used to wish would toss me high up in the air like Matt. Or carry me on his shoulders like Matt. They grabbed me and held me, and I cried until I couldn't breathe, cried for Matt, cried for all the wasted years, cried until I was empty.

"Christ, will you put on some clothes? This is getting weird," Dad muttered into my hair when my sobs finally slowed.

I was in a hospital on a suicide watch, in a fucking dress, but my dad was here, and damn if it wasn't the best day I ever had.

***

An hour or so later, after Dad got me sprung from the hospital, we were driving home when he asked me the bonus question.

"So what did Steve say about your video?"

I braced myself for Dad's wrath. "I didn't show him yet. I waited for him, but he had stuff to do, and then I got admitted to the hospital."

"You didn't show him? Jesus, Reece! That could be crucial evidence in his investigation."

I spread my hands apart. "I tried, Dad. I was in his office, but he said he had to interview the guys on-scene first. And then—"

"Then what?" He looked at me with a frown when he stopped for a light.

"Amanda saw the video."

"Yeah, I remember. You think she knows this kid?"

"I know she does. He's her foster brother."

"Holy shit. Did you tell Steve all this?"

Slowly, I shook my head. The light turned green. Dad drove through town, impatience sweating out of every pore. "No. I didn't get the chance. Amanda asked me to wait—"

"Oh goddamn it, Reece!"

"I know. But I owed her one, Dad. Amanda's a foster kid. Did you know?"

By the unsurprised look he shot me, I figured he did.

"Anyway, she and the kid in my video, his name's Larry Ecker, live with the Becketts. She told me how bad it's been for her, for him, and how much they love it there. She asked me to wait to report to Steve, wait until she had a chance to see for herself what Larry's been up to."

Dad was silent for a moment, but when I looked over, I could see the muscle clenching in his jaw. "I knew Amanda was a foster kid. The Becketts are good people, so life can't be that bad for her."

"She loves the Becketts, Dad. She wants to stay with them. So does Larry. She said they could be sent away like that." I snapped my fingers.

"Oh," he said. "So Larry starring in your video could be enough trouble for the big adios?"

"Yeah." I looked away. "Like I said, I thought I owed that to her. Time, I mean."

Dad pulled up to the curb in front of our house—well, Mom's place—and cut the engine. "Reece, everybody who steps into that firehouse has to do one thing, the *same* thing, and that's do the job—period. What if this kid is guilty? What if he set three more

NOTHING LEFT TO BURN

fires since Saturday and you could have stopped him? What if one of us got—"

I shot up a hand. "I get it. She asked me for time."

Understanding dawned, and he nodded. "Okay." He slapped my leg and unfastened his seat belt. "I'll call Steve."

"Dad, what about Amanda? I don't want to mess things up for her—with the Becketts."

Dad's lips went thin. "That's not on you, Reece."

But it *was* on me. I'd demanded that she trust me, but did I give her that same trust back? No, I acted like she'd betrayed me when all she was trying to do—all she was still trying to do—was keep her own family together.

Cursing, he shoved himself out of the car. "Okay, look. I'll make some calls, see what we can do. The Becketts aren't the only foster family in town."

I opened my door and joined him on the sidewalk. "What if...what if it's not enough? What if she never forgives me?"

He turned, faced me directly, and put a hand on my shoulder. "Could you live with it if he sets another fire that kills somebody? One of us, a civilian, somebody close to you?"

Somebody close to me...like him?

Tucker practically leaped into my arms when I walked in the door, followed by Mom. "Jesus, Abby, let the kid breathe."

"I'm okay, Mom."

"Reece, I—"

Dad's hand squeezed her shoulder, and she left the thought unsaid.

"I'm gonna take a nap."

They nodded, and Tucker followed me up the stairs and curled up on my bed next to me. Under us, hidden in an old iPod box, was something that could show everyone I was a liar.

I left it where it was. For now.

***

"And you shot this footage yourself?"

Steve, the fire marshal, sat in our living room, watching the video on my phone.

"Yes, sir. On-scene."

The fire marshal took off his glasses and stuck one end in his mouth, a frown creasing his forehead. A moment later, he looked up at me. "Okay, Reece. I blew you off the other day, and I'm sorry for that. This is good work. Scoping out the scene on arrival is good, solid firefighting practice. You looked for the things that stuck out, and you found something. This, by itself"—he returned my phone—"well, it wouldn't stand up as evidence. But it gives us a direction to look in."

Steve put his glasses back on, opened a file folder, and handed me some sheets of papers.

"These are reports from the investigation—not just of Saturday's fire, but of three others. I'm showing these to you because your dad says you're sharp."

I looked at my dad, and he nodded. My mother, who hadn't stopped hovering over me since Dad brought me home, sat on the couch next to me. She made a sound that she tried to cover with a cough, but I knew it was one of frustration, and the glare that went with it was aimed straight at my dad.

"You and your friend Bear were first on-scene and reported the fire, correct?"

"Yes, sir."

"Tell me exactly what you saw."

"Uh, well, I was driving," I began and recounted the entire event. When I finished, Steve's eyes snapped to mine.

"Your dad tells me you have a perfect memory. Is that true?"

"Yes. If I consciously look at something, I remember it."

"Let's go back to the beginning again. You got out of your car. What did you smell?"

As soon as he said the word *smell*, it hit me, like I was right there. But I didn't know how to describe it. "The smell was bad. Melting plastic. Rubber. Burnt sugar. Noxious—something chemical, because I felt my throat go tight. Not gasoline or kerosene. I know those odors."

"You had no gear, correct?"

"Um, not exactly. I had practice gear in my trunk but an empty tank. Bear and I moved across the street, just two hundred feet away, and we could breathe better."

"You did not see flames?" he asked again.

"No, only smoke. But we could feel it. The heat in front of the house was intense. You could see the heat waves at the roofline."

"When did you see flames?"

"Not until Truck 3 vented the structure. Flames shot out at the front and back of the house."

"Front *and* back?"

When I nodded, Steve jotted something down on his notepad. "Go back to the smoke. Describe it."

I shut my eyes and imagined the moment when I pulled over to the curb. "It curled out from under the eaves. It was thick and moving fast."

"What color was it?"

"Light. It didn't turn black until after the trucks arrived and vented."

Steve wrote more notes. "I want you to take a look at these summaries. See if anything there reminds you of Saturday's fire." From a folder, he took out three sheets of paper.

I read the papers. Three other fires this year, all empty and boarded-up homes. "He's practicing."

Steve angled his head. "Why do you think that?"

"Three previous fires—Saturday's makes four. All residential homes. All were empty. Foreclosures. And the flames—each report states flames were colored. Purple, blue, green. Rainbow fire."

At Steve's raised eyebrow, I elaborated. "Something I learned in J squad. Metals burn in color; that's the principle behind fireworks. At Saturday's fire, I saw green flames."

"Were all the flames green?"

"No. No, they weren't. Only the first flames I saw were green, after the truck crew ventilated the roof. You'd need a lot of chemicals to produce that much green fire, right?"

"Correct."

"I saw Larry Ecker leave the chemistry lab at school. The lab was empty and should have been locked. He's not even taking chemistry. Coloring fire is possible with metals—metal salts, right? The chem lab would have those. Blue fire could be butane or copper chloride. And the purple flame could be created with potassium chloride. This isn't about destroying property. He just likes the colors."

Steve and Dad exchanged a look, and then Steve put all his reports back in the folder. "Reece, thank you for talking to me. I think the Ecker boy is a good lead." He smiled, revealing that gap between his teeth, and left.

Mom shut the door after him and then stood awkwardly in the living room. "Well, thanks for bringing him home, John."

"Yeah, no problem." Dad stood up and looked back at me. "Reece, I get why you gave Amanda some time. But you can't do that anymore."

"I know." I hoped Amanda and me could be more than friends. But she didn't—or couldn't—trust me. "I wonder if the only reason she showed you guys my note was to get me off her foster brother's back."

Dad shoved his hands into the pockets of his jeans and made a face. "Maybe, maybe not. I really get the sense that she cares about you. A lot. But she doesn't want to. She gave it to me pretty good about the way I treat you."

Mom snorted. "Smart girl."

Dad shot Mom a look. "Reece, could you do me a favor? Could you give me and your mom a few minutes to talk alone?"

My eyes narrowed. He didn't look pissed off, but he could be sneaky about it sometimes. I nodded and walked upstairs to my room. I left the door open so I could run interference the minute I heard raised voices, but there weren't any. In fact, I didn't hear anything at all until the front door shut an hour later.

Chapter 30
Amanda

"I need your help," I said in a breathless rush the second Bear opened his front door.

"No way, Man." Bear waved both hands. "You got Reece kicked out."

I stuck my foot in the door before he could close it in my face. "I can get him back in, if you help me."

Bear crossed thick arms over his chest and angled his head. "Okay. I'm listening."

I smiled my thanks. "I want to fix things." I sucked in a deep breath. "Okay, here's the thing. The letter? Lieutenant Logan called Reece's mom and told her to take him to a hospital."

Bear dropped his arms. "*What?*"

"That's why nobody's heard from him. He's been in the hospital. Psych eval."

"Jesus, Man." Bear sank to the porch steps and scrubbed a hand over his hair. "Shit. You ruined his life. They're never gonna let him come back now."

"They might if his friends defend him. Talk about how great he's been, how much he loves J squad. That kind of thing."

"Aw, fuck." Bear dropped his head and blew out a heavy sigh. "I can't believe this."

"Bear, I'm sorry. I thought I was helping. His dad hates him. When I saw that note—I don't know." I lifted my hands. "His pain was just so *raw*, you know?"

"Okay, so what are we supposed to do? If they put Reece in a hospital, they must believe that too. How are we supposed to change that?"

"I don't know. But we have to try. Can you talk to the other guys? I'm going over to his house now to talk to his mom. Maybe, if we all talk to the chief, he'll listen."

Bear raised his head and shook it. "I'll give it a try. But what if it's true? What if Logan's really sick?"

"If he is, then he needs friends. He needs to know he's liked and respected and—and—"

"Wanted," Bear supplied, and I nodded.

"Yeah. Wanted."

***

By the time I got to Reece's house, it was dinnertime. I was going to be in trouble when I got back to the Becketts'. Mrs. Beckett was strict about mealtimes, but I couldn't worry about that now. I had to talk to Mrs. Logan, tell her what I knew about Reece and his stupid note. Why had he bothered to show it to me in the first place?

I straightened my shoulders, took a deep breath, and pressed the doorbell. The door opened, and instead of Mrs. Logan, it was the lieutenant.

He frowned. "What are you doing here, Jamison?"

"John! Don't be rude." Mrs. Logan slapped his arm and opened the door wider.

"Um, Mrs. Logan, I wanted to talk to you about Reece. Could I come in?"

John rolled his eyes and stepped aside. I followed them into the living room. "I'm Amanda Jamison, from the junior squad."

"Yes, I know. Have a seat." She waved a hand at the sofa that faced the big window at the front of the house. She sat on the love seat next to it. To my total shock, John sat beside her. I took off my backpack and sat on the edge of the sofa.

"What do you need, Amanda?" John's tone was abrupt.

I swallowed hard. "Um, okay. I wanted to apologize for making trouble for your family. I thought I was helping Reece. I'm no expert, but when I recognized that one line in his note, I got scared."

Mrs. Logan waved off my concern. "I'm glad you said something. I read that note, and honestly, I'm still worried."

John flung up his hand and rolled his eyes. "Abby, will you stop? The kid's fine, I told you."

"John, you talked to him for an hour. Would you even know if he lied to you?"

The lieutenant's lips tightened into a line. "I talked to him, Abby. I apologized. I even hugged the kid. What more do you want?"

I shifted, uncomfortable with the accusing tone. I was trying to fix things, not make them worse, and that seemed to be all I was doing. I jumped up. "Um, so would it be okay to visit Reece?"

"Yeah, go on up." Lieutenant Logan waved his hand, happy to be rid of me.

"John!"

"What? He's probably up there missing her. Give the kid a break."

Um, yeah. Upstairs? Okay. I'll just walk slowly away and jog up the stairs while they argue over it.

At the top of the stairs, I hesitated in front of the open door to Reece's room. There he was, sitting at a desk with one hand petting a big black-and-white dog, the other clicking through some online search results. He still wore the hospital bracelet around his wrist. I tapped on the door and stepped inside. He looked over his shoulder and, when he saw me, broke into one of those huge grins I didn't deserve at all.

"Hey," I said lamely.

His smile disappeared. I figured it was because he just remembered to hate me. "What are you doing here?" The dog sat up and twitched his ears at me.

Where do I start? "Uh, well," I stammered, trying to find the right words. "Everybody misses you. Especially Bear. He's sent you, like, a dozen texts."

Reece swiveled in his chair, faced me directly, and folded his arms. "And what about you? Do you miss me, Amanda?"

God, yes. More than I can ever tell you. "A little."

He snorted. "Right. Well, thanks for stopping by." He swiveled back to his laptop.

What? No, I was not about to let him get rid of me that fast. "There's more."

The chair squeaked when he shifted back to face me. I stared down at my hands, clenching and unclenching them. I unzipped my backpack and took out the container I'd rescued from the trash that morning. "I've been watching Larry for days. He's acting strange. Nervous. I've caught him sneaking out twice. This morning, he was helping Mr. Beckett do yard work, and I watched him steal this from the garage, then bury it under a pile of trash at the curb."

Reece stood up and took the plastic jug. "What is it?"

"No idea. Chemistry's not my strong suit."

He uncapped the top, took a sniff, and frowned. "Maybe it's just water?"

"No way Larry would have risked getting in trouble for just water."

"So if it's a chemical, why would he throw it away?"

I shook my head. "I think he was stealing it. It's probably something Mr. Beckett got from school. He doesn't let us in the garage. Ever. Not even when he needs yard help. It's like his man cave or something. He's got a TV and a big chair out there, plus a ton of chemicals he uses to design lab exercises. But Larry knew right where this was. I think you were right, Reece. I think he's been taking stuff from Mr. Beckett…you know, to play. I think he hid this with the trash, hoping to rescue it as soon as his chores were done so he could play some more."

Slowly, deliberately, he angled his head and stared at me for a long moment. "So let me get this straight. You're basically saying everything I said was right and that I didn't need to spend the last couple of days strapped to a hospital bed getting my head shrunk?"

"Reece, please. I—"

"What, Amanda? You want to take another kick at me? Go ahead. Can't possibly do any more damage." His voice rose, and the dog's ears went back.

Tears burned my throat. "I'm sorry! I should have listened to you. But I'm not sorry about the note."

"I trusted you!" He kicked at his chair, sending it skidding across his room. "You were the only one I showed that fucking note to, and you ratted me out to protect a kid who isn't even your brother. Tucker, quiet!" He pointed a finger, and the dog stopped his mad barking.

"Reece, I—"

He flung up a hand. "My mother hasn't slept in days. And me—they pumped me full of so many drugs, I'm still whacked, so excuse me for saying there is no reason, no excuse, you could possibly tell me to make up for that."

"I can't lose you."

The words bounced around the small bedroom and hung in the air. I clapped a hand over my mouth. How had they escaped? I was afraid to think them, let alone form them, and suddenly, they'd exploded from me like verbal diarrhea. Judging by the sneer on Reece's face, they smelled as bad.

"Lose me? Are you fucking kidding me? All you do is push me away," he said.

"Because I have no idea how long I'll be here, not because I want you to die," I shouted back. "Jesus, Reece. Anybody who looks in your eyes after you and your dad go a round can see it. But those words! They're from a suicide note. I—Jesus, Reece—" I broke off when my voice hitched on a sob. "I had to do something before you—" I couldn't say it, didn't want to think of him lifeless, in a box in the ground next to Matt. I didn't want to imagine never seeing that breathtaking smile again, or never seeing that little boy joy when the trucks rolled out. My lungs constricted, and I couldn't breathe, and suddenly, he was there, right there, his arms holding me.

"Hold on, Amanda. Just hold on to me. Hold on."

I wrapped my arms around his neck and tried to remember how to breathe.

He gripped my arms and held me back. "Look at me. I'm not going anywhere." He ran his hands over my hair, my shoulders, and my back, and my heart just flipped over.

Oh crap.

I'd done it. I'd done the one thing my foster parents and my social worker and my guidance counselor had cautioned me—warned me—not to do.

I'd fallen in love with a boy.

No. Not just a boy.

Reece Logan. The only boy.

"I'm sorry," I croaked when I could talk. "For everything. I didn't think about what they'd do to you. I only wanted to save you."

"Save me," he echoed and smiled. "But you've been treating me like crap."

"Yeah, about that." I sat on his bed, my back up against the wall. "I was trying to not fall in love with you." His eyes nearly popped out of his head, so I rushed on. "If I can just hold out with the Becketts until

I'm twenty-one, I've got a good shot, Reece. A really good shot. The state will pay my way for college, but I need a car, rent, books, clothes. And Mr. Beckett has a strict no-boys policy. You have no idea what it's like living with the constant threat of reassignment over your head."

His eyes narrowed. "Yeah. Guess I don't."

"But all of that's just an excuse." When his eyes went wide, I rushed ahead before I lost all my courage. "Love scares me, Reece. It scares the fucking hell out of me."

He let out a snort. I shot up a hand and continued. "My mom got stuck with me because she loved a guy who didn't love her back enough to stick around and take care of the kid he made. And then she got sent to prison when I was barely nine years old because she loved another guy who didn't deserve it. She left me, Reece. She loved someone else more than she loved me, and I—oh God! I just couldn't stand if that happened with you." I folded my legs and leaned forward. "I tried as hard as I could to stay away from you, but you have those puppy-dog eyes and that smile that makes me think of Christmas morning, and you're so devoted to your father for no reason except that he's your dad and—and—damn it, I didn't want to love you. I didn't want you to matter."

He sucked in a sharp breath. "Wait. Are you telling me that all this time—"

"Yeah. I love you."

"Say it again," he whispered.

"What—oh. Once wasn't enough?" My face burned.

"Only three people in my entire life have ever said that to me before, and one's dead. Say it again."

"Only one person in my entire life ever said it to me, and she's in prison, so, okay. I love—"

His mouth was on mine before I finished talking, swallowing the words like they were food. My heart sped up so fast, I could hear it beat. His hands on my face warmed me all the way to my toes, and when I felt his lips part, I forgot all about the no-boys rule and aging out of care and the statistics and the note. This kiss was all there was, and I never wanted it to stop.

Until a tongue licked me from neck to temple and I squealed.

"Jeez, Tucker. Get your own girl." He pushed the dog's head away from mine. I giggled.

"Tucker?"

Reece blinked at me, idly rubbing his lips. "Oh, um, yeah. My buddy. And apparently yours too," he added when Tucker put his head down on my lap, staring up at me with adoring eyes. "My dad bought him when Matt said he wanted a dog. But Matt never really had enough patience to train him, play with him, and stuff."

"He's pretty." The dog's thick coat was snow white and jet black. If he stood on his hind legs, he'd be as tall as I was. When he looked up at me, I swore he was grinning.

"So are you."

My already-hot face burst into flame, and I looked away in frustration. A boy finally noticed I was a real girl, and I choked.

Reece took my hand, his thumb making quiet little circles on the back of my hand that weirdly had the same effect on me as his kiss. His other arm came around my shoulders, hugging me closer. "I'm sorry. I get why you've been so determined to help me with my dad now though."

"You do?"

"There wasn't much to do, strapped to a hospital bed, except think. So I thought. A lot. And I realized that this whole thing with your mom and her boyfriend and foster care—J squad is your family. And you shared it with me."

Crap. Do not cry. Not now. I was a sixteen-year-old foster kid who still believed in fairy-tale magic. There should be a pill for that or something.

***

Steve Conner held a long slim lighter to the glass dish that held the mystery fluid I'd rescued from the trash along with a little fuel.

It ignited and burned—green.

"Boric acid." He took off his gloves and safety glasses. "You say your foster brother took this out of the garage?" He wiped his hands on his pants and picked up a piece of fried chicken from a plate he had left on the table.

"Yeah. Well, maybe. He might have been throwing it out. I can't be sure."

"But he knew where to find it." Steve squinted at me. "You live with this kid. Do you believe Larry could have set that fire?"

I sank into a chair in the conference room we used for junior squad lessons and spread my hands apart. "I don't know, Steve. The thing is he's a pretty good kid. I've met my share of messed-up kids, and he's just not like them." I watched Steve devour the chicken leg.

"Oh, um," he said with his mouth full. "Want some? Ken fried up a huge batch. There's lots left in the kitchen. Help yourselves."

I shook my head. I wasn't sure I could eat. The green flame fizzled out. Reece put down the fire extinguisher he held and waved a hand at the glass dish. "Was boric acid used at all the fires?"

Steve looked at the pile of file folders on the table but didn't open them. "No."

Reece waited a beat. "Okay, so what *was* used at the other fires?"

Steve scrubbed a hand over the stubble on his chin. "Reece, you're a cadet. I shouldn't be talking to you at all, but you two are my best leads right now."

"Hey, Conner." Ken Tully stuck his round face in the door and jerked his chins toward the hall.

"Be right back."

Reece and I watched Steve talk to Ken for a few minutes. Reece elbowed me. "He left the files right there. I mean, *right there*."

I'd noticed that. I shifted my eyes to the door, but Steve and Ken were deep in conversation. When I looked back to the files on the table, Reece already had them open.

"Different accelerants. Different metals. All foreclosed properties. Huh. The same charred wood fragments. Mulch, maybe. I don't see any analyses of the wood…" Reece muttered.

Mulch. Hmm. I remembered the charred piece of wood I'd stepped on the night Larry woke me up making his midnight snack. He swore he hadn't been outside that night. I'd found more of it last week after the fire. Larry hadn't been home, only—

"Got chromatograms though. Acetone, toluene, xylene, and—Jesus—potato chips?" Reece muttered the results under his breath.

Potato chips.

"Don't touch Mr. Beckett's potato chips."

I froze when the outrageous thought arrowed through my brain and then lunged to my feet. "I have to get home. Will I see you in school Monday?"

"What?" Reece looked up. "Oh right. Yeah, I'll be in school." He narrowed his eyes. "You okay? You're really pale."

"Yeah." I smiled. "Fine. I have to run before I get in trouble. I'll, uh, text you later. Bye."

"Yeah. Okay." Reece had his face buried in the files and never noticed the way my hands shook when I waved. I turned and ran from the firehouse.

***

I jogged all the way to the Becketts' house, where I found Larry home alone, huddled on a corner of his bed.

"Potato chips," I said, gasping for breath.

His eyes snapped to mine, and all the color faded from his face. "Don't tell, Amanda. Don't."

"Oh God! You *did* know. Jeez, Larry, why didn't you tell me?"

"This is our house now. I had to protect it." And then his eyes shut and his shoulders sagged. "And because he'll say it was *me*. Us."

The blood chilled in my body. In front of me, Larry was shaking, and I was abruptly mad. Furious. We *liked* it here. Mr. Beckett wouldn't do that. He couldn't. He was…nice. God. Goddamn it.

"Did he tell you that?"

"You know how it works. If there's trouble, they'll blame *us*."

Jesus, he was right. "We won't let that happen, Larry. I promise. Where are they anyway?" Their cars weren't in the driveway, and the first floor was dim.

"Mrs. Beckett had car trouble. He went to help her."

I grabbed Larry's arm and pulled him off the bed. "Come on. We have to move fast."

"Move where?"

"The garage. The man cave. If we can find proof, we can use it against him before he can use it against us."

Larry shook his head violently, his hand tightening around mine. "And then what? Where are we gonna go?"

I blinked and tried to find something to say, but I had no answers for him. "I don't know. But we have to do *something*."

"They'll send us back. I'll never see you again."

His voice was low and steady and shot straight to my heart. "You *will*. I won't ever forget you." Slowly, I sat next to him on the bed and wrapped both arms around him. "So how long have you known?"

Against my shoulder, I felt him shrug. "Couple weeks."

"How? How did you know?"

"I got hungry." He laughed once and shrugged against my shoulder. "I got up in the middle of the night and saw Mr. Beckett out back in the garage. He had…bottles, so I figured he was just gonna get drunk and watch a movie out there."

Made sense. Mr. Beckett had a TV and a couch in the garage.

He wriggled out of my arms. "I made myself a sandwich and watched out the kitchen window. There was this, this—" He broke off and then *poofed* his hands apart. "Flash of light. No sound, just the light." Larry hunched over his knees and stared at the floor. "I thought he got shot or something. I went out just to see, I guess. He had on those goofy chemistry glasses and was holding a lighter to a bunch of those potato chip bags. He lit them up, one at a time. That's why we're not supposed to have any. He um…*uses* the bags."

Holy crap. Mrs. Beckett bought *cases* of those single-serve chip bags.

"That's not all, Amanda. He poured out some of whatever's in that bottle. He takes it from school. You should have seen him. God!"

"What'd he do?"

Larry lifted his face with a look of such horror, my stomach clenched. "He clapped his hands and giggled. Like a little kid."

"Oh God, Larry."

"Yeah. I know." He looked down again and sniffled. After a moment, he swiped a hand under his nose and looked around. "Shit, I really liked it here."

"Me too," I admitted on a sob. I pulled in a deep breath and stood up. "Did he set Saturday's fire?"

Larry nodded. "Yeah. When I saw him with the bottle, I followed him. He was there. Watched the whole thing from down the street, inside his car."

He sniffled again, and then his entire body curled up. A great big hiccuping sob came out of his mouth, and then he was crying, and so was I, because it was gone, everything that we had.

Gone.

And we both knew it.

Tears dripped, and I knew we didn't have time for them. I wished my mom were here and that we were back in the little apartment where I grew up before Dmitri came along to fuck it all up. *God!* I hated her for letting him.

Larry straightened, grabbed a backpack from the chair at his desk, and started stuffing his few belongings into it. "Let's do it," he said, his voice flat.

Out back, the garage was dark and the door was locked, but Larry knew how to get around that. He led me inside, unfolded his phone, and held the faint blue light over the worktable in the back. There was a funk over the room, more than the stale ash from Mr. Beckett's playtime. A whiff of alcohol—where was that coming from? Oh. The open Sterno cans. On a shelf over the table, jugs of chemicals, judging by their labels. There was a beat-up metal trash bin beside the table, half-filled with the remains of things he liked to burn. Jesus, it was a pyro playground. Did Mrs. Beckett *know* what he did back here at night?

I unzipped my own backpack and grabbed some of the potato chip bags, the ashes, and a bottle of boric acid from the shelf. "Take pictures, Larry. We're gonna show the fire marshal."

"It's too dark."

"Give me your phone and turn the light on and stay by the door. Turn it off the second you hear the car pull in."

Larry tossed me his phone and flipped the switch by the door. I snapped pictures of the trash can, the chemical bottles, the charred dishes on the worktable—all of it. I switched to video mode and—

"You broke the rules."

At the sound of Mr. Beckett's voice, we both whipped around.

"Run, Larry!"

We grabbed our packs and ran from Mr. Beckett, ran from the best foster house we'd ever had.

Chapter 31
Reece

When I'm at the firehouse, missing Matt doesn't hurt so much. Oh, it always hurts. But it hurts just a little less.

I skimmed through all the reports in Steve's files. Chemical after chemical. Larry must have been sneaking stuff out of Mr. Beckett's lab for months. I didn't understand how Mr. Beckett hadn't noticed his stock dwindling. The labs at school have to be kept locked, though Larry had a key. He was robbing them blind, and nobody noticed. Nobody did inventory checks? I shook my head. This smelled funny.

I grabbed a whiteboard marker and drew a time line on the board. The first suspicious fire was seven months earlier. I added the date and address to the line and then plotted the rest, ending with last weekend's fire a few blocks away from Amanda's foster home. Where was Larry Ecker on those dates and how did he travel to these locations? Long Island wasn't exactly a hub of public transportation. In fact, the closest county bus stop from the school was over a mile away, on Main.

He could easily have gotten a ride with a friend or biked, so that wasn't what bugged me. I stared at the board, and it hit me. The date of the second fire was the week of standardized tests at school. I couldn't be sure Larry had actually been in school, but based on what Amanda said about him being a good kid, a good student, and doing whatever it took to *not* get booted out of the Becketts' foster care, I'd be willing to bet he hadn't skipped.

I put a big question mark over that incident. I studied the next fire, barely a month later. Larry couldn't have started this fire either. Larry's grade had a field trip to New York City. I remember it distinctly because it was only the second time in our school's history that one hundred percent of the class participated. Usually, you had a handful out sick. I put another question mark on the board and blew out a frustrated breath.

He had the means but not the time. Which could mean only one thing. It wasn't Larry. I took out my phone and rewatched the video I'd shot, carefully watching Larry's face. I played it again. Then I scrolled through all the stills I'd shot of Bear directing traffic.

There it was. The reason Larry Ecker was anxious.

Holy fuck.

"Well. You've been busy."

I turned and found Steve standing in the doorway, arms crossed. "Yeah, I know. Take a look." I indicated my question marks on the board and explained why I'd marked those events.

Steve let out a low whistle. "If you're right, the kid couldn't have done it." He tossed the files on the table and cursed. "Does Amanda know this? She sure left in a hurry."

Maybe. Maybe she did.

"Steve, sit down," I began. "I want you to listen to this theory. I admit, it's—" I broke off. No sense editorializing it before I'd even pitched it. "Forget that. Just listen." I walked over to the far right of the board, where last week's fire was plotted. "This address is a few blocks from the Becketts' home. Bear and I witnessed Larry Ecker on-scene and acting strangely." I handed Steve my phone and cued up the video again. "What got my attention in the first place is this. See how he isn't watching the fire the way everyone else is? He was watching something—or someone—else."

Steve's eyebrows shot up. "You think he has a partner?"

I shook my head. "Look at his face." I pointed. "Larry's anxious. Worried. I thought it was because he was afraid he was gonna get caught. But now I think it's because he was afraid someone else—the real firebug—would."

"The real firebug?" Steve repeated. He grabbed the phone and replayed the video. "You think he's protecting somebody." He stared at me hard.

I showed him the photos I'd snapped.

"There's Bear, directing traffic, and—" Abruptly, he broke off, pressed his lips together, and shook his head. "Reece, you're reaching."

Maybe. But what if I was right? "All the fires this year, four fires, four different chemicals, and by the reports in those files, in quantities a lot higher than your typical household usage. All were in houses that were empty."

"But what about Larry stealing chemicals from the school lab? You saw him yourself."

"Maybe he wasn't *stealing* them. I think he was *returning* them."

"Why would—" Steve broke off when the answer kicked him in the teeth. "Oh my God. He was protecting him."

I shook my head. "Not just him. He's protecting his whole family." Amanda told me over and over again how much she and Larry liked living with the Becketts.

Steve considered that for a moment. "So that's why Amanda practically bolted out of here."

I frowned, thought about that for a long moment, and couldn't deny it. "Yeah. I think she figured it out while we were reading your files."

Steve grabbed his plate of chicken bones, tossed them into the trash can near the door, sank back into his seat, and hung his head. "Hell, Logan. I don't know what to do with this. There's no evidence to support it—any of it." He pressed his lips into a grim line. "We need more. Speculation and opportunity aren't proof."

The tones sounded.

The PA system began broadcasting. *"Engine 21. Truck 3. Rescue 17. Structure fire. 1097 Southern Street."*

I watched the crew members who were in-house don gear and roll out, followed by Chief Duffy in his vehicle. Steve stayed behind. He didn't respond to routine calls, only the suspicious ones. He turned on the radio he wore on his belt. We listened to the trucks respond.

"Dispatch, Engine 21. We are 10–8 and proceeding to alarm."

"Engine 21. Acknowledged."

The sirens faded, and the bay doors rolled back in place. We turned to walk back into the conference room. We'd taken no more than a few steps when the lights cut out and even the always-present current that hummed inside the house faded until there was nothing.

***

"Why haven't the emergency lights kicked in?" My voice echoed off the corridor walls.

"Give it a minute," Steve replied.

We stood there for a full minute, but the emergency lights never illuminated.

"Hell," Steve muttered. "You got your phone?"

I pulled out my smart phone, tapped a button, and we had light. Steve did the same.

"Logan, let's go check the generator." Steve led us to the closest exit, which faced the front of the firehouse. We hurried around to the rear entrance that led to the kitchen. "Jesus, you can still smell the fried chicken."

The generator was in a green utility box, and that was inside a cage on the side of the building near the kitchen. Steve opened the gate and then popped open a panel on the box. He held up the light from his phone and frowned. Abruptly, he stood and scanned the area. "Reece, somebody deliberately interrupted this circuit. I want you to call 911, tell them that LVFD is on fire, and the fire marshal suspects arson. Tell them no one is here except me and you."

The bottom fell out of my gut, and my heart plunged straight to the ground. "Uh, right. Copy that, Captain." I called in the 911 report just as he'd directed. Steve moved to the rear door, the one that led directly to the kitchen, and jiggled the handle.

We heard screams.

Steve looked at me. "Did you hear that?" He banged on the door. "Hello!"

"Steve! We're trapped!"

My stomach dropped to my feet. "Amanda. Oh God, that's Amanda!"

"Reece, stop!" Steve grabbed my arm when I ran. "Look. This door's hot." He put my hand over the kitchen exit, and I felt the heat.

Okay, okay. I could do this. *Think!* I tried to remember my training. Smoke wisped out from the top of the door. I dragged both hands through my hair. "We can't wait. We have to help her."

Steve nodded and ran back to the front of the station house to the main entrance. The doors wouldn't budge. He rattled them, but it was no use. "Look." Someone had chained them together.

"The apparatus bay," I suggested.

Steve clapped my back. "Good thinking. Let's go." We ran around the building and tried to pry up one of the bay doors. "What I wouldn't give for a Halligan right now," Steve said.

"How about this?" I grabbed a long branch.

Steve grabbed it and wedged it under the door. Frantic, I searched the area and found a cinder block someone had left near the Dumpster. I hefted it up and hauled it to the door. Together, we pushed the branch down on the block, and inch by inch, the door lifted.

Teeth clenched, Steve held the branch down. "Can you shimmy under, hit the control?"

"Copy." I dropped to my stomach, army-crawled under the edge of the door, and hit the control panel. Nothing happened.

"Use the manual!" Steve shouted.

I cursed. The power was cut; of course the controls wouldn't work. I grabbed the chain and hauled the door up so Steve could enter.

"Okay, Logan, listen up. The panel out back was sabotaged, and there are chains on the door. What does that tell you?"

Jesus, did we really have times for guessing games? "He's here. Mr. Beckett. And he's got Amanda."

"And there's smoke in that kitchen. So you and I are going to suit up in full PPE, and you are going to follow every one of my instructions to the letter, is that clear?"

"Yes, Captain."

We ran to the storage room on the side of the apparatus bay. Steve unlocked the door and handed me gear. I kicked off my shoes, stepped into the boots, and snapped on the suspenders. He did the same. In two minutes, we were fully dressed.

"Tank level?" He spun around so I could see his gauge.

"Green, sir."

"Turn around."

When I did, he slapped my back. "You're green too." He moved down the wall and grabbed some fire extinguishers. "Take this. And this." He handed me a can and a Halligan tool, then grabbed an ax for himself. As we left the storeroom, I grabbed another bunker coat.

Amanda had no gear.

I swallowed down the terror that nearly paralyzed me at the thought of her burning and followed Steve.

We flipped on the flashlights clipped to our bunker coats and headed down the main corridor. Steve waved a hand at the smoke wisping at the ceiling.

"Conserve your tank. Got it?"

I nodded and slowed down my breathing, the way Amanda and the guys had taught me.

We checked the conference room. Empty. We proceeded down the main corridor, crouched low, my hand on Steve's shoulder, just like in practice.

When we reached the kitchen, he stopped, put the back of his hand against the door, and nodded.

I gulped. Oh God. *Amanda.*

Steve pushed the door open, and we stepped into hell.

Chapter 32
Amanda

Mr. Beckett shut the door that led from the kitchen to the main corridor and rolled a utility cart in front of it to block it.

"You think I'm a monster, but I'm not. I never hurt anybody. I never let the fire get out of control, and I never caused injury to anyone. All you had to do was just leave it alone. Now, we're all going to get hurt. I already called your social worker, told her what I just discovered you were up to." He moved around the kitchen, eyes wild behind his wire-rimmed glasses. He turned on the stove top burners—all six of them. An enormous pot covered two burners. Someone had fried a ton of chicken in here earlier.

I could smell it, and my stomach rolled over.

He searched through the trash and piled up papers in little bundles in a trail leading from the stove to the table…right where Larry and I sat. My hand tightened on Larry's.

He found a huge jug of cooking oil and started pouring it on the floor. From his pocket, he took out a folded-up potato chip bag and a long, slim lighter—the kind he used to light the barbecue grill. He turned to us with a grin. "Watch this!"

He flicked the lighter, held it up to the bag, and laughed like a little boy when it whooshed into a fireball, which he threw at the pot of oil on the stove.

I had just enough time to shut my eyes and fold my body around Larry's before the room lit up.

Chapter 33
Reece

So that's why I'm doing this, Dad. For Matt. For me. And yeah, even for you, because even though you're too tough and macho to admit you have any feelings, I love you. But this isn't about love anymore. It's about living without guilt. So just in case you haven't figured it out yet, I'm saying good-bye. Maybe someday, you'll miss me.

Letting you go,

Reece

My mind shut off.

Click.

What was I supposed to do? What the hell was I supposed to do?

"Logan! Do not pant." Steve shoved a cart away from the door.

Don't pant. Don't pant. Right. Right, okay. Deliberately, I slowed down my breathing and followed Steve into the kitchen, eyes sweeping the scene. The first thing I found was fire.

A lot of it.

Then my eyes found Amanda. She and Larry were sitting at the table, arms wrapped around each other, faces tucked into the collars of their shirts. I hurled the extra coat toward her. Fuck! I wished I'd thought to drag another tank in with us.

"Rear exit blocked," Steve shouted. I squeezed his shoulder to acknowledge that. First order of business was to kill the fire at the stove. The pot was fully engulfed, sending a tower of flames to the ceiling, which had already ignited. When those flames started crawling, the whole room would go, and us with it.

Steve moved for the stove and aimed his fire extinguisher at the base. I remembered the cart he'd rolled away from the door. It held large pans—giant cookie sheets the guys used as serving trays.

I tapped Steve's shoulder, pointed to the cart and made a gesture to indicate smothering a fire. He nodded. I grabbed a tray and got ready to drop it over the fire. Just as I did, a figure moved out of the smoke and tackled Steve.

Amanda screamed. "No!" She'd managed to get both Larry and herself under the bunker coat.

I dropped the tray on top of the pot. The plume of flame immediately died, but it did little to stop the rest of the fire. I felt my skin crisping like buns in an oven. Jesus, the heat was unholy. Pieces of ceiling rained down on us, some pieces in flames, others in melted drops, all of it hotter than my mind could grasp. I had to get them out of here; they had no oxygen tanks.

I looked at Amanda and saw fear in her eyes, but not panic. I took a step, and a wall of fire suddenly erupted between us—a circle trapping her and Larry in the center of the room.

Mr. Beckett, pinned under Steve Conner, held a lighter in one hand.

Steve's eyes met mine, and I saw his look of horror turn fierce. With one punch, he knocked out Mr. Beckett and grabbed for his fire extinguisher, meeting me at the wall of flame. Together, we aimed streams from both fire extinguishers at the floor, directing them away from Larry and Amanda. We'd gotten the floor fires out, but the flames at the ceiling were rolling. Smoke, black and thick as tar, coiled and billowed inside the room—the inside of a dragon. Amanda and Larry coughed and gasped. Steve and I ran to them. He whipped off his mask and held it to Larry's face while I did the same for Amanda.

My throat immediately constricted and burned. It was like trying to breathe on the sun.

"Come on! Let's run for it!" Steve urged.

"No! I can't leave Larry!" Amanda choked out. And then we saw the tape holding him to the chair. Frantically, I searched the pockets of the coat I was wearing—maybe there was a knife? No such luck.

I grabbed Steve's hand, put it on the chair next to mine, and lifted. He got the hint. Together, we hefted Larry's chair up and made our way toward the interior door.

The room was pitch black now.

Amanda pressed my mask back to my face, and I hungrily gulped down cool air. How the hell were we going to manage this? She needed my air, and I needed both hands on Larry's chair. Inch by painful inch, we made our way to the door, then crashed into something blocking our path.

The utility cart!

I swiped everything off the top of it and put Larry's chair on top. I wrapped my free arm around Amanda, then gave her the mask again. She sucked down air. My tank's warning alarm rang, and my heart stalled. This was it. It was over. We were done. I aimed my light toward Amanda and saw her cheeks hollowing with every breath.

Matt. I'd get to see him after all. I'd decided to live after that whole incident with the note and the hospital. I wouldn't give in to the pain then, and damn it, goddamn it, I wasn't ready to give in to it now either. If we got out of this alive, I would prove that.

I swear.

I held my breath and shoved the cart holding Larry's chair toward the main hallway. Suddenly, air and light rushed into the room, and there was a second—less than a second—before that air and light got sucked into the dragon's belly, powering the fire's second life, and I could see it. I could see through the tarlike smoke, two flashlight beams breaking through.

The cavalry was here.

Hands lifted me and strapped another mask to my face, and cool oxygen flowed again.

"Reece! Jesus Christ, Reece."

That voice, I knew. Dad grabbed me in arms strong enough to crush iron. "They wouldn't let me in. I didn't think we'd get to you in time."

I wasn't sure if it was desperation in his voice or the smoke that made my eyes burn and tear, but I hugged back until the oxygen mask was strapped to my face again. The cool air was heaven after the apocalypse we'd just survived. I blinked up, only peripherally aware of the lights blinking and sirens wailing. An ambulance drove off, tires squealing, and a surge of panic nearly choked me.

I pulled the mask off. "Amanda!" I croaked out.

"She's okay, Larry too. They just pulled out in the ambulance," Dad replied into the hair that was matted to my head with sweat.

I sat up and took off the turnout coat.

"Beckett."

"Yeah. We know." Dad pulled away and looked across the parking lot. Rescue 19 from the next town was working on Mr. Beckett. One of the techs looked up and shook his head. I panned across the lot and found Steve Conner rinsing out his mouth with a bottle of water. He saw me and flashed a thumbs-up.

"It was a ruse to get us out of the station house. He started a small fire, kept us busy for about an hour. And then the calls came over the radio about a fire at LVFD. And we all knew. It took the truck crew forever to vent that roof so the guys could move in. And all I could do was watch." He grabbed me again, shaking as he held me. I tightened my arms around him. I didn't have a lot of memories of my dad holding me. I wanted this one to last for a long time.

"Dad, please." My voice was rough. "Please don't hate me anymore."

"Jesus, Reece, I love you. I love you so much, and if I—" His voice cracked, broke. Tears fell from his eyes in streams. "I swear to God, if

I have to put another son in the ground, I won't survive it." The last of that was shoved out on a sob, and my dad—my big, tough, macho dad who never had the right words—cried in my arms in front of the entire Lakeshore Volunteer Fire Department, and it was okay, because he wasn't the only one crying. I looked around and saw big Chief Duffy mopping his eyes too.

"Love you too, Dad. So much."

***

"Stop fidgeting or you'll wilt," Alex said, rubbing sunscreen on his arms.

Four weeks had gone by.

Despite Alex's warning, I couldn't stop fidgeting under the blazing sun, trying not to sweat through my station uniform. Dad held Mom's hand and chatted to Chief Duffy. Someone waved to me. I squinted and recognized Ken Tully. The entire battalion was here at the training facility, wearing their dress blues.

"Hey, Logan."

I turned to see Gage Garner and Max Tobay approaching. Max wore shades with his ear stud and turned every female head on his way over to me. I smirked because he knew it. Gage held out his hand. "Congrats, man."

"Oh, uh, thanks."

"Hey, guys! Hey!"

I spun around and found Kevin and Ty running over, followed by Bear doing his typical shuffle.

"Dude, I heard the chief talking to your dad. Eight kids signed up for J squad since the fire. Can you believe that? We haven't had that many at one time since our first year," Ty gushed.

Gage grinned like it was his squad.

"Check it out. The county executive is here." Max jerked his chin at the tall man who'd just left the backseat of a chauffeured car.

Great. Everyone was here, except Amanda.

"Where the hell is Amanda, Alex?"

He shrugged. "She'll be here." His expression turned solemn—no small feat given the stripe of sunscreen down his nose. "It occurs to me I never congratulated you on your achievements—both personal and professional." He thrust out his hand.

I grasped it and, in a moment of profound emotion, pulled him in for a tight hug. All that sunscreen made him smell like a piña colada. When I went to pull away, he thumped my back a few times and whispered in my ear, "If you ever feel that desperate again, I'd better be the first to hear of it—not the last."

I laughed. "They overreacted—"

Alex's grip tightened. "This is *me*, Reece. You're lying, and they're not overreacting."

He let me go, and I just stared at him. "How the hell—"

Impatient, he waved me off. "I know every one of your tells, Reece. I've known you since you were nine. I know you lied to them, probably because you're lying to yourself." His eyes focused on something over my shoulder. "Your girl just got here. We're going to talk about this later."

I nodded. I'd lied to my parents, to the shrink, to the chief. Nobody knew what used to be under my bed. But I couldn't lie to my best friend. I'd tell him all of it. Later.

The air changed, and I knew Amanda was here. I found her standing anxiously at the edge of the field, flanked by Mrs. Beckett and Larry Ecker, and wearing her station uniform. Her hair was free from its usual tight twist and gleamed in the sun like molten gold. She turned, saw us on the dais, and started walking. I had to remind myself to breathe while she strode up the steps, took her seat right next to me, turned, and smiled, damn near inducing cardiac arrest.

She'd had a tough time since that night—she and Larry both. They'd both healed from some burns and smoke inhalation. After Mr. Beckett's death and, of course, public disgrace, the county wanted to move them both into new youth facilities immediately. But Mrs. Beckett had protested.

Loudly.

She'd already lost her husband and saw no reason why she had to lose "her" kids too. There had been hearings and social worker appointments and surprise visits but still no final ruling on the situation. Amanda and Larry had been living out of their backpacks for the last month, dreading every knock on the door.

The public address system crackled, and a voice asked us all to find our seats.

"Showtime," Bear said with a grin, holding out a fist. I bumped it, and we headed up a short flight of metal stairs to the dais and took our seats. The sun was vicious, but after what we endured in that kitchen last month, it was a cinch. Dad winked at me right before he kissed Mom, left her with Alex, then strode up the dais steps to sit across the aisle from me.

"You look hot," Amanda murmured as she sat beside me.

My jaw fell open. "Oh, um, thanks," I stammered as I felt my face burn.

"No, not *hot* hot." She frowned at my embarrassment. "I mean you look really uncomfortably warm."

My shoulders fell. "Oh."

"No, no!" She waved both hands. "I didn't mean that you're not *hot* hot. You totally are, and you're weather hot, and I think I'm just gonna shut up now."

On her other side, Max snickered. "Smooth, Man."

"Shut up, Max," she snapped.

I snorted out a laugh, and before I could say anything, the music started and we were all on our feet for the color guard marching in, bearing the American and the LVFD flags, proudly announcing our motto—PROUD AND READY. We saluted the flag, recited the Pledge of Allegiance, politely clapped for the various visiting dignitaries, and did our best to not show how anxious, embarrassed, and—okay— bored we all were.

Finally, Chief Duffy took the podium and cleared his throat, his gruff voice making the microphone whine and squeal. "Sorry about that," he muttered to the laughing audience and cleared his throat once more. "The news is full of stories about teenagers in trouble. Drunk driving, robbery, parties gone wild, vandalism. You seldom hear about the teens who do good solid work in your community, and that, ladies and gentlemen, is why we're here today. The Lakeshore Volunteer Fire Department began our junior squad program seventeen years ago. In the years since then, we've grown some mighty fine cadets, many of whom continued in the fire service in both volunteer and career capacities. I got my start in a similar program when I was a boy, and I'm proud to tell you it made me the man I am today.

"Behind me on this stage is a group of teens you can—and should—be proud of. Our junior squad cadets practice with trained firefighters and study fire service principles in carefully controlled drills. Most importantly, our cadets forge the bonds of brother- and sisterhood that will make them the kind of firefighters who will walk *into* danger instead of away from it, who embody the words printed on our uniforms—PROUD AND READY."

Chief Duffy had to pause here for thunderous applause.

"I'd like to ask several people to join me at the podium. Captain Steven Conner, Lieutenant John Logan, Cadet Captain Amanda Jamison, and Cadet Reece Logan." The crowd applauded again while Dad, Steve, Amanda, and I flanked the chief.

"Captain Conner, our fire marshal, has been with us for fifteen years. Lieutenant Logan, a decorated volunteer, is the instructor responsible for training this talented group of teens. Amanda Jamison, a two-year cadet, is their acting captain, an honorary rank that's awarded by an election of peers. And Reece Logan is our newest cadet, having joined junior squad in April.

"Last month, after a suspected arsonist took two teens hostage, Captain Conner and Cadet Logan went in after them. Applying the two-in/two-out tactics cadets learned in training, they donned personal protective equipment, armed themselves with tools, and proceeded to the station house's kitchen, where they found the teens restrained in a room already partially engulfed. Although he'd never practiced in a real fire, Cadet Logan applied what he'd been taught and saved two lives that day."

More applause. I twitched and squirmed. Amanda tucked her hand into mine, and I didn't hear another word said after that. I watched her, and those eyes that weren't quite blue, weren't quite green, shone back at me, and then everyone was on their feet, cheering. I shook hands with Chief Duffy and Steve Conner, and then Dad put a leather case into my hands with a wink and a public hug.

He'd gotten really good at those.

Finally—finally!—the photographs were taken and the congratulations accepted. It took forever due to the traffic, but we were all back at LVFD for the after party. Someone hung streamers off the apparatus. A few tents covered folding tables piled with food in the parking lot near the rear door. The kitchen was still blocked off, but the guys who volunteered to repair the damaged kitchen and roof had made a lot of progress already.

My parents were sitting under one of the tents, chowing down on a portion of a six-foot sandwich. I caught up to my crew around a cooler of bottled water, because Max tried for the beer and now that cooler was under Chief Duffy's butt.

"Hey, Logan! Check it out." Bear pulled a piece of paper folded up into quarters from his pocket.

I unfolded it and grinned. It was his report card. "Holy crap, you got an A!"

Smiling wide, Bear grabbed me in a hug worthy of his nickname. "I never got an A in biology before. It was thanks to you, bro."

Bro. The word wrapped around my heart and squeezed. I hugged him back and then went in search of Amanda. I found her, leaned over, and murmured into her ear, "Walk with me?"

She grinned and took my hand. We strolled out of the parking lot behind the station house and walked down the road that circled the lake.

"So, that was—"

"Awkward," she finished. "Glad it's over. And you are *hot* hot. Just so you know."

My tongue suddenly felt too big to operate. "So are you." We walked to the water, holding hands. "Still, it was kind of cool. You must have a whole collection of those medals."

She shook her head, her hair spilling over her shoulders. "Nope. Not a one."

I stopped walking and turned to face her. "How is that possible? Everything I did was the stuff you taught me."

"Bullshit. You taught yourself," she said with a snort.

I laid my hands on her shoulders. "I'm not sure I'd have stayed past that first day if not for you."

"But you did."

"Yeah, I did." I ran my hands along her shoulders and up into her hair, then pulled her in for a slow kiss, enjoying the way that strong lean body went weak when I did. "Come on. Let's sit by the water."

I led the way down over rocks and sand and pebbles and plopped down. Amanda grabbed a handful of rocks, skipped them over the surface, and sat next to me.

"God, I love to watch you move. The way you walk—Jesus, Amanda, you could start a fire."

She snorted and rolled her eyes. "Yeah, right."

I tugged at my shirt collar and rubbed my palms on my legs, and the weight of what I had in my pocket shifted. I took a deep breath, opened my mouth—and choked. Amanda gave me a sideways look.

"What is up with you, Logan? It's like you're still up at that stupid podium. Relax. It's just me."

Laughter exploded out of me. "Oh God, Amanda, you have no idea."

"No idea about what?"

Crap, this was not going well. I hung my head and sighed. I wanted this to be perfect, and I ended up making it more awkward.

"Hey, hey, come on. Tell me what's wrong."

"Nothing." When she frowned, I quickly added, "It's right. Everything's actually right."

"Oh. You mean you and your dad."

"No. I mean, yes—that's part of the stuff that's right. But not all of it." I paused and tried to find the perfect words. "My dad and I are okay, I guess. Or we will be. But I was thinking of you."

Her eyes went soft. "Me?"

"Yeah. It's good, right? That you get to stay with Mrs. Beckett? That you get to stay with us?" *With me.*

"Completely. Mrs. Beckett's great. She's teaching me stuff like cooking. She really likes to cook. And she talks to me, you know? Like she's interested in me not because I'm a case, but because I'm me."

"That's great," I said quietly. And it was great, but it wasn't what I'd hoped to hear.

"And Larry's allowed to stay too, which is even better, because it's like he's really my brother now. That night, in the ambulance, when he was scared I might die, he told me he loved me." With a laugh, she added, "Of course, he denies that now." Still laughing, she shook her head. "Nobody's loved me since I was nine years old, and now, I have a brother."

"That's not true." I smiled down at her. "I love you." A second went by. And then another. And then it was clear she wasn't planning to say the words back to me. "You know how I knew? That I love you, I mean?"

She angled her head, waiting.

"I don't have a lot of experience with love. Not much to compare it to. There was this one thing I wanted, wanted more than anything else in the world. And when I got it and it wasn't you, that's when I knew, you know?"

She sobered up, scrambled off the sand, came up behind me, and wrapped her arms around me. "Yeah. Yeah, I do know."

I shut my eyes and cursed myself for forgetting—even for a second—that I wasn't the only person in this world with a few problems. I reached up and dragged her down into my lap. "I'm sorry. I didn't mean—"

"I know what you meant." She curled an arm around my neck, tugged me lower, and kissed me. "Just for the record, you're a hell of a firefighter. Nobody will worry with you at their back."

I sat there, her sugar and lemon scent tickling my nose, making my mouth water, and shrugged. "I belong here now. Thanks to you. And to Matt. And Alex. It was his idea, you know."

"I belong here too." She smiled, and my stomach flipped. God, she was beautiful. "Now, come on. Let's go get rid of a few weights."

What the—? I followed her to the edge of the lake. From her pocket, she took out a key.

"What's that?"

"This is the key to Mr. Beckett's home chemistry lab. Everything's gone now. It's just a plain old ordinary garage again." I watched her wind up and pitch the key long and far until it splashed with a heavy *plunk*. Then she turned to me, her smile fading. "Your turn."

My eyes bulged. My muscles coiled. "What?"

"Reece, I know what's in your pocket. And I know you don't need it anymore."

I stared at her with my heart thudding in my goddamn throat. "How? How could you possibly know?"

She wrapped her arms around me, pressed her cheek to mine, and rested her hand on my chest, right over my tattoo. "I know *you*. I know when you're nervous, when you're pissed off, when you're scared. I know you've got it in your pocket right now. I know you don't want it there anymore, because you don't hover over it the way you used to—like an animal protecting her cub."

I still didn't know how, but Matt had known too.

"Don't you give up, Reece! Promise me."

"No, Matt, hold on! Help is coming. I hear sirens. I'm sorry. I'm so sorry. Please!"

"I can't. It hurts. Reece, listen to me. I know! I know what's under your bed. I found it. Don't you do it. Promise me you won't do it!"

"I can't!"

"You have to! Can't breathe, Reece. Have to go. Hurts. Hurts so bad. Love you so much. Promise me."

"Jesus. Oh Jesus Christ, Mattie. I promise. I promise. I promise…"

When Amanda shifted, I shoved my hand in my pocket and pulled out an envelope with that stupid note sealed inside, and Amanda grinned.

"Ready?" she asked.

"Oh hell yeah." I crumpled the envelope into a ball, cocked my arm, and let it fly. It made a bigger splash than Amanda's key.

"Huh," she said, frowning. "It's like it was weighted down."

It was. It was weighted down with a single .38 caliber bullet I'd carefully etched Matt's initials into. Matt had found Dad's gun under my bed—the one I'd taken from the shelf in his closet. I didn't need that anymore either. I wasn't sure I ever needed it. Maybe that's why I was never entirely finished with that damn note.

I watched the ripples fade until the water was still. In the distance, we heard the alarm blare at the station house. For a second, Amanda and I stared at each other. Then we ran, holding hands, making it to the corner just in time to watch the crews on big red trucks speed down the street to battle another fire, wishing we were old enough to be on the trucks with them, striding into the belly of the beast and knocking it down.

It's what we do.

It's what we *are*.

Discussion Guide

Before you read the story:

1. Can you describe a time in your life when you felt guilty and responsible for something that was an accident? What skills did you use to cope? What would you tell a friend experiencing a similar struggle?
2. Have your parents ever been seriously disappointed in something you did? How did you make things right again?
3. Has there been a time in your life when you felt like nothing you did was ever good enough? How did you overcome this feeling?
4. Consider what being a hero means to you. Who are the heroes in your life?

After you read the story:

1. What do you think is the main theme of *Nothing Left to Burn*?
2. Reece believes his father hates him. Do you think that's true? Why or why not?

3. Which person was most influential in Reece's life—his dad or his brother?

4. In the beginning of the story, Reece tells his friend Alex he's writing his father a note. Do you think this was a good way to share his feelings? What could Reece have done differently?

5. Midway through the book, Reece and his father paint a room together. Why was this a significant moment for them?

6. At the fire when Bear and Reece were allowed to stay and help, what would you do if you'd been the fire chief?

7. Do you think Amanda did the right thing by reporting Reece's note to his father and the chief? Why or why not? If you discovered a friend wrote a note similar to Reece's, what would you do?

8. How did *Nothing Left to Burn* change the ways you might approach your friendships?

9. How do you think Amanda and Reece's story continues after the book ends?

10. Now that you've read the story, did your perception of what it means to be a hero change in any way? Why or why not?

Acknowledgments

It's funny...I live on Long Island and hear the fire alarm ring nearly every day, but I'd learned to ignore it. To never wonder about the brave men and women who voluntarily rush into hell for nothing more than sheer love of the job. It wasn't until I was sitting on a quiet beach during a weekend getaway that the sound of the fire alarm truly made me gasp out loud at the bravery of the people who battle those blazes.

And that's when Reece Logan and Amanda Jamison were born.

But to make them real and believable, I had a *lot* of research to do. For that, I need to thank a number of people who volunteer their time and service fighting fires. They invited me in to see what they do and spent countless hours on the phone or via email with me, answering scary questions like "If you wanted to set a fire, how would you try to get away with it?"

To firefighter Terence Keenan, thank you for your patient answers to my plot questions, to my junior program questions, to everything I asked. My vision of Reece is as a mini-Terence. You're awesome! Thanks also to your lovely wife for letting me "borrow" you *big grin*.

To Steve Krol, thank you for the hours on the phone, telling me your experiences investigating arson. I used so much of what you shared with me.

To Karen Blackburn, thank you for all of your emails and insight and patience at the early stages of this novel as I tried to flesh out my characters.

For Chiefs Ed J. and Ron S. on Long Island, thank you both for your advice and insight and for letting me visit the fire station. The mental map I made of that visit became the setting for the Lakeshore Volunteer Fire Department station house.

These brave folks are masters at what they do, so any firefighting mistakes you find in the novel are mine, not theirs.

Huge thanks go to all the book bloggers, because without them, I'd have a voice that no one would hear. Thank you for all that you do, Alyssa-Susannah, Amy Del Rosso, and Lorelei! Big hugs and thanks to Voule Walker, who read an early draft of this manuscript in record time and provided priceless feedback. I am so glad I met you!

Enormous thanks to the sisters of my heart—Jeannie Moon, Jennifer Gracen, Jolyse Barnett, and all of the members of Long Island Romance Writers RWA Chapter 160 who have advised, guided, and supported me during this book's long journey from blank page to publication.

Thank you to my family, Fred, Rob, and Chris, who pitched in and cooked dinners, cleaned the house, and did the shopping whenever I had a deadline. Thank you also to Bonnie and Augie Caruso, who not only gave me time to write after Thanksgiving dinner but let me borrow their border collie, Tucker, who really is a giant puppy at heart.

A huge hug and massive thanks go to Amanda Pitcher for leaving such thoughtful and extremely complimentary Post-it notes on my desk at work whenever she visited her dad—that's how you feed and care for an author! I hope whenever you read this story, you're proud to know you inspired Amanda Jamison.

PS I've kept every one of those notes.

DON'T MISS PATTY BLOUNT'S

SOME
BOYS

Chapter 1

Grace

No Monday in history has ever sucked more than this one.

I'm kind of an expert on sucky days. It's been thirty-two of them since the party in the woods that started the battle I fight every day. I step onto the bus to school, wearing my armor and pretending nothing's wrong, nothing happened, nothing changed when it's pretty obvious nothing will ever be the same again. Alyssa Martin, a girl I've known since first grade, smirks and stretches her leg across the empty seat next to hers.

I approach slowly, hoping nobody can see my knees knocking. A couple of weeks ago during a school newspaper staff meeting, Alyssa vowed her support, and today I'm pond scum.

"Find a seat!" Mrs. Gannon, the bus driver, shouts.

I meet Alyssa's eyes, silently beg her for sympathy—even a little pity. She raises a middle finger. It's a show of loyalty to someone who doesn't deserve it, a challenge to see how far I'll go. My dad keeps telling me to stand up to all of Zac's defenders, but it's the entire bus—the entire *school*—versus me.

I gulp hard, and the bus lurches forward. I try to grab a seat back but lose my balance and topple into the seat Alyssa's blocking with her leg. She lets out a screech of pain.

"Bitch," she sneers. "You nearly broke my leg."

I'm about to apologize when I notice the people sitting around us stare with wide eyes and hands over their open mouths. When my eyes meet theirs, they turn away, but nobody *does* anything.

This is weird.

Alyssa folds herself against the window and shoves earbuds into her ears and ignores me for the duration of the ride.

The rest of the trip passes without incident—except for two girls whispering over a video playing on a phone they both clutch in their hands. One of them murmurs, "Six hundred and eighteen hits," and shoots me a dirty look.

I know exactly what she means and don't want to think about it. I look away. As soon as the bus stops, I'm off. On my way to my locker, most people just ignore me, although a few still think they've come up with a clever new insult. An elbow or the occasional extended foot still needs dodging, but it's really not that bad. I can deal. I can do this. I can make it through school unless I see—

"Woof! Woof!"

My feet root themselves to the floor, and the breath clogs in my lungs. And I know without turning who barked at me. I force myself to keep walking instead of running for home, running for the next town. I want to turn to look at him, look him dead in the eye, and twist my face into something that shows contempt instead of the terror that too often wins whenever I hear his name so he sees—so he *knows*—he didn't beat me. But that doesn't happen. A foot appears from nowhere, and I can't dodge it in time. I fall to my hands and knees, and two more familiar faces step out of the crowd to laugh down at me.

"Hear you like it on your knees," Kyle Moran shouts, and everybody laughs. At least Matt Roberts helps me up, but when Kyle smacks his head, he takes off before I can thank him. They're two of *his* best buds. Nausea boils inside me, and I scramble back to my feet. I grab my backpack, pray that the school's expensive digital camera tucked inside it isn't damaged, and duck into the girls' bathroom, locking myself into a stall.

When my hands are steady, eyes are dry, stomach's no longer threatening to send back breakfast, I open the stall.

Miranda and Lindsay, my two best friends, stand in front of the mirrors.

Make that *former* best friends.

We stare at one another through the mirrors. Lindsay leans against a sink but doesn't say anything. Miranda runs a hand down her smooth blond hair, pretends I'm not there, and talks to Lindsay. "So I've decided to have a party and invite Zac and the rest of the lacrosse team. It's going to be epic."

No. Not him. The blood freezes in my veins. "Miranda. Don't. Please."

Miranda's hand freezes on her hair. "Don't, please?" She shakes her head in disgust. "You know, he could get kicked off the lacrosse team because of you."

"Good!" I scream, suddenly furious.

Miranda whips back around to face me, hair blurring like a fan blade. At the sink, Lindsay's jaw drops. "God! I can't believe you! Did you do all of this, say all this just to get back at me?"

My jaw drops. "What? Of course not. I—"

"You *know* I like him. If you didn't want me to go out with him, all you had to do was say so—"

"Miranda, this isn't about you. Trust me, Zac is—"

"Oh my God, listen to yourself. He breaks up with you, and you fall apart and then—"

"That is *not* what happened. I broke up with him! I was upset that night because of Kristie, and you know it."

She spins around, arms flung high. "Kristie! Seriously? You played him. You wanted everybody to feel sorry for you, so you turned on the tears and got Zac to—"

"Me? Are you insane? He—"

"Oh, don't even." Miranda holds up a hand. "I know exactly what happened. I was there. I know what you said. I figured you were lying, and now there's no doubt."

Lindsay nods and tosses her bag over her shoulder, and they stalk to the door. At the door, Miranda fires off one more shot. "You're a lying slut, and I'll make sure the whole school knows it."

The door slams behind them, echoing off the lavatory stalls. I'm standing in the center of the room, wondering what's holding me up because I can't feel my feet…or my hands. I raise them to make sure I still have hands, and before my eyes, they shake. But I don't feel that either. All I feel is pressure in my chest like someone just plunged my head underwater and I tried to breathe. My mouth goes dry, but I can't swallow. The pressure builds and grows and knocks down walls and won't let up. I press my hands to my chest and rub, but it doesn't help. Oh, God, it doesn't help. My heart lurches into overdrive like it's trying to stage a prison break. I fall to the cold bathroom floor, gasping, choking for breath, but I can't get any. I can't find any. There's no air left to breathe. I'm the lit match in front of a pair of lips puckered up, ready to blow.

Minutes pass, but they feel like centuries. I fumble for my phone—my mom's phone since she made me switch with her—and call her.

"Grace, what's wrong?"

"Can't breathe, Mom. Hurts," I push out the words on gasps of air.

"Okay, honey, I want you to take a breath and hold it. One, two, three, and let it out."

I follow her instructions, surprised I have any breath in my lungs to hold for three seconds. The next breath is easier.

"Keep going. Deep breath, hold it, let it out."

It takes me a few tries, but finally I can breathe without the barrier. "Oh, God."

"Better?"

"Yeah. It doesn't hurt now."

"Want me to take you home?"

Oh, *home*. Where there are no laughing classmates pointing at me, whispering behind their hands. Where there are no ex-friends calling me a bitch or a liar. Where I could curl up, throw a blanket over my head, and pretend nothing happened. *Yes, take me home. Take me home right now as fast as you can.*

I want to say that. But when I glance in the mirror over the row of sinks, something makes me say, "No. I have to stay."

"Grace—"

"Mom, I have to stay."

There's a loud sigh. "Oh, honey. You don't have to be brave."

Brave.

The word hangs in the air for a moment and then falls away, almost like even it knows it has no business being used to describe me. I'm not brave. I'm scared. I'm so freakin' scared, I can't see straight, and I can't see straight because I'm too scared to look very far. I'm a train wreck. All I'm doing is trying to hold on to what I have left. Only I'm not sure what that is. When I say nothing, she laughs too loudly. "Well, you're wearing your father's favorite outfit, so just pretend it's a superhero costume."

That makes me laugh. I glance down at my favorite boots—black leather covered in metal studs. My ass-kicking boots. Ever since Dad married Kristie, Mom lets me get away with anything that pisses him off, and wow does he hate how I dress.

"Grace, if you feel the pressure in your chest again, take a deep breath, hold it, and count. Concentrating on counting helps keep your mind from spiraling into panic."

"Yeah. Okay." But I'm not at all convinced. "I missed most of first period."

"Skip it. Don't worry about getting in trouble. Where are you now?"

"Bathroom."

"Why don't you go to the library? Relax and regroup, you know?"

Regroup. Sure. Okay. "Yeah. I'll do that."

"If you need me to get you, I'll come. Okay?"

I meet my own gaze in the mirror, disgusted to see them fill with tears. Jeez, you'd think I'd be empty by now. "Thanks, Mom." I end the call, tuck the phone in my pocket, and head for the library.

The library is my favorite spot in the whole school. Two floors of books, rows of computers, soft chairs to slouch in. I head for the nonfiction section and find the 770s. This is where the photography books live—my stack. I run a finger along the spines and find the first book I ever opened on the subject—*A History of Photography*.

I pull the book off its shelf, curl up with it in a chair near a window, and flip open the back cover. My signature is scrawled on the checkout card so many times now that we're old friends. I know how this book smells—a little like cut grass. How it feels—the pages are thick and glossy. And even where every one of its scars lives—the coffee ring on page 213 and the dog-eared corner in chapter 11. This is the book that said, "Grace, you *are* a photographer."

I flip through the pages, reread the section on high-key technique—I love how that sounds. *High-key.* So professional. It's really just great big fields of bright white filled with a splash of color or sometimes only shadow. I took hundreds of pictures this way—of Miranda, of Lindsay, of me. I practiced adjusting aperture settings and shutter speeds and overexposing backgrounds. It's cool how even the simplest subjects look calm and cheerful. It's like the extra light forces us to see the beauty and the flaws we never noticed.

I unzip my backpack and take out the school's digital camera. It's assigned to me—official student newspaper photographer. I scroll through the images stored on the card—selfies I shot over the last few weeks. Why can't everybody see what I see? My eyes don't sparkle. My lips don't curve anymore. Why don't they *see*?

I shove the camera back in my bag. With a sigh, I close the book, and a slip of paper floats to the floor. I pick it up, unfold it, and my stomach twists when I read the words printed on it. A noise startles me, and I look up to see Tyler Embery standing at one of the computers. Did he slip this paper into my favorite book? He's had a painfully obvious crush on me forever. Every time he gets within five feet of me, his face flushes and sweat beads at his hairline. Tyler volunteers at the library during his free periods and always flags me over to give me the latest issue of *Shutterbug* that he sets aside for me as soon as it arrives. He grabs something off the desk and walks over to me. I smile, thankful there's still one person left in this world that doesn't think Zac McMahon is the second coming of Christ. But Tyler's not holding a magazine. He's holding his phone.

"Six-eighty-three." There's no blush, no sweat—only disgust.

I jerk like he just punched me. I guess in a way he has. He turns, heads to the magazine rack, and places this month's issue, in its clear plastic cover, face out, in a subtle *fuck you* only I'd notice. I stuff the paper into my backpack and hurry to the exit just as the bell rings.

I make it to the end of the day. At dismissal I make damn sure I'm early for the bus ride home so I can snag an empty row. I plug in my earbuds to drown out the taunts. *It's not so bad*, I tell myself repeatedly, the taste of tears at the back of my throat familiar now. I don't believe me.

Once safely back in my house, I let my shoulders sag and take my first easy breath of the day. The house is empty and eerie, and I wonder how to fill the hours until Mom gets home. Thirty-two days ago I'd have been hanging out after school with Miranda and Lindsay or shopping at the mall or trying to find the perfect action photo at one of the games. In my room, I stare at the mirror over my dresser, where dozens of photos are taped—photos of me with my friends, me with my dad, me at dance class. I'm not welcome at any of these places, by any of these people anymore. I don't have a damn thing because Zac McMahon took it all. I think about Mom killing all of my online accounts and switching phones *just until things settle.* But now that the video of me that Zac posted on Facebook has 683 Likes, it's pretty clear that waiting for *things to settle* is a fantasy.

I rip all the pictures off the mirror, tear them into tiny pieces, and swipe them into the trash bin next to my desk. Then I pull out the slip of paper I found in the photography book, and after a few minutes of staring at it, I dial the number with shaking hands.

"Rape Crisis Hotline, this is Diane. Let me help you."

SEND
Patty Blount

All Daniel Ellison wants is to be invisible.

It's been five years since he clicked Send, five years since his life made sense. Now he has a second chance in a new town where nobody knows who he is. Or what he's done. But on his first day at school, Dan sees a kid being picked on. And instead of turning away like everyone else, he breaks it up. Because Dan knows what it's like to be terrorized by a bully—he used to be one.

Now the whole school thinks he's some kind of hero—except Julie Murphy. She looks at him like she knows he has a secret. Like she knows his name isn't really Daniel.

TMI

Patty Blount

Best friends don't lie. Best friends don't ditch you for a guy. Best friends don't post your deepest, darkest secrets online.

Bailey's falling head over heels for Ryder West, a mysterious gamer she met online. A guy she's never met in person. Her best friend, Meg, doesn't trust smooth-talking Ryder. He's just a pictureless profile.

When Bailey starts blowing Meg off to spend more virtual quality time with her new crush, Meg decides it's time to prove Ryder's a phony. But one stupid little secret posted online turns into a friendship-destroying feud to answer the question: Who is Ryder West?

About the Author

Powered by way too much chocolate, Patty Blount loves to write. She's written everything from technical information to poetry. After writing her first novel in an ice rink on a dare by her oldest son, Patty's debut novel, *Send*, was the first in a series of Internet issues novels for teens. Patty adores happily-ever-afters and frequently suffers from a broken heart when her love affairs with fictional heroes keep getting ruined by real life. Patty is an RWA member and vice president of her local chapter, and when she's not reading, writing, or volunteering, she likes to hang with her family in their Long Island home, even though it doesn't have nearly enough bookshelves...or chocolate.